WINTER'S REDEMPTION

WINTER BLACK SERIES: BOOK THREE

MARY STONE

To my husband.
Thank you for taking care of our home and its many inhabitants
while I follow this silly dream of mine.

DESCRIPTION

He's killing again. He's killing Winter...over and over.

The Preacher—the sadistic serial killer who slaughtered Winter's parents—has come out of retirement, leaving the bloody evidence in his wake. Special Agent Winter Black has spent her entire life preparing for this moment, and she intends to see it through—no matter the cost. When she's taken off the case, that cost just might be her FBI career.

She doesn't care.

Winter won't stop until she ends the man responsible for destroying her family. And since she isn't sure who she can trust anymore, she plans to do it alone.

It doesn't take Winter long to discover that The Preacher isn't after just another victim.

He's after her. And he won't let anything get in the way of his sadistic plans.

Welcome to book three of Mary Stone's debut crime fiction series. If you love a page-turning thriller with nail-biting suspense, Winter's Redemption will keep you guessing until the end.

Grab your copy of Winter's Redemption to find out if Winter can stop the killer who took everything from her and solve the disappearance of her little brother.

1

Tala Delosreyes outlived her mother's dire predictions.

At only ten, Tala's mother had wholeheartedly believed she'd never survive childhood. Even as a very young girl, she was too fearless and headstrong. An adrenaline junky, many had claimed. Tala rode BMX bikes all the way into her late teens, even racing in a Red Bull competition, and never broke a bone.

After surviving her teens and early twenties, Tala's mother's optimism didn't increase. She tearfully claimed that her daughter would die young if she joined the New York Fire Department at the ripe old age of twenty-five. Tala survived 9/11. And not only that, she was one of the lucky few firefighters to experience no devastating health effects in the years after that terrible day.

Even then, Tala's mother warned her that she'd never live to see forty if she joined the Washington, D.C. Metropolitan Police Force. At forty-one, Tala was awarded a Medal of Valor for preventing an active shooter incident near the Washington Mall. The President of the United States personally presented the award as her mother sobbed into a tissue beside her.

Tala's mother stopped making predictions after that.

She shouldn't have.

"GOT ANY PLANS AFTER WORK?"

Braeden Carpenter never seemed to take no for an answer, but not in a creepy way. He was too cute to be creepy, with those big brown eyes and that earnest face. But, unfortunately for Braeden Carpenter, Tala had what she'd always considered a very firm rule. She didn't date co-workers.

But the man in front of her was tempting.

"No plans that involve you, Brae." Tala shot him a bright smile to take the sting out of her words, putting on her heavy coat. She tugged her thick braid out of the back and picked up her purse. "I have a date with my mom. She's luring me home with beef *kaldereta*. Says I don't have enough time for her lately."

Braedon picked up his own bag and followed her toward the doors of the station. "I'm pretty sure I like beef *kaldereta*," he said, hope in his voice.

Tala laughed, the sound snatched up by the December wind and flung away. "You wouldn't know *kaldereta* from *kawalie*, and you know it."

He grinned, unashamed. "Maybe I'm an expert in Filipino food." She raised a skeptical eyebrow, and he laughed, lifting a shoulder in an easy shrug. "I know it's got beef in it. Besides, if your mother makes it, I'm sure it's great."

"Maybe next time," Tala promised, realizing after she said it that she'd meant it. "My mother is afraid of change. I'll have to ease her into the idea that I might bring a man home to dinner."

She reached her aging Durango and pulled her keys out of her pocket with fingers that already felt numb. The night-time temperature had dropped into the low thirties, but the wind made it feel colder. Brae was parked next to her, but he made no move to go to his truck. He stepped closer so that his broad shoulders blocked the chilly gusts.

"*Maligayang Pasco*, Officer Delosreyes," he wished her in Tagalog, butchering the accent adorably.

He gave her the cute, dimpled grin that had been making her toes tingle since he joined her unit in June as he leaned forward to kiss her. She didn't have time to back away or question whether she *wanted* to kiss him. She was too busy noticing how warm and firm his lips were. And remembering how long it had been since she'd broken up with Josh. Two years ago? Three?

Brae's lips only touched hers for a moment before he backed away and winked. "Maybe when you're back from vacation, we can talk about that dinner."

"Maybe we can," she responded, feeling a little out of breath. "Merry Christmas."

Some co-workers, Tala thought on her way home, maybe weren't such bad dating prospects. She had a feeling that even her mother would agree when it came to Braeden Carpenter.

2

I wandered around the apartment, getting a feel for the gal who lived there. I took my time, enjoying myself, but there was a pep in my step that hadn't been there for a while. A certain anticipation. Coming out of retirement had been a good idea.

I picked baby Jesus up from his little cradle in the crèche and held him up so I could see him better with my bifocals. His porcelain face was perfect and serene. Children had such purity. The boy ones, anyway.

The blue eyes of the Lord's son looked back at me, and I didn't see any judgment there. He knew that I was on a mission. I knew he approved.

I set Jesus down in his cradle and moved on. No Christmas tree, I noticed, but a police officer's schedule likely didn't allow for very much time spent at home. Maybe she had family nearby. She had a pretty place, but it didn't look like a home. There were a few pieces of tan-colored furniture, a TV, and a coffee table. None of what my momma would have called knickknacks or personal things. Except the crèche.

That meant she was probably religious. Not that that would save her.

I wandered down the hallway, running my gloved fingers down along the wall. No family pictures. But I knew the gal was a loner. I'd been watching her for a couple of days now. Learning her habits. Getting a feel for what she was like.

The joint in my shoulder snapped and popped as I reached up to the cheap apartment light fixture and unscrewed the globe. The LED bulb inside took just a couple of twists before it was loose enough so that the light went out. Working by feel, I screwed the plastic fixture back into place.

Then, I headed to her room. That was where all the joy would happen. I couldn't wait to unbraid all that gal's pretty dark hair and spread it out on her pillow. I wanted to see if it was as soft and shiny as it looked. "But if it is disgraceful for a woman to have her hair cut off or her head shaved, let her cover her head," I preached to the woman's picture sitting on the nightstand. Then looked away. Religious or not, she was a sinner. Just like the rest of them.

And just like the rest of them, she would pay her retribution.

I dropped the old canvas tool bag I'd slung over my shoulder on the floor and sat down on her bed. It was all covered up with a nice, colorful quilt. I gave the mattress a couple of test bounces. It was built so solid that the head-board didn't even bang on the wall. How many other men had this knowledge too?

Sinners. I was so tired of them.

It had been a while since I'd baptized a sinner. My old pecker wasn't what it used to be, but at least the neighbors wouldn't hear me when I gave it the college try. "Smite them with my sword," I murmured as I unscrewed her bedroom lightbulb. "Baptize them with my holy water." Even knowing the good Lord wouldn't approve of such musings, I chuckled at my humor, but only for a moment.

The scrape of a key drew my attention. I was glad my eyes had adjusted to the darkness of the apartment, and I stepped into an even darker corner as the slight squeak of the door told me it was being opened.

My heart jumped up into a double-time beat, and to my dismay, I actually got a little nervous. It had been so long since I'd fulfilled one of my missions, but I didn't like the feeling of insecurity running through me. I didn't like it at all.

I sat down on a nearby chair, the wood only creaking a little underneath me.

Having the calling was like riding a bike, I reminded myself. The know-how would all come back to me as soon as I got started.

The buttons on the gal's security pad beeped as she punched in her code. I grinned. She'd probably paid a boat-load out of her measly cop salary to get the thing installed. But when the person breaking into your place had worked for twenty-six years as a security alarm technician, all the keypads and buttons and cameras in the world wouldn't do you any good.

I pulled my pistol out of my tool bag and set it on the nightstand next to me. I wouldn't need it unless she'd changed up her routine in the last day, but it wouldn't hurt her none to see that I had it.

That done, I waited for her to come to me.

Listening hard, I heard the rustle of her coat and a click that was probably the door of the closet closing where she hung up her cold-weather things. The thunk and clatter of her belt hitting the table. I'd watched her for a couple days now. She was a creature of habit, always dropping her work things at the door before she came in the bedroom to change into something more comfortable.

Today was no different.

I pictured her opening the fridge. Heard the clatter of bottles. Inhaling a calming breath, I could almost see her leaning over to grab a beer.

I'd punish her for that later. It was unladylike for a woman to drink alcohol.

She drank Miller Lite. The same brand as me. When I'd seen her making the purchase at the local grocery store, I'd known she was to be my next target. It was just another sign. Just like that pretty dark hair she wore in a braid. She was meant to be punished, and God had chosen me to do it. He wouldn't have put her in my path if that truth wasn't so.

The fridge door closed. I closed my eyes in response, inhaling a noiseless breath. I heard a hissing pop as she opened up the bottle. She'd be taking a long, thirsty drink right now, that dark head tipped back. But it wasn't her tanned, slightly foreign-looking face I was seeing in my mind.

It was Winter's. My girlie's.

3

The end of Tala's workday always tasted like hops and fizzy bubbles.

She allowed herself one beer a night and damned the calories while she let go of the worries of the day shift. The weight of her belt around her waist loosened. The weight of a mostly thankless job shifted off her shoulders. Today, those worries slid away a lot easier. She was still seeing Braedon's dimples. Still feeling the imprint of his lips on hers.

She licked her lips to see if the kiss had lingered but tasted only beer.

Tala set down the bottle on the counter and undid the buttons on her uniform. She pulled the tails free from her waistband, leaving the shirt to hang open on either side of the white tank top she wore beneath.

It was only five-forty. She had time to change into a pair of comfy leggings and a t-shirt and do her nightly yoga routine before she headed to her mom's house for dinner at six-thirty. The dress code at Mom's was lax. Mom didn't care if she looked like a bum, as long as Tala showed up.

The first niggling feeling that something was wrong didn't hit Tala until she went to flick on the hallway light. Nothing happened.

She moved the light switch again. If the bulb had burned out, she would have seen it flash. Or didn't the new LED bulbs do that? Not letting the burnout dim her mood, and even thinking it was probably yet another electrical issue that the building maintenance would take six weeks to get to, Tala headed down the dark hallway to her room.

Her bedroom light wouldn't turn on either.

It wasn't a power outage. The fridge worked. Had a breaker blown somewhere?

Unease crept over her, but she pushed back the childish stab of fear she felt in the darkness.

Stupid winter months with their early sunsets. Stupid light-darkening curtains. It was black as pitch in her bedroom. She fumbled in the darkness for her bedside lamp. Finding the switch took her a second, and she knocked a picture frame off her nightstand by accident. It hit the carpet with a soft thud just before she registered the rustle of movement behind her.

She had no time to react.

A spasm of pain hit between Tala's shoulder blades just before a sharp cramp locked her muscles. A quiet grunt of air escaped her lips as the rest of her limbs seized, and she felt something catch her as she fell toward the floor.

She recognized them for what they were...callused hands.

Having your body taken over in what felt like one giant charley horse made thinking hard. The mind was funny that way. She'd been tazed during police training three times, and the effects on the body were unmistakable.

Even as she fell, she remembered the instructions she'd learned that terrible day. Your body stiffened as it tried to absorb fifty-five thousand volts of electricity—not lethal, but highly unpleasant—and most people were completely incapable of doing anything but mentally freaking out until the tazer was turned off.

Tala was disappointed to realize that she was no exception.

Seconds ticked by in agony as one long electrical shock gripped her. Ten. Twenty. She started to think this was it. Her heart would explode. There was no way her body could withstand this kind of torture. Just as she prayed for the end to come quickly, the stun gun was turned off with abrupt suddenness.

"Fuuuck," she groaned. Even the sound was involuntary.

Hard hands hooked beneath her armpits as she twitched and jerked and tried to get her motor skills to cooperate.

"Ladies shouldn't swear."

The comment was made without any inflection at all. Almost casual sounding, with an accent that labeled her attacker as a man from the deep South.

"I'm gonna have to punish you for that, Winter."

Winter?

Tala tried to speak. She really did. She knew she needed to communicate. Negotiate. Plead. Cry. Something. Anything to buy her more time, make herself more human to this monster.

But when she opened her mouth, sounds she didn't recognize escaped her lips.

"Shhh…" her attacker soothed, his voice barely a breath of air. "Eternal life is nothing to fear. I will save you from the sins of the earth and release you into heaven."

This man was crazy.

She opened her mouth again, willing all her strength into a single word.

"Please…"

When the prongs affixed to her back lit up again, her body twisting and her teeth grinding together at a fresh onslaught of electricity, Officer Tala Delosreyes knew her time on this earth was truly over. And she realized something else. She wasn't going to die in the line of duty. She was going to die—a predator's victim—in her own home.

4

It was beginning again.

Like a poisonous spider, The Preacher had finally crawled out of whatever dark hole he'd tucked himself into in the decade since he'd destroyed her family.

In the darkest hours of the night, just before she would wake drenched with sweat, Winter sometimes saw her mother's face. Jeanette's dark blue eyes were always wide in surprise and accusation, staring back into Winter's.

Where is your brother? they seemed to ask. *You know you're supposed to keep an eye on Justin.*

Her mom never said the words out loud, even in her dreams. In those dark subconscious moments, The Preacher had severed her vocal cords when he slit her throat. When she was fourteen, a counselor had claimed Winter would never hear her mom's voice again, even subconsciously. It would be lingering punishment of the trauma she'd received by witnessing the immediate aftermath of her parents' deaths.

The brake lights on Noah's big red truck flashed a warning on the highway in front of her. Winter shook herself mentally and eased off the accelerator. She had to stay out of her own head. Aiden could be mistaken. It was too soon to tell if this recent murder had been committed by The Preacher, or if the crime merely had similarities.

Would there be a Bible verse? Or just a simple cross on the wall, crudely drawn in the victim's blood?

She cracked a window, letting in a stream of chilly air that smelled like exhaust and wet pavement. In front of them, traffic going into Richmond stretched for what looked like miles. Taillights glimmered in a stubborn mist that refused to dissipate. It was nearing two in the afternoon, but the gray sky could have belonged to an early morning hour.

It was Christmas Day, she thought in irritation. All these people should've been home with their families, not cluttering up I-95. Frustration clawed at Winter as traffic puttered forward, inch by inch.

Aiden Parrish, head of the FBI's Behavioral Analysis Unit, had called that morning, interrupting a peaceful holiday vacation with her grandparents with news of the murder. Despite still recovering from a gunshot wound in his leg, Aiden had promised to meet them at the Richmond office while Max, Special Agent in Charge of the Richmond Violent Crimes Task Force, briefed them on the case.

And they were meeting ASAP. Having already been on the road for an hour and a half, Winter couldn't wait any longer. She eyed the distance to the next exit, estimating it was probably a quarter of a mile. When Noah's truck inched forward far enough with the traffic in front of him, she whipped the wheel to the right and squeezed between his truck and the concrete lane divider on the shoulder of the highway.

Ignoring the honking of other drivers and the gravel that spit up against the undercarriage of the Civic with metallic pings, Winter made her way off the highway. She sent an apologetic look back toward where Noah's truck was still stalled out by traffic. Noah would be irritated by the risky maneuver, but he'd also understand what the delay was doing to her. Noah wasn't just a fellow FBI agent. He was a friend.

He was also one of the only people in the world who knew her secrets.

THE TWELVE-MAN VC unit office was sparsely populated because of the holiday. Winter had to hold herself back from sprinting down the empty hallway between cubicles. The briefing was already happening, and she didn't want to miss any more than necessary.

She narrowed her eyes as she saw Noah's broad-shouldered silhouette coming down the hall right behind her. She hadn't beaten him to headquarters by much after all. When she pushed the door open to the conference room, Max, who was reading out loud from his laptop, looked up at her in surprise.

"What are you doing here, Black?" Max grated out the question in his rough voice, his thick gray eyebrows drawing together in a heavy scowl.

Winter froze, her glance darting around the room. Noah's face was drawn and tight. His green eyes were sympathetic on hers. Bree, another agent in their unit, appeared puzzled. It was Aiden's face, though, that caught her attention. His patrician features were composed, his lips curved in a cool smile, but there was something in the intensity of his stare that made her uncomfortable.

He looked watchful. Was he just waiting to see how she'd handle herself when faced with the opportunity to capture her own nightmare?

"SSA Parrish called me in," Winter replied, her eyes fixed on Aiden's in challenge. His expression didn't change.

Max shot Aiden a loaded look that promised retribution. He obviously wasn't happy to have her there, and Winter's intuition tingled. Something wasn't right here. Surely everyone knew that this was going to be her case.

Max gave a brusque nod. "Fine. Sit down, Agent Black."

Winter settled next to Bree, who smiled at her in welcome. "Merry Christmas, huh?" she whispered.

Winter didn't reply but returned the smile with a small one of her own. She liked Bree. They'd both been part of a team assigned to the same case several months before. Winter's first, after she and Noah were hired straight out of Quantico.

Bree's friendly, outgoing nature was an effective cover for her fierce intelligence and analytical mind. Anyone who made the mistake of underestimating the woman, either because of her effervescent attitude or her curvy-cute looks, only had to spend a few minutes with the agent to realize the error of their ways.

Max pushed a pair of bifocals up higher on the bridge of his nose and sent Winter a hard look over his laptop, but she wasn't cowed. Max Osbourne acted like a jerk, but he was a good guy.

"I'll back up a little for those of us who came late," he growled. "We have a female victim, age forty-four, from Washington, D.C. She was murdered in her apartment two days ago. No suspects. A red flag went up in the system when their lead investigator entered the info into ViCAP. Aspects of the killing match up with one of our serial killers gone dormant. The Preacher."

Winter felt eyes turn her way but kept her gaze firmly on the paper in front of her, where she had been jotting notes. She didn't talk about her history, but it wasn't a secret. Noah knew. Aiden Parrish was the case agent on her family's investigation. Bree probably knew, too, along with everyone else in their tight-knit unit, but they hadn't asked and she hadn't told them, aside from Noah, about her bloody history.

The murder of her family had been sensationalized, making national headlines for months, and Winter wasn't a common name. Plus, she worked for the FBI. The background checks she'd had to go through had been extensive, to say the least. Any information that wasn't on an episode of *Dateline* could be easily found by the FBI.

"The victim, Officer Tala Delosreyes," Max went on, "returned home after her shift briefly before she was supposed to be to her mom's house for dinner. When Delosreyes didn't show, the mother called the police. It was initially treated like an overreaction, but when an off-duty officer headed over to check on her, he found her apartment door unlocked and ajar."

Winter's pen stilled. The memory of her own parents' open door flashed into her head. The arm that hung over the side of the bed, pale and white, almost touching the floor. The small puddle beneath the index finger, slowly expanding as blood dripped from above.

"From marks on the body, it looks like the suspect used a tazer on Delosreyes to subdue her. She was tied down and brutalized. Ligature marks on her wrists show that she struggled."

Jeanette Black had ligature marks on her wrists. They'd been raw and angry looking. Winter imagined that her mom had swallowed back screams as she'd struggled with the ropes that tied her down, hoping to keep Justin from waking up. His room had been just down the hall.

She'd probably been just as silent in the last moments of her life as she would be in death.

"Her throat had been slit."

Winter didn't realize she'd spoken the words out loud until Max paused. She kept her eyes lowered, her face flushing. There was the sound of papers shuffling.

"What was the scripture?" Noah asked, turning the attention to himself, and Winter blew out a shallow breath.

"Yet we know that a person is not justified by works of the law but through faith in Jesus Christ," Max said, not even looking at his notes. "Galatians 2:16."

Winter took notes, staring at the words on the paper. It still galled her that the man who'd killed her family believed he was righteous in their murders.

"I'll just pass out the case notes. You all can read the details there." His voice was gruffer than usual, and Winter looked up. His eyes were on her, and she wondered if he was trying to spare her the gory details that would sound so familiar.

"Stafford." Beside Winter, Bree tensed. "You're case agent on this one. Dalton, you're the assist. Pull in anyone you need. Two of SSA Parrish's BAU agents are at your disposal as well. Keep me updated. Officer Delosreyes wasn't just a random cop. You'll see from her file that she was a fucking hero. We'll get you whatever resources you need. Dismissed. Black, you stay."

Winter blinked and looked up. Noah was avoiding her eyes, tucking his laptop away. Bree shot her an apologetic look and headed for the door.

What the hell?

She looked at Max in disbelief, but Max was glaring at Aiden as the other man pushed a

little awkwardly to his feet.

"Call me if you need anything." Aiden ignored Max's dirty look. "I'm heading home."

He'd said it to her boss, but the words seemed to be directed at Winter. She didn't look at him as he headed for the door. She was busy staring down SAC Osbourne. The expression on his grim face eased back from pissed off into just a deeper-than-usual scowl. He was obviously uncomfortable with the situation.

"Parrish called you in without letting me know first. I didn't want you here." Max's words were blunt. "You're not assigned to this case."

Winter struggled against the urge to respond with knee-jerk fury. She didn't need to get herself fired. She just needed to convince Max that he was wrong. She bit her lip as he went on.

"I know why you became an FBI agent." His voice gentled a little. His expression was serious as he took off his glasses and folded in the earpieces, setting them down in front of him carefully. "I don't have to be a profiler like Parrish to understand why you'd dedicate your life to becoming an FBI agent."

"Then," she said, her voice sounding choked to her own ears, "you should understand why I need to be in on this."

Max ran a hand over his thinning gray buzz cut. He looked regretful, his face sympathetic. "I can't let you. You're too close."

"So what if I am?" she burst out. "Probably because I'm the *closest to him*. The only survivor The Preacher ever left behind. You'd be an idiot not to use that." His face reddened, and she regretted her choice of words. She tried to dial it back and went on anyway, her voice quieter. "I can catch him. You need to give me this chance, Max."

"Answer me one question," he ordered, his gaze nearly pinning her to the seat. "Say I put you in on this. You're already a talented investigator. And you're right. There's something to you being his only victim. Say you track this fucker down and you're face-to-face with the man who butchered your family. Will you really be in the right frame of mind to slap a pair of handcuffs on his wrists and read him his Miranda rights?"

Winter opened her mouth to give him the answer he wanted to hear.

But she pictured it. The face of the man she'd seen in the vision. The innocuous-looking smile stretching across a rounded face with a neatly clipped white beard. The balding, grandfatherly appearance, as comfortable as if it had been designed to put victims at ease with one glance.

The black eyes, deep and fathomless. Empty and dead. Completely free of remorse.

She'd kill him without a second thought, like the evil, conscienceless shitbag deserved.

Max understood her silence.

"We can't compromise the investigation by making emotional decisions that will come back to bite our asses when he gets his day in court. We need to make sure the monster *gets* his day in court. It's our job to uphold the rule of law. So, answer my question."

"A conviction is what I'd be working for. Don't you think I'd be more likely to take care? Dot the i's and cross the t's?" The words sounded weak, and her heart sank as she saw Max's expression shut down.

"You can't promise me that if you had the chance to kill The Preacher, take vengeance for his dozens of victims or preserve his life and put it in the hands of the imperfect justice system, that you wouldn't be tempted."

The statement wasn't a question. A cold, numbness settled over her. Winter's fate in this was already sealed.

"You're right. I wouldn't Mirandize him. I'd gut the bastard."

5

"Can you focus for a sec here? We just got handed a huge case, and we should probably start working on it." Bree's voice was laced with humor. "It's a little too soon for you to be stressing. We haven't even read the file yet."

"That's not it." Noah couldn't sit. He couldn't focus, either. He leaned up against the wall, glancing down the hallway. The conference room door was still closed. "You got here before me. Did they say anything about Agent Black not being assigned to the case?"

Which wasn't his biggest worry. Right now, Winter could be losing her job.

He'd never thought about what would happen if The Preacher came out of hiding. It had been more than ten years since the murder of the Black family. Since that time, not a single case had been tied to the notorious serial killer. Honestly, he'd hoped the guy was dead. It would have made things simpler for everyone. Especially Tala Delosreyes and her loved ones, he thought with a deep grimace. And any future victims.

"There were some weird vibes between Parrish and

Osbourne when I got there," Bree said. "They were having a pretty heated discussion, but quit when I came in." She made a face. "I was bummed to miss out on whatever beef they had. It would have been an interesting fight. Osbourne is a seasoned agent who takes no shit. Parrish looks like such a straight-edge, but there's something about him that makes me think you wouldn't want to tangle with the guy."

In the conference room, Noah caught a glimpse of Winter rising to her feet. She was leaning over the desk, and he could hear the volume of her voice rising from where he stood. He winced. She really was going to get herself fired.

Bree's face softened. "She couldn't have expected that they'd let her work this case."

He looked at her, feeling more than a little guilt. "You know?"

She stood up from her desk and rounded the cubicle wall, laying a hand on his arm.

"Everybody knows. You can't work in such a small group day in and day out and keep a secret like that."

"No, I guess not."

"And you can't help her with this, either. She's got to face it herself."

Bree watched him with compassion. Her brown eyes were bright, her dark coffee with cream complexion smooth and ageless, even though he knew she was older than he was. Probably in her late thirties or early forties.

"You care about her." Bree said the words without judgment.

"Winter and I are friends," Noah admitted.

She lifted an eyebrow. "Friends who spend Christmas together, even though they drive separately?"

"Her grandparents invited me." He didn't want to sound defensive, but there was a thread of it in his voice. She was nosy.

Bree smiled. "Sure. And you spent the holiday there for just them."

Bree saw more than he'd like, Noah knew.

Before he could argue her out of her too-accurate assessment, the door to the conference room flew open and slammed against the wall with a hollow bang that echoed through the office. Jackson, Ramirez, and Sandovar, the only other three agents working on Christmas Day, popped their heads over their cubby walls like gophers to see what was going on.

Winter stalked out, her dark blue eyes flashing, a pink flush of angry color high on her cheekbones. Noah wanted to call out to her, say something. Hell, he wanted to apologize for being assigned to the case she'd always seen as being hers alone, but she walked by them without a word. There were tears in her eyes as she swept past, and he backed off. She wouldn't want him or Bree to see them.

Max Osbourne left the conference room a moment later, heading for his office. His steps were brisk and his face stormy. It was a typical look for Max when he was on the warpath about something.

"Wanna bet that SSA Parrish is about to get a nasty phone call?" Bree asked. "Or do you think Max will jump him out front by the flagpole after school?"

That got Noah the only grin he'd had since he left Fredericksburg early that afternoon. He'd pay money to see Aiden Parrish get a fist in the mouth. He'd pay even more to punch the guy himself.

NOAH KNOCKED on Winter's apartment door. He half-expected no answer and was surprised when she pulled it open right away. She was dressed in jeans, black boots, and a leather jacket, her bag slung across her shoulder. Her face was pale but composed.

"You got a minute?"

"Not much more than that. I was on my way out."

She stepped away from the door to let him in. He'd only been in her apartment countless times. It wasn't much different than his, just a few doors down. Same small floor-plan. IKEA furniture. Gym equipment in the dining room instead of a table. Empty pizza box on the counter.

Their apartments reflected who they were. Federal agents who threw everything into their jobs and didn't leave much time for anything else.

She sat down on her cheap couch and folded her hands on her lap, staring down at them. Her dark braid slipped over one slumped shoulder.

"This isn't like you." Seeing her so defeated-looking, Noah scrapped the beginnings of what he'd planned to say. "You look like a whipped dog, darlin'."

Winter's head shot up, and she glared at him. "Why are you here, Noah? To tell me you talked to Osbourne? Got me a place on the investigation?"

He sighed. Reached into his pocket and pulled out a deck of cards. Leaning back in a chair across from her, he watched her closely. The cards whispered as he deftly shuffled.

"No. Osbourne's mind is made up."

Her face went from bleak to bleaker.

"Is there anything I *can* do for you?"

"No."

This was driving him crazy. He was used to Winter taking on every challenge. Bucking convention and rolling with the punches. Getting shit done with that unique way she had of seeing things and not letting anything faze her. Right now, she looked pale and insubstantial. Like a stiff breeze would knock her over.

She was a mystery wrapped in an enigma most of the time, but Noah knew what buttons to push to get her going.

"Look, I know how you're feeling." He deliberately injected a little patronizing, mansplaining tone into his voice. He needn't have. "I know how you're feeling," was a trite phrase, never accurate, and guaranteed to get a reaction.

Winter shot to her feet, finally exploding.

"You have *no idea* how I feel, Dalton. This is what I've been focused on completely since I was thirteen years old. This is *why* I'm here. What the fuck have I done with my life if I can't even be part of the takedown?"

"Maybe you started out with The Preacher's capture as an end goal," Noah pointed out. "But you graduated at the top of your college class. You earned the highest marks at Quantico and were recruited straight out of graduation. You're an agent, and you're a damn good one. Look at your apprehension record. That is why you're here. You were made for this."

She shoved her hands through her hair. "It doesn't matter. None of that matters."

"It does matter. It matters to the women who were brutally attacked by the serial rapist you nailed. It matters to the families who were used as guinea pigs by a soulless child killer with money and ambitions. It matters to Agent Ming and to me and everyone you work with."

"But, I—"

Now, he was getting pissed. "Quit feeling sorry for yourself, Winter. You can't have reasonably expected Osbourne to put you on this. You'll be a liability. What lawyer wouldn't point out to the jury that one of the investigators on the case had a conflict of interest? Namely that The Preacher targeted her family? You could jeopardize the whole thing."

"I don't care." Her mouth set in a hard line as she paced the floor. "I've earned this."

"That's bullshit." He stopped shuffling, winding a rubber band back around the deck. Standing, he crossed the living room to Winter in two long strides and stopped her, taking her by the arms.

"Let me do this for you. Let me get him."

She tried to shake loose from his grip, but he held on with gentle pressure.

"You can't do this. You know you can't. Not through the right channels. Let me."

Winter stopped struggling, but her eyes still sparked.

"We're friends, Noah. Good friends. I don't make them easily. You want to talk about putting something in jeopardy? Don't try to be my white knight, because I don't need one, and I'll only resent you for it."

"What you need is to stay far, far away from this," he countered. "You were The Preacher's only victim to survive in what might have been decades of killings. You think he doesn't know that? What do you want to do? Use yourself as bait?"

She didn't answer, but he could see it on her face. That's exactly what she'd intended.

Fury burned hot for a moment, but Noah sighed, letting it —and her—go. He took a step back before he gave in to the urge to shake some sense into her.

"Think rationally. Your last encounter with him put you in a coma. You have those...migraines now, or visions, or whatever the hell they are. You didn't have them before. It's like he left a mark that's still affecting you, every day. A wound that won't heal. Whoever takes him down needs to be able to separate personal feelings from professional. It can't be you."

Her face went cold, her deep blue eyes freezing over. "You've gotten to know me pretty well since we met. I expected you to understand."

"I do." He was losing her. "I understand. It's just not possible."

"Did you even go to bat for me?"

He didn't even hesitate. "No."

"Did it occur to you that we can work around this? That I can assist in an unofficial capacity?"

That had occurred to him. He'd rejected the idea. Even knowing the words might break something fragile, he had to say them anyway. "I *won't* include you. I want you as far away from him as you can possibly be."

He could almost hear the connection they'd been forging between them shatter like an icicle dropped on the pavement.

"Then I guess there's nothing more to say, is there?" Her voice was flat. She went to the front door and opened it. "Goodbye, Noah."

The words sounded so final.

Noah told himself as he headed to his truck that he could fix this. It wasn't the end of anything between him and Winter. They could fix it. He just had to catch The Preacher first.

He also told himself he was a damned liar.

6

After Noah left, Winter dropped down on the couch again, her head in her hands.

Damn him for being so chauvinistic, so overprotective, so *Texan*.

Noah had been her shadow since Quantico. Competing with her. Hovering over her. Teasing. Flirting. Having her back when she needed him. Making her laugh and punch him within seconds of each other. Just being…Noah. He infuriated the shit out of her with his overbearing attitude and huge ego. He also constantly tried to charm her with his dimpled grin and wicked green eyes.

The hell of it was, *that* had started to work.

Lately, he wasn't just Noah anymore. A friend she could actually count on, for the first time in her sorry history of friendships. He was a sexy, caring, funny guy, and she couldn't have asked for a better partner if she tried.

Now, though…chalk up another reason for retribution on The Preacher. Because of the case, she was looking at the end of a friendship and maybe something more.

Winter huffed out a breath and stood up, pacing the short

length of her living room with restless quickness. The cheap Venetian blinds that hung over her sliding glass door swung as she passed. What she'd told Noah was true. If she wasn't on this case, all the work she'd done to get to this point was a waste.

She had to get assigned to The Preacher case. There was no other option.

If she didn't, she might as well quit. Leave the FBI.

Even the thought of doing that knocked the wind out of her. She couldn't imagine leaving. She'd only chosen her career path with one thought in mind. Vengeance. But she was *good* at being a special agent. She'd taken down suspects that her colleagues never would have caught. She knew things that none of them ever could. Without her, the cases she'd been on might never have been resolved.

The irony in that was that she was probably only as good as The Preacher had made her.

The night of the murders, she'd seen her parents only for a second, slaughtered in their beds. In the next moment, she'd been hit over the head so violently that the killer assumed she was dead.

Winter spent the next couple of months in a coma. When she came out of it, she did so with heightened observational skills. Sometimes, she could tell if an item was connected to a violent crime. Other times, she caught quick glimpses or snapshots of events that had once taken place or might soon happen. While that all sounded like handy traits to possess for a law enforcement official, those particular skills came along with severe headaches, unconsciousness, and nosebleeds.

The observational and sensory sensitivities had surfaced first. She'd been a fascinating puzzle for the doctors and psychologists she'd seen. They'd been relentless with CT scans, MRIs, analyses, and interrogation until she and her grieving grandparents had enough and moved to Fredericks-burg, cutting off all treatments.

The other skills came later, when she was in college. Identifying things connected to crimes was great. Being at the mercy of what were basically random, debilitating seizures was not.

Thinking about her migraines, Winter tried to calm down. She already had a tension headache and had wondered whether being stressed out made her more susceptible to the visions. With the shoulder muscles at the base of her neck knotted so tightly and her forehead throb-bing with low-grade pain, she was basically begging the universe to let her test that theory now.

She took off her jacket and hung it on the back of a chair. She wasn't in any frame of mind to go anywhere anyway. She pulled open her refrigerator. She wasn't hungry either, which was a good thing, since the only edible items inside were some shriveled-looking grapes and a questionably aged carton of yogurt. Instead, she grabbed a bottle of Rolling Rock.

She'd started keeping some around in case Noah came by, she realized as she popped the top. When had he become such an integral part of her life? She'd always kept her focus narrowed. Eyes on the prize. Taking a bitter swallow from the bottle, she also realized the chances of Noah dropping by now were slim.

She dropped the mostly full beer in the sink, where it landed on its side with a clatter. Pale liquid foamed out, yeasty-smelling and sour. The scent seemed to intensify, assaulting her senses, and she winced.

Abruptly, the beer smell became more cloying, choking and heavy, until she had to gasp for air. Then, a shock of pain rolled over her out of nowhere, like a tsunami. Her vision went dark and bright all at once, like an overexposed photo.

Winter cracked her forehead against the edge of the laminate countertop on her way down to the floor, but she didn't feel it.

HER EYES FLEW open as Winter sucked in a gulp of air. A soft, Southern-sounding voice still echoed in her head.

"This is what happens when ladies drink alcohol."

Winter's stomach twisted, and she rolled to her side in her narrow, galley kitchen. Bringing her knees up to her chest, she closed her eyes and counted slowly, trying to keep from throwing up.

It had been worse this time. Different.

Somehow, she'd felt the bindings around her wrists, she thought, tucking her cold hands underneath her arms. She hadn't seen Tala Delosreyes tied down to her bed with rough twine. She'd experienced it.

She'd also seen the face of the killer. Again.

As soon as she felt steady enough, she made it to her feet and stumbled to the bathroom. The headache and nausea were gone like they'd never been, but Winter grimaced when she caught sight of her face.

Her eyes were wide, shadowy, and haunted-looking, and her face was so pale it was practically transparent. She also had the dark hint of a bruise forming high on her cheekbone. The skin had split with the force of impact with whatever she'd knocked it against, and a trickle of blood had run back into her hairline, where it dried in a sticky mess. There was more blood on her face, some of it still wet, from a nosebleed. Tears had left salty tracks on her cheeks, and her eyes were swollen from crying.

She looked like the shell-shocked survivor of some kind of natural disaster.

Grabbing a cold washcloth, she removed as much evidence of the experience as she could. The abrasion on her face was deep enough that it reopened when she dabbed at it with the washcloth, leaking blood sluggishly. She put a butterfly bandage on it and dismissed it. There would be a scar, but it didn't matter.

Her heart was pounding with a quick urgency and the need to do something. Now.

In the bedroom, she pulled on a clean gray t-shirt and grabbed her coat again. She slung her messenger bag over her shoulder and headed for the door but stopped by the kitchen on her way out.

Where was she going?

She leaned against the doorjamb and closed her eyes, trying to control her instinct to move now and to move fast. Noah wasn't going to fight to bring her on. Max had dismissed her. From what she'd picked up on his personality in the last year, once he made up his mind on something, that decision was etched in granite.

She had to get on this case. Not because of her mom and her dad, or her missing little brother. Or her elderly grandma and grandpa, who still grieved. Not because it meant catching the specter that had taken dozens of lives over the years, or because of the loved ones they'd left behind.

It was because she'd felt the fear of Tala Delosreyes.

This had been different than seeing the aftermath of a serial killer's bloody bacchanal. The gore and loss of life in her visions could be processed. It was disturbing and horrible, more graphic than the worst slasher movie, because the scenes were Technicolor-real. They'd happened. She'd seen them in vivid detail, almost as if she'd witnessed them with her own eyes, but she could handle that.

This last experience had been entirely different. It was like Winter's panicked lungs were struggling to take in air.

Her wrists were chafed and bleeding. *Her* heart had fluttered with fear like a trapped bird in her rib cage. Winter had been in Tala's body. Her head.

She could smell the stale, old-man breath of The Preacher. She could imagine Tala's mother, a small, dark-eyed Filipino woman with a sweet smile and nervous hands. She'd seen a man's face. A little rounded, attractive laugh lines, sandy brown hair, a wise-ass, boyish grin on his face. She didn't know who he was, but Tala had been thinking about him in the moments before she died.

Winter was no bystander in this vision. She'd been in the victim's head. During that quick flash, she *was* Tala. A fearless woman with an adrenaline addiction who'd done incredible and selfless things with her life. A badass, who'd stayed strong until the end, fighting against the ropes that held her until the killer's knife had pierced her throat. Tala had faced her death like the hero she was.

The bone-deep grief and loss Winter had felt for Officer Delosreyes when she'd awoken on the kitchen floor had shaken her to her core.

She needed to get the woman's killer before he snuffed out any more lives. And Max was right. She wouldn't settle for an apprehension. Winter would give him no chance to walk free, get off on a technicality, and continue his grisly work.

When Winter found him, she'd kill him.

She'd go to Aiden. The Supervisory Special Agent of the Behavioral Analysis Unit was brilliant, cold, and sometimes unpredictable, but they had a history together. He'd require careful handling, but with some clear-thinking negotiation and a little manipulation, maybe she could get his help.

Straightening up, destination decided, Winter dug in her bag for her car keys. She was about to head for the door when a wide stain on the tan linoleum caught her eye. She hadn't cleaned up the floor after her episode. The sight of the blood was startling—like she'd brought it back with her from the vision.

But it was hers. She'd blacked out without warning and ended up on the floor, bleeding on the tile. Slowly, Winter slid the keys back in her purse and pulled out her phone instead.

Noah had expressed his concerns about the unpredictable nature of her "migraines" before. She hated the thought of not driving, and more, hated to admit he was right, but she'd been lucky so far. She couldn't push that luck. If an episode came down on her like the last one, she'd have no warning. Like Noah pointed out, it was no different than epilepsy in the respect that she could experience a seizure and be physically unable to drive. The decision left her feeling trapped, but Winter called for an Uber pickup.

As she cleaned up the kitchen floor and waited for her ride, she started planning how to handle SSA Parrish. He and the Assistant Deputy Director of the Richmond Office, Cassidy Ramirez, hadn't been able to catch The Preacher when they'd been in charge of the case, earlier in their careers. Bree had twelve years as an agent and Noah had been an experienced police officer before he'd applied to the FBI, but it wouldn't be enough. They wouldn't be able to do it, either, instinct told her.

Winter had to convince Aiden to help her get into the investigation. Otherwise, she would have to do it alone.

7

S he hadn't called him, but he was expecting her. In fact, he was surprised she hadn't already shown up.

Aiden looked out the window of his top-floor apartment at the wet streets below. Traffic was light, and the streets were empty. Most people were probably at home, celebrating Christmas with their families, or just staying in because of the dismal weather. Streetlights made indistinct puddles of light in the cold, thick fog.

Headlights cut through the gloom, and a gray minivan pulled up in front of his building. A tall, slim figure got out. She was far away, but Aiden still reacted at the sight of Winter, her face a pale oval and her hair so black it seemed to absorb the glow from the streetlights.

His muscles tensed for the fight ahead, and a bolt of pain shot down his thigh, reminding him that he was still supposed to be recuperating. He rubbed at the cramped muscle absently as he watched her walk toward the front doors.

He didn't know why she'd pay for a ride when she normally drove a beat-up little Honda Civic everywhere, but he was glad to see she had. He worried about her driving with her condition. She'd apparently come to the same conclusion. It wasn't safe anymore. That let him off the hook. He hadn't looked forward to having the conversation with her, and now, it wouldn't be necessary.

He'd been trying to put some emotional distance between them, but old habits died hard.

Putting the issue out of his mind, he sat down in his chair, easing the weight from his wounded leg as he waited for her to come to the door. Security buzzed him to let him know she was on her way up.

At her knock, he drained the rest of his Scotch and set the glass down on the table beside him. A lot depended on how this conversation went. He smiled grimly.

"Come in."

She did, but without the easy familiarity that she'd adopted in the last couple of months. Seeing her had become an almost nightly routine when she'd stop in to check on him after he was released from the hospital.

Tonight, she entered the room slowly, like she was expecting a trap. She pulled off her black jacket and hung it on the back of one of the barstools at the kitchen counter. He could smell the rainy outdoor scent she brought with her.

Her face was hard, tight with stress, and her dark blue eyes looked haunted. A fresh bruise was blossoming just underneath her right eye, a bandage in the center. He squashed the instant wave of concern.

"What brings you out on a night like this?" Aiden asked instead, his tone faintly sardonic.

She dropped down in a chair across from him. Not her usual one that was beside his, where she'd taken to eating Chinese food with him while she talked about her latest case. He wasn't the only one distancing.

"I need you to get me in."

He laced his fingers together and leaned back in his seat. Letting a little sympathy show on his face, Aiden shook his head slowly. "Listen, I'm sorry about today. I'm afraid Max has his mind made up. I invited you to that meeting because I thought I could change it." He shrugged. "I was wrong."

Her eyes narrowed in suspicion, and she stared at him steadily. "Why do I feel like you're lying to me?"

He'd have to be careful. She was intuitive and quick.

"Why would I lie? I know how much this means to you." He reached down to a shelf on his side table and picked up a piece of paper. Holding it up, he watched her face.

"Would you have given me this if you didn't trust me to help you?"

It was a drawing of The Preacher, near sketch artist quality. Winter hadn't told him what was behind the creation of it, or how she could be sure it was him, but Aiden didn't doubt for a second that it was an exact likeness of the killer. With pencil and paper, she'd captured a man, approximately sixty years old, with a short white beard. He had a smooth, innocuous face and thick glasses. Behind the lenses, she'd shaded black eyes that looked almost hungry. The face of a beloved grandpa with the eyes of a ruthless predator.

"And what have you done with it since I gave it to you?" Winter asked, her voice low.

Aiden just smiled, a slight twist of his lips. "Your trust is fleeting, isn't it?"

"You had plenty of time to tell me whether you'd found anything after my team wrapped the Presley heists. I was on vacation after that, but last I knew, you had no problems calling me."

She was referring to the calls he'd made to check on her when she was a teenager. As the case agent on her family's murder, back when he was younger and more idealistic, he'd taken on the responsibility of keeping tabs on her over the years. Partially to atone for failing her and partially to protect her. She'd been The Preacher's only surviving victim.

He admired her tactic. Reminding him of their previous relationship and laying the foundation for a counter-argument with a big dash of guilt. He pretended to consider her words, letting the moment draw out.

"I don't have anything new," he finally said. "But I have something else you need."

Winter's tension seemed barely leashed. She didn't move from her position, leaning forward, elbows on her knees. Her braid fell over one shoulder, brushing against her folded hands.

"You're going to go over Osbourne's head? To ADD Ramirez?"

Aiden shook his head, pasting a regretful look on his face. "Ramirez won't budge, either." It wasn't a lie. He didn't need to talk to Cassidy to know that she'd agree with Max Osbourne. Besides, getting Winter included on the VC investigation wasn't what he was after.

But he had to dangle a carrot. This would be the tricky part.

"What if I told you I can give you access to my personal files. Information, case notes, handwritten docs that the violent crimes unit hasn't even seen yet." He gave her a significant look. "It would be up to you whether you shared that information or kept it to yourself."

Aiden couldn't read her face. She'd sat back and was now just outside of the circle of light cast by his tableside lamp. When she spoke, her face was in shadow. Even as a trained observer of human behavior, he couldn't tell what she was thinking.

"And what would you get?" Her words were casual. She betrayed nothing in her body language. "As admirable as your character is, SSA Parrish, you always seem to have an endgame in mind. If you were being altruistic, you would have already given me everything you have. A gift isn't just a gift with you."

"Sometimes it is," he murmured, thinking about the impulsive gift he'd given her a week ago, before she'd left for Fredericksburg. A mistake.

"In this case, let's assume I'm right."

"I want you."

That managed to startle her. Winter's eyes widened. Reminding himself that he was doing this by any means necessary, he lowered his voice a fraction. He had to keep her off-balance. Take advantage of the awareness that had sprung up between them in the last several months. He had to use any feelings she might have for him.

"I mean," Aiden clarified in a honeyed tone, "I want you in the BAU."

Winter was already holding herself very still, but at that, she seemed to freeze. When she spoke, her words were frosty. "I think you already tried this once, Parrish. Not as creatively, maybe."

He smiled, aiming for charm. "And it didn't go well. I was doing it for the wrong reasons. Now, I think—"

"I don't care what you think. Let me remind you how that ended." The words were clear and spaced slowly, so he'd be sure to understand. Winter leaned forward so he could see the cold blue fire that burned in her eyes. "I would rather quit the FBI than put myself behind a desk. Specifically, under *your* control," she added. "I haven't changed my mind about that."

"I don't blame you," he replied, his voice smooth and soothing, not even hinting at the sting her words had produced. "If I were in your position, I'd feel the same way. By all means, quit the FBI. With your talent, you could track The Preacher. Hunt him down. Kill him." Aiden paused, letting the seconds draw out. "But, under my terms, you'd have access to more than just a sketch. You'd have a complete psychological profile. Evidence. The ability to catch him *before* he goes into hiding again. Maybe you'll find him before he targets anyone else."

Self-loathing was secondary to satisfaction, he found as he watched her face. He saw hatred, temptation, strategy. Soon, he'd see the resignation he was counting on.

But the silence stretched out. He was well-versed in its value during negotiations, but she was so quiet, it started to get to him.

"I'll give you a year." She didn't look up at him.

"It's a permanent move or no deal." He was irritated to realize he'd been holding his breath. Beside him, he picked up the transfer documents he'd already completed. His hand shook the slightest bit, which pissed him off. It was steadier when he held the packet of paperwork out to her.

Not a carrot, maybe. But she would have to come to him.

"Fine." She pushed to her feet and gave him a hard look, tinged with betrayal as she took the final step toward him and snatched the papers from his hand. The last rosy glow of hero worship had finally been extinguished. She saw the man he was now, and not the FBI agent she'd idolized as a child. Without another word, she headed for the door. It slammed behind her, hard enough to rattle the glass bowl on his foyer table.

A normal man would feel guilt right now. Almost smiling, Aiden levered painfully to his feet and headed for the liquor cabinet. He felt satisfaction. Mostly.

In the kitchen, he refreshed the ice in his glass and picked up a prescription bottle from the counter. Washing down Norco with Scotch was probably against doctor's orders, but as he waited for the room to go pleasantly blurry, Aiden hoped he'd be able to blur the hurt he'd seen in Winter's eyes too.

It made him think of the first time he'd put that look there.

Winter had been tall for a teenage girl, and coltish. She'd showed hints of maturing, but she was still miserably awkward. Much more a kid than a young adult.

Her vibrant eyes were watchful, and she'd worn her hair loose back then. Hiding behind the glossy black curtain, in her black boots, jeans, and a gray, hooded sweatshirt, she'd still managed to project the vulnerability she was trying to hide behind angsty teenaged attitude.

When he'd shown up at the restaurant where her grand-parents had taken her to celebrate her seventeenth birthday, Beth McAuliffe had seen him first. Her sharp eyes had narrowed quickly with recognition, followed by dislike and suspicion. He couldn't blame her. He was the FBI's failure to capture her daughter's family's murderer, personified. Winter's Grampa Jack, a bluff, straightforward old guy, had just given him an inscrutable look.

Winter, though, lit up when she looked up from her menu to find him at their table. He handed her the gift he'd picked out and wrapped before he'd driven up from Richmond.

Aiden sat down at their table when Beth made the sweet but probably grudging offer before waving off the waitress. He wouldn't stay. He was interrupting their family time. Bringing up memories that should be put aside on a kid's birthday.

Winter ripped off the paper with childlike greed and opened the box. Holding up a stuffed cat dressed in a gradua-tion outfit, she grinned widely. The smile lifted the shadow that lingered around her, and for a second, she just looked like a normal kid. One that didn't carry a stain that lingered long after her brush with death.

"You're so predictable, Parrish," Winter teased. Her eyes gleamed as she smiled wider. "I love it." Despite the sarcastic tone, she rubbed her cheek against the stuffed animal's soft head.

"It's a little early," he admitted, "but you'll be graduating high school before you know it. Happy birthday, kiddo."

Aiden reached out without thinking and tousled her hair affectionately.

The sparkle in her eyes went out. Her smile disappeared as she sat back quickly. She dropped the stuffed animal back into the box.

"Thanks." Winter picked up her menu again, holding it in a white-knuckle grip. Her hair fell forward to shield her face.

Shit. He realized what he'd done almost immediately. He wasn't the only one. Beth was biting her lip, looking at Winter's bent head with sympathy. Jack just winced and made eye contact with Aiden, shaking his head.

Mortified, he'd made his excuses and left.

He'd quit making his periodic calls after that disaster. It was uncomfortable to realize that he'd accidentally broken a teenaged girl's heart, totally oblivious to what had obviously been a strong crush.

Aiden had been working on his dissertation for his Ph.D. in Psychology at the time. The lingering self-disgust with his inability to read basic human emotion kept him from sending another birthday gift or making any attempt to check up on her in person. Even after he quit any direct contact with her, he'd still get the occasional hopeful-sounding emails. Eventually, he'd gotten an invitation to her graduation. He didn't respond to it.

She'd seen him there, at the end of the ceremony. Winter had grown out of the awkward stage and looked much more mature at eighteen. Her emails had finally stopped months before, and she'd only acknowledged him with a nod. Her grandparents never noticed him.

After that, he kept tabs on her remotely, and with decreasing frequency. Winter had finally begun to slip off his radar. He'd been in a serious relationship at the same time, and it ended badly. He'd turned his considerable focus toward his career instead, throwing himself into advancement. Aiden created a new purpose for himself, and if The Preacher case still haunted him, he was the only one who knew.

Until Beth McAuliffe called him one day, out of the blue. She'd told him, her voice brisk with worry, that Winter'd been serious when she'd started saying at fifteen that she was going to be an FBI agent. She was about to graduate with a double master's and was already talking about applying for Quantico. Beth had hinted heavily that he should try and change her mind.

So, he made one more appearance in Winter's life. He'd owed Beth that much. But at twenty-three, he hadn't expected her to be...such an adult. She'd seemed determined, bright, and less vulnerable. If she held any resentment against him for embarrassing her all those years ago, she didn't let on. Instead, she talked enthusiastically about her plans. She was dead set on achieving her goal of joining the FBI.

She'd changed. He'd changed, too, but Winter hadn't noticed. He hadn't allowed her to.

He wasn't the same young FBI agent she'd known. No longer idealistic and hopeful, making the world better, one bad guy at a time. He was selfish and ruthless. Controlled. He'd moved up the ladder in the BAU, but he had his eye on Ramirez's spot as the Associate Deputy Director, whether his former colleague had to move up—or out—for that to happen.

Aiden didn't let on. After focusing on her again, he'd discovered Winter's secrets. He wasn't afraid to turn them to his advantage. By penning her in the BAU, she'd be behind a desk, and she'd stay safe.

It was just an added bonus that she'd be spending her time using her considerable intuition to create incisive profiles, increase their apprehension rate. If any of that helped him into the ADD spot, so much the better.

Having Winter in the BAU would erase the only black spot on his record. She'd track down The Preacher. He hadn't lied about his confidence in her ability. He was sure she could do it.

But Aiden would never let Winter take the killer down solo. Instead, he'd use Winter to get *him* to the killer, putting an end to an ugly story that should have been shelved years before.

8

Noah had witnessed the bloodiest, most gruesome crime scene of his law enforcement career only a month ago. Heidi Presley, a vicious sociopath bent on carving her mark in the world with a string of heists modeled after the most famous robberies in history, had lost her temper with one of her victims. She'd slaughtered a man in a fury, rather than simply executing him, breaking from her previous MO in a spectacular show of violence.

Heidi had mutilated the body afterwards, careless of the blood that had spattered the ceiling, floor, and walls of the hotel suite. With her vengeance finally satisfied, she'd left the hotel room, tracking gore nearly twenty feet down the hallway. Her victim had been left behind in his bed, an unrecognizable mess.

That had been nothing compared to The Preacher's latest crime scene. The similarities between the two stopped at the victim being killed in bed. The differences were chilling.

Detective Bardo, a slim, gray faced man in his late fifties, led them to apartment 218. His face was grim, and he kept conversation minimal. He didn't need to tell them, though.

Noah had known it would be bad. Bree stayed close to Noah, silent, as they donned gloves and booties outside the door.

They'd been given some warning ahead of time. They'd both read the reports on Officer Delosreyes. It was impossible not to personalize the victim, knowing her background and getting a feel for who she was. It was especially hard when the local law enforcement officers in charge of her case were so obviously grieving her loss.

The smell hit them first. Overpowering and coppery, it reminded Noah of the meatpacking warehouse his grandpa had used to process deer during hunting season.

Beside him, Bree swallowed audibly, her face visibly pale.

"If you're going to puke, do it outside," Bardo snapped. "This is still an active crime scene."

"I've *never* puked on scene," Bree countered evenly, without heat. "It disrespects the victim."

The detective's aggressive expression eased a little when he saw that she meant what she said. He nodded with a degree more friendliness than he'd shown since they arrived and led them to the bedroom at the back of the apartment.

Noah had never puked at a crime scene either, but this time, it was close.

Unlike the Presley murder, The Preacher hadn't been in a rage when he murdered Tala. He'd been thorough in his destruction. Meticulous. Devoted.

The remains had already been autopsied, but the white sheets and cheery yellow comforter where they'd lain were stiff and dark. Noah grimaced. The average body had a capacity of about a gallon and a half of blood. Looking around, anyone would think that the killer'd brought extra along with him.

Preliminary reports labeled cause of death as cut throat. That only accounted for some of the victim's massive blood loss. Ritualistic post-mortem mutilation was responsible for the rest. Along the walls, in tight, neat rows, was handwriting. Filling every available surface, the words began at one end of the room and stretched to the other side along the apartment's beige walls. Dripping crimson letters that formed words and phrases that spelled out the Bible verse that somehow was crystal clear in the suspect's twisted mind.

"How many hours would it take someone to do this?" Beside him, Bree's voice was hushed. Her face was tipped back, eyes almost blank with disbelief as she studied the serpent that had been painted to look like it had slithered up one wall and was moving on to the ceiling. And then there was the cross, dripping blood in zagged lines.

"Days?" Noah had a hard time imagining it.

"Try a couple of hours," Detective Bardo corrected. "Based on the approximate time of death and the time the body was discovered."

He tried to fathom how fast a person had to move to create something of this magnitude within that amount of time. It would take manic, nearly boundless speed.

The Preacher had been killing for decades. He had to be an older man by now, at least in his sixties. How had he managed to overpower an experienced police officer in her own home, maneuver her unresisting, dead-weight body into the bed, secure her so that she wouldn't escape, kill her, and then do *this*?

A young man would have a hard time accomplishing it all. The Preacher was either extremely spry for his age—or possessed.

"I've just started looking into some of these Preacher cases since you all called with the ViCAP flag," Detective Bardo said. He ignored the screed on the wall, facing Noah squarely. Either he'd seen enough of the crime scene, or he couldn't take seeing it anymore. "I haven't gotten far. Is this type of thing normal for the sick fucker?"

Bree responded, tearing her gaze away from the serpent. Consciously or not, she turned her back to it as she replied to Detective Bardo.

"We know a pitiful little more than you do at this point. Even though The Preacher killings fueled a long-running investigation, we don't have a lot on him."

Senbk woiev kw ksklwe asowek, Noah read silently. *WWINEN KSJF FIWNEF!*

The jumble of letters felt sinister, especially below the more clearly written Bible verse. Was it Satanic? They'd email high-def pictures to Agent Goldsboro, Richmond's top resident code cracker, in case it could be deciphered, but instinct told him the meaning was something murky and ominous, clear only to the suspect.

"There's always a Bible verse left behind, written in the victim's blood," Noah put in as he scanned the ranting, indecipherable messages. "There have also been jumbled letters before. Usually a word or phrase in whatever...language this is. Sometimes as much as a sentence but nothing like this."

They spent the rest of the afternoon closeted with the task force Officer Delosreyes's precinct had put together. He studied so many glossy, detailed photos of the victim that they began to blur together in his mind. Naked, tanned limbs splayed. Cuts and slices made with careful precision. Sightless eyes, and long, black hair.

Noah shook off the fatigue that dogged at him long enough to reach for several of the full-body shots of the victim.

"Her hair," he said hoarsely. Conversation in the room stilled. "How did Officer Delosreyes normally wear her hair?"

One of the officers, a petite redhead with sad hazel eyes, spoke up. "She told me one time in the locker room that it was a pain in the ass to take care of such gorgeous waist-length hair like hers. It's…" She stopped. Cleared her throat and collected herself. "It was so thick. She always said it would kill her mom if she cut it, so she wore it back in a braid about as thick as my wrist." She held up one slim hand, pale and freckled. It visibly trembled.

He had to get out of here. He wasn't normally an intuitive guy—though he did get the occasional hunch—but the press of emotion coming from all sides of the small conference room was making it hard to think. If her strained expression was any indication, Bree felt the same way.

Noah lined the pictures up, facing away from him, toward the other members of the team.

"Does anyone notice anything about the victim's hair in these pictures?"

Detective Bardo immediately saw what Noah was talking about. "Unbelievable. Did anyone else notice this?" He looked around the table, almost accusingly.

Faces in various stages of disbelief looked back at him.

In each photo, despite the gory chaos of the body, the victim's hair was carefully arranged. Loose and black and flowing over the pillows, like it belonged to a fairy tale princess instead of a mangled figure that could have doubled as a horror movie prop.

"Has he done this before? Targeted women with black hair? Or avoided women with short styles?"

"Not that I can tell," Noah admitted. "Not specifically. I haven't noted a trend in his past victims, and our profile of him from the BAU isn't as filled out as I'd like. But this is too careful not to have been significant."

That's what worried him.

"How far back have you gotten with Tala's case files?" Bree asked. "We can help with that."

Before the ViCAP flag had given them the possible identity

of the killer, the team had already gone back six months. They'd looked through arrest records at suspects, interviewing many of them in case the act had been spurred by a need for revenge, but had come up empty. They'd covered an incredible amount of ground in just a few days, but with no success.

Noah and Bree agreed to go over them again, as a fresh pair of eyes, and highlight any older cases that might look like a possibility. They headed back to the hotel, both of them relieved to be out in the cold, chilly night.

"I should have been prepared for this." Bree broke their subdued silence as they pulled up in front of the hotel they'd booked. "I knew it would be intense, but I had no idea it would be this bad."

Noah had to agree.

They ordered a pizza to split and spent the evening holed up in one room with their laptops. Neither one of them caught anything noteworthy that had been missed in the initial run-through. The local LEOs had been understandably thorough.

Bree yawned, and the sound nudged him out of his concentration as he tried to read case notes that blurred in front of his eyes. The digital clock next to one of the two twin beds he occupied read 1:36. He rested his stiff neck against the pastel-patterned wall behind him and closed his eyes. He was tired, his thoughts getting mushy. The whole process felt futile.

A thought occurred to him, and he sat up in a rush, startling Bree.

"Can I help you?" she asked wryly.

"You and I are looking at this the wrong way," Noah said, thinking quickly. "The Preacher isn't new at this. He's avoided capture for so long, he won't be in any of these arrest records. That's not how he targets his victims."

"We don't know *how* he targets his victims," Bree pointed out.

"Maybe not, but we do know he's not going to risk being *arrested*, identified, or fingerprinted to go after a victim he's selected. Let's assume he chooses at random. Tala Delosreyes had long, black hair. You don't have to be a profiler to know he admired it. Look at the care he took with her to keep it from getting messed up."

Bree's eyes glowed, understanding the point he was getting at. "We're looking at the wrong cases. We need to switch our focus to anyone Tala might have encountered during a normal day. She went nowhere but work and home, most nights. That narrows our focus to witnesses or bystanders and subjects of routine traffic stops."

Noah lifted his eyebrows. "Bingo."

They went back to work with renewed energy. In a short amount of time, this case had begun to feel personal to them both. Bree identified with the victim. A friendly loner, a caring daughter, and a hardworking female LEO, serving up badassery daily in a male-dominated field.

It hit much closer for Noah. He wanted to nail the sonofabitch for the victims and their families' closure, and for the future innocent lives he could be saving. That was a given, and the way he approached any case.

What made solving this one so vital was Winter. She and Tala Delosreyes had something in common that made him uncomfortable. Beautiful, long black hair, thick enough to pull back into a braid as thick as a woman's wrist.

9

W inter ended up with the same Uber driver she'd gotten for the drive downtown to Parrish's luxe apartment building. Now, she made attentive noises as the guy chattered on the way back to her place like he'd encountered a long-lost friend. He seemed so young as he talked about a concert he'd been to the night before, naming some artist she'd never heard of.

He was cute, with tousled dark hair and a slightly crooked grin. He had on a Virginia Tech hoodie and played '90s grunge on the radio. He was also about the same age as she was, she realized, feeling jaded, depressed, and three decades older.

Would she have been like this if it hadn't been for The Preacher? Carefree and confident? Worried only about making rent money and not about stopping a long string of brutal killings? The kind of twenty-five-year-old girl who'd never imagine herself in the role of a tragically damaged anime protagonist, existing only to avenge her family?

When the Uber driver—Sameer, he'd said his name was— glanced at her and winked, his eyes a warm, deep shade of brown, she realized with a little shock he'd been flirting with her. She returned the smile with an automatic one of her own, and he grinned before he turned his attention back to the road.

She winced at his enthusiasm. He seemed like a nice guy. It wasn't his fault she wasn't a normal girl.

"You hungry?" he asked. The hope in his voice penetrated her funk as she stared out of the passenger window of the minivan into the night.

"Not really."

"Are you sure?" he asked, keeping the pressure light. He was persistent and didn't seem to notice or care that she wasn't the most cheerful person he'd ever given a lift to. "My uncle has an amazing restaurant near here. They do takeout, and you won't find much else open this late on Christmas. Not asking for a date or trying to drum up business here," he added. "You just look like the kind of person my aunt is always trying to fatten up with her awesome *kabob soltani*."

Maybe a Winter from an alternate timeline would have said yes. But she just smiled and shook her head in a firm negative.

"No problem." Sameer shrugged, seemingly unoffended. "It's called Zooroona, off Staples Mill Road." He handed her a cheap business card. "Call me if you need a ride and somebody to have a meal with."

"I'll stop in sometime," she promised, avoiding the companionship part of the offer as he pulled up in front of her apartment building. "That's not far from where I work."

"Performance Food Service?" he guessed, putting the car in park and half-turning in his seat. He waved off the bill she tried to hand him.

"No," Winter answered. "FBI."

"Sweet." His eyes widened, and he looked boyishly

impressed. "Are you an actual agent, or like an analyst or a janitor or something?"

"Special Agent in the Violent Crimes Division." Winter opened her door and pulled her official ID out of her pocket.

Sameer's eyes went wide, like he was afraid he was about to get busted in some kind of Uber driver flirtation sting.

The FBI badge carried a certain amount of inadvertent intimidation.

She put the ten-dollar bill on the front seat and grinned at him.

"I catch violent offenders for a living. Thanks for proving that there are still nice, normal people in the world, and not all of you random strangers are into murder and mayhem, Sameer. I needed that. And I'll be sure to check out your uncle's kabob."

Winter walked into her apartment feeling better than she had when she'd left, despite it all. She dropped her keys on the kitchen counter and flicked the light on, chasing the shadows into the corners.

But dammit, now kabob was sounding good.

Instead, she changed into a loose sweatshirt and a pair of leggings and heated up a bowl of soup from a can to eat in bed. She wasn't tired—couldn't imagine sleeping—but she needed the warmth. Her visit with Aiden had left her feeling as cold as his arctic blue eyes.

She'd seen the potential in him for Machiavellian manipulation a long time ago, and he'd made it clear when she was hired that he wanted her in his unit from the beginning. It was guilt and her genuine liking for him that made her drop her guard with him. Aiden was recovering from the two gunshot wounds he'd taken on her behalf, and she felt the responsibility for that every day.

The blackmail aspect to Aiden's move wasn't unexpected, but it was still upsetting. There had been something different between them in the past year. It had begun when she'd faced off with him after her first case and slowly intensified as the months went by. A few days before Christmas, she'd stopped by to check on him before heading to her grandparents' house for the holiday. Aiden had been missing some of his characteristic sardonic edge—making him seem almost human for a change. He'd also surprised her with a gift.

She glanced toward her dresser. The stuffed tabby cat in the police officer's uniform he'd given her stared back owlishly. It was the kind of thing he'd have done without thinking when she was fourteen or fifteen. To receive one again after all these years felt significant.

Winter wished she could talk it over with Noah, even though he'd made no secret of the fact that he couldn't stand Aiden. Noah always gave good advice and was an impartial listener. She spooned up chicken broth and sipped, hearing raindrops beginning to spatter against her bedroom window. Noah was holed up in D.C. with Bree somewhere, working on the case.

She felt a pang of regret, thinking of him. Tall, good-looking, caring, and protective. Alternate Timeline Winter would probably adore him. This Winter had done her best to alienate him, forgoing friendship for personal gain.

Was she really any better than Aiden? Noah had never done anything to deserve that. She had the uncomfortable feeling that she was about to irrevocably crush more than a friendship. He'd kissed her a couple of weeks ago, out of anger, but the heat in it had been real.

He had feelings for her. She wasn't sure of hers for him and couldn't—wouldn't—parse them out now. She had more important things to think about than the men in her life. If Noah was the rock, Aiden was the hard place. She'd sort them both out when this was all over.

Besides, the decision she'd all but made would only push

Noah further away and necessitate keeping as much distance between herself and Aiden as possible. She was going to make the transfer.

Before she could second-guess herself, she sent a brief text to Aiden, accepting the terms he'd laid out. He replied after only a minute, telling her to consider it effective immediately. He'd talk to Ramirez and Osbourne and have the transfer in progress by the following day. She was to show up at his office in the Behavioral Analysis Unit in the morning.

Right or wrong, it was done. She couldn't change her course now.

Shaking out her shoulders to try and relieve the tension in them, she decided to put her yoga pants to their intended use. She needed to stay loose and as relaxed as she could, impossible as that sounded.

Winter set her empty bowl on the nightstand and shifted from her cross-legged position to climb off her bed. Her head spun dizzily with the movement, and she stopped for a moment. Like a distant wave coming closer, she heard a rushing sound in her ears.

Then, with a stab of pain that shot from the top of her head to her toes like a lightning strike, she went under again.

Aiden's face. His eyes locked with hers. Such a pale blue they were almost colorless. His lips formed words that she strained to hear. She studied the shape of them, the movement of his mouth, trying to translate.

Trust no one.

Blinking, she was in her room again. There was a splashed dot of red on the back of her hand, and she reached for a tissue from the box at the bedside. Slowly, just in case. Her head, though, was clear. She blotted at her upper lip. The stream of blood was minimal.

She'd never had two episodes in a day. This one wasn't bad, but it left her feeling weak and shaky. Exhaustion dropped over her like a weighted blanket. Leaving the bedside light on, she crawled back under the covers until their warmth soothed her chills.

Aiden's warning wasn't necessary. She didn't trust anyone completely. Especially him.

THE NEXT MORNING, stiff from being curled up all night and grumpy from lack of sleep, Winter left her apartment earlier than usual, coffee in hand. The fog hadn't gone anywhere overnight, despite the showers, and she glanced longingly at her Civic on her way to the bus stop at the entrance of the apartment complex.

Her contemplation of the joys of public transportation was interrupted when a flash of red caught her eye. At five o'clock, it wasn't light yet, but the mailboxes at the end of her block of apartments glowed red like someone had covered them with reflective tape. The closer she walked, the more focused the glow became. When she reached the box, a five-by-five-foot elevated cube, only Apartment 2A's number was illuminated.

She pulled out her keys and opened the box.

Inside was an envelope. It was addressed to Winter Black, and she recognized the blocky scrawl immediately. She didn't worry about pulling on gloves as she opened it, her hands only trembling slightly. The Preacher never left fingerprints.

Two Polaroid snapshots fell into her hand. One was an indoor shot, washed out from the brightness of the camera flash. Her stomach twisted as she recognized what remained of Tala Delosreyes. The body was ravaged, laid open to the bone in some places. She slipped it back into the envelope, trying to control the knee-jerk pain and rage that was almost overwhelming in its intensity.

Winter's only comfort was that Tala had been dead before he'd started cutting into her. Cold comfort, but better than nothing.

The other photo was older. The colors had faded a little, but the identity of the boy in the picture was clear. Justin, her baby brother, sat in the dirt near what looked like an outdated RV. His head was downturned, and there was only the partial view of his face, but what she could see was sad. There was no fear there, only resignation.

He wore clothes that she'd never seen on him. Denim overalls, boots that looked too big for him. A dun-colored, button-down shirt beneath. And he wasn't six in the photo. Her heart thudded in her chest. Here, he looked to be at least eight.

He'd been taken when he was six. Investigators had tried to keep her hopes alive, and those of her grandparents, but she knew they all thought he was dead, abandoned in a shallow grave somewhere. It wasn't until she was an adult that she'd received the first indication that he might not be. That photo, too, had come from The Preacher, but in it, Justin was still wearing the SpongeBob pajamas he'd disappeared in.

If what she thought she was seeing was correct, this photo proved that he'd been kept alive. At least for a couple years after his abduction. Fierce hope gripped her as she slid the envelope and photos into her messenger bag, and she continued down the sidewalk to the bus stop, her steps quick, almost running.

Public transportation or not, Winter had to get to the office. She had work to do.

10

"What do you mean Winter's gone?" Noah demanded. "Where is she?"

He'd come straight to the office after three days in D.C. He was tired, hungry, and badly needed a shower and shave. He wasn't in the mood to deal with Sun Ming's guessing games. Instead of elaborating, she gave him a pointed look and crossed her arms.

He recognized the look. There had been drama in the office when he and Bree had been out. Sun knew the details. Noah didn't.

"Please," he said with exaggerated calm. "Tell me what you know, Sun."

Satisfied, she didn't hold back on the details.

Word had come down from Ramirez that Agent Black was to be immediately transferred to the Behavioral Analysis Unit. After their meeting on Christmas Day, she'd never come back to VC. An intern with a cart had stopped by to clear her desk. No one in VC had seen Winter since.

Sun didn't look terribly sorry about the news. She'd

pitted herself against Winter before. Both women were competitive. Neither would back down.

He couldn't resist poking a hole in Sun's triumphant attitude. "I'm surprised you're not sorry she's gone. Winter one-upped you on the Presley case. I'd figure you'd want to get even, but you won't be able to do it from here."

Noah left her fuming and checked in with Osbourne, who refused to talk about it. Winter's defection was an obvious sore spot. He updated his boss on their progress with the case and headed home to clean up.

His first instinct had been to call her and light her ass up for not even telling him what she was doing. But once he was clean and had demolished a half a box of cereal and three cups of coffee, he realized that cornering her this morning would have been a bad idea.

He'd already said things to her he hadn't meant. In his fatigue, he'd have probably blown it.

Noah settled for texting.

Does your new boss allow lunch breaks?

He wasn't sure if she was ready to talk to him at all, but he didn't have to wait long for a response. He'd missed her.

Getting coffee at 12:30.

It wasn't exactly an invitation, but Winter didn't look surprised to see him when he showed up. She was working on her laptop but closed it when he sat down.

"Secret BAU stuff?" he asked, nodding toward the computer.

She sat back in her seat and folded her arms, watching him coolly. Then he realized that her hair was down. It jolted him how much her hair looked like Tala Delosreyes's. If he closed his eyes, he'd be able to superimpose Winter's face over the victim's ruined body.

"What?" she asked as he stared at her, tucking part of it behind her ear self-consciously.

Noah was about to reply, but the starburst bruise on the side of her face caught his attention. "What the hell happened to you?"

He shoved away from the table, the metal legs of his chair screeching. Ignoring the glances of other customers in the coffee shop, he rounded the table and dropped down to his haunches beside her. Gently, he ran his fingertips over her cheekbone, where purple faded to green and sickly yellow. In the center of the bruise was a small, scabbed cut.

"Sit down, Noah. It's fine. I bumped it the other day." She nudged his hand away impatiently and picked up her mocha.

"It looks like someone wearing a diamond solitaire punched you in the face."

She snorted. "No one punched me."

He studied her as he retook his seat, looking closer this time. She was always pale. He'd seen a kid ask her if she was Snow White one time because her black hair was such a startling contrast with her fair skin. But now, her eyes were tired and shadowed. Her skin looked so translucent, he could see the delicate tracery of veins beneath.

"Is it the case, the transfer, or me? You look like shit, Winter."

She fluttered her thick black lashes sarcastically. "You do know how to flatter a woman, Dalton. You don't think I have a reason to look stressed?"

She didn't try to argue about her rights to the case with him again, for which he was grateful, but he hated this awkwardness between them. Then, something occurred to him. He pushed aside his coffee cup and leaned forward on his elbows, pinning her with a look.

"You've been having migraines. Did you hit your face on something?"

"I'm fine, Noah," she repeated, her cheeks flushing with

color. It wasn't a healthy glow. It was a pissed off one. She didn't want to talk about it.

"Would you tell me if you were having problems?" He'd seen what her episodes could do to her. They were scary.

She laughed, but it was bitter. "Not your circus, Dalton. Not your monkeys."

In other words, butt out. Irritation rose, and his retort came out sharper than he meant. "Of course you wouldn't tell me if your migraines were getting worse. You didn't find time to drop me a phone call or a text, letting me know that you were transferring units. Did SSA Parrish make you an offer you couldn't refuse?"

"This was a mistake." She stood up, slid her laptop into her bag. "I need to get back to work. For all of Aiden's faults, at least he trusts me to be a professional and not let my past get in the way of my present."

"Winter. Don't go."

It was too late. She was moving toward the door. He stood up to follow her and saw the moment her knees buckled. She was halfway through the inside door when she stumbled. A college kid who was holding the outer door for her stepped forward, clearly concerned, but Noah made it to her side in time to steady her. Under his hand, her bones felt birdlike. She was thin, but up close like this, he could see she'd gotten thinner.

Winter's face was leached of color again. "Get me out of here. Please." The whisper didn't carry far, but he heard it.

He thanked the kid holding the door for them and hurried Winter out to where he'd parked his truck.

She held on until he lifted her bodily into the passenger's seat. By the time he'd rounded the truck to climb in the driver's side, she'd gone blank. This time seemed worse. Her eyes were half-open, rolled back in her head so that only the whites showed. Every muscle in her body seemed seized up when he tried to take her hand.

A constant trembling vibration ran through her body. He opened the glove box and took out a handful of fast-food napkins to hold against the blood that streamed from her nose.

He was terrified.

It seemed to go on and on. Before, Winter's outages had only lasted a few seconds, leaving her shaky, but fine. She'd usually have a little bit of warning. This was different. It struck with little notice, completely debilitating her. The seconds stretched out into a minute. Then, two. He monitored her heart rate, made sure she was breathing and didn't swallow her tongue.

At two and a half minutes, Noah was reaching for his phone to call for an ambulance when Winter came out of it. She gave a last hard shudder before her breathing started to even out and her eyes cleared. "That was something," she said, breathless.

"You can't drive anymore."

Noah was so worried about her he felt sick. She saw it, and closed her eyes again, leaning back against the headrest.

"I'm not. Public transportation."

"I have a truck," he stated flatly. "I live four doors down from you, and I work in the same building. Don't take the bus."

"We're not exactly copacetic enough to be carpooling right now, Dalton."

"Take a drink of this." Noah popped the top on a can of Mountain Dew. "Maybe the sugar and caffeine will help."

She took a sip. Made a face. "It tastes like battery acid."

"Have you seen a doctor yet?"

"No." Her eyes locked steady on his. "No doctors."

"Dammit all to hell, Winter," Noah exploded. He slammed

a fist down on the dashboard. "You can't keep this up. You brag about being this professional agent who can handle her shit? You can't even handle your own health issues. Max was right. You are a liability."

"I told you," she replied, her voice going cold. "Not your circus." She reached for the door handle, and Noah hit the lock button. She slowly turned her head until she was facing him again. "Open the door." Her voice was like ice now.

"Talk to me."

"No."

He was handling her wrong. She wasn't going to give, and he was too fucking tired and frustrated to get through to her right now. "Fine, Wonder Woman. Handle your shit all by yourself."

Winter left, and Noah dropped his head to the steering wheel. He sat in his truck for almost twenty minutes, fighting the urge to chase her down. To shake sense into her. To explain to her *why* he was so worried. He cared about her— too much—and the fragile connection they'd made was on the rocks.

After another twenty minutes of debating with himself, he came to a decision that could backfire on him and wreck things with Winter for good. He'd weighed it out, though, and had to take the risk.

Noah picked up his phone and pulled up Google.

WALKING BACK TO THE OFFICE, the chilly air was bracing, but her legs felt like lead. Winter was glad Noah hadn't tried to follow her. She had too much on her mind. She was trying not to focus on the fact that this recent vision had happened less than twelve hours after the last one. The episodes were getting closer together, striking with less warning. They were also becoming more intense.

She couldn't worry about that, either, right now.

She had to figure out if what she'd seen during her blackout was a vision of the past or the future. Either Winter had just had a flashback to when she was a thirteen-year-old girl, the same age she'd been when her parents were killed and her brother taken, or she'd been in the head of another of The Preacher's victims.

The vision was vivid, like all the rest had been. She'd been gossiping with a group of girls she was walking home from school with. Winter—or the victim—was looking down at the pavement as she walked. She hadn't seen any of the other girls' faces so she couldn't tell if they were people she'd known in real life.

She'd physically felt like a teenager again. It had been a weird feeling. She had been shorter, her limbs lithe and missing the strength that she'd gained as an adult through regular training. If it was a flashback, it was a detailed one. She'd felt the fitful wind that grabbed at her unbraided hair. The faint warmth of the sun that didn't do much to penetrate the mostly cloudy sky. One canvas Converse sneaker rubbed against a blister that was forming on the back of her right heel.

Behind her, a voice called out. "Hey, girlie. I've been looking all over for you."

The tone was friendly, but the smooth Southern drawl made the hair on her arms rise. As she—the girl in the vision —had turned, Winter's connection with the vision broke loose, and she'd come back to awareness in the front seat of Noah's truck.

She quickened her steps. The chances of this being a flashback were unlikely. She'd never had one before. Besides, this experience was more like when she'd gotten into the head of The Preacher's last victim. It was scary, intrusive, and fascinating. If it wasn't a memory—Winter herself as a child —did it mean that The Preacher was about to target a teenage girl?

She picked up the pace, hitching her bag higher on her shoulder. Her body felt drained, and her head throbbed vaguely. It had seemed like a good idea to walk at noon. She'd wanted to get away from her desk. The mostly friendly scrutiny of everyone on Aiden's team. The sharp eye of Aiden himself.

Now, she just wished she'd stayed at her desk.

11

She was a hard worker.

The woman had been bent over her desk for the last hour as she scribbled on a notepad next to her and tapped at the fancy little computer on her ugly desk. Her office was prissy, decorated in some kind of modern style, with lots of glass and chrome. It had proven to be kind of tricky to get to since she lived in a gated community, but I poked around in the woods a bit and found a broken-down piece of fence. There was a little clearing close by where local rich kids probably came to drink alcohol and fornicate around a devil-worshipping bonfire.

The thought bothered me more than it usually did. There weren't enough people like me, tasked with punishing sinners. Not that I was arguing with God or anything.

I hitched up my coveralls and didn't bother to tinker with the air conditioning unit by the window. I didn't need my regular disguise. No neighbors were going to see me. The woman's office was at the back of her house. Plus, the swanky, rich-folk neighborhood had been carved out of some woods. You couldn't see through the trees from one big, expensive house to the next.

I watched as she took a slug from a bottle of water next to her computer. She wasn't very pretty. Her brown hair was cut boyish short and dyed an unnatural purple color. She looked like a lesbian, but she had a husband. Go figure. The husband had left the house earlier in the day, probably to go bang a real woman and not one trying to ape his fellow menfolk. Unless the "husband" was one of them wrist-wavers that married women just to cover up their sinner ways.

I thought about that for a bit and got heated up mad about it. Men were superior to women, and it was ordained for them to be able to do whatever they wanted to do. But some men didn't handle their women right, raising their wives and daughters to be a holy credit to their gender. That's why He picked out folks to take up the calling of punishing those who deserved it. God had chosen others to take care of the prissy boys of the world. I'd focus on the girls. That's where my calling was.

Still. I felt like maybe this husband deserved to be punished too. I'd never thought like this in all my years, and I wondered if it was because of my age. With age came wisdom. Maybe I'd been thinking about it wrong all my life. The thought was disturbing.

Images of what I could do to a man to punish him took hold of me, and I sat down next to the house and hunkered up beside a bush to think of it for a spell. My knees crackled and popped, but I ignored them. Maybe I'd wait for him to come home and punish him too. But I'd never punished a man before.

A little uncomfortably, I wondered if it would make me a sinner. To do the things I did to the girls on a man seemed a little unnatural. I had to ponder the thought for a while before I decided since the husband wasn't home, I wouldn't have to worry about him now. Maybe the next time, I'd decide.

A fat raindrop hit my nose, and when I looked up, it was dark. Like somebody had speeded up a movie from daytime to nighttime. I'd been daydreaming again. Gathering wool, as my grandpa used to say. Shaking the cobwebs out of my head, I stifled a groan, trying to straighten up my legs. I was all bent-up from sitting the same way for too long.

Rheumatism. I didn't know if it ran in the family since my ma and pa were dead long before they got old like me, but my doctor said I had it for sure. My knuckles were still all knotted up from all my holy writing I'd done at Winter's house a few nights ago. I hoped the Lord wouldn't ask me to do so much of it tonight.

Stretching up on my toes, I looked in the window again and saw the girl still hunkered over her computer. The things some women's husbands let them get away with was downright disgusting. The woman should have been dressed in soft, pretty colors. Feminine, like God made her. This one was dressed all in black. A bulky sweater hung off her like a potato sack, covering up her breasts so a man couldn't get a good look at what she was selling, which would have been a virtue if the covering had been more attractive.

The way she was letting herself go to fat was shameful too. She dropped a pen, and when she bent over to grab it, I could see that her ass was wide under the tight black pants she wore.

All black, like for a funeral. I shook my head in disapproval. She sure needed punishment, but I wasn't ashamed to say that I liked the prettier ones. Lessons were fun to teach when the sinning harlots you were teaching to were pretty.

This one's fate had been sealed when she'd glanced over at me from the counter where she was paying for fuel for her big Mercedes SUV in Roanoke. A man's car, I thought in disgust. But in that quick second, before she looked away, went back to what she was doing without even registering me, I'd seen her eyes.

They were my girlie's eyes.

Framed with black lashes, they were deep, quiet blue like the Smoky Mountains from a distance. It didn't matter what the rest of her looked like. She'd be my next. It was a sign. She had Winter's eyes, and that was enough to tell me that God wanted me to punish her. Because, the more I thought on the matter, Winter deserved to be punished more than any other female I'd ever culled before.

Maybe when I finally got around to her, she'd be my last project. I'd have to make it perfect. I went woolgathering again, just imagining it.

Time skipped again on me, and then it was late at night. I wondered how long I'd been standing still. If anyone were driving by, they'd have seen me and probably thought I was a fancy statue in the fancy yard. Chuckling at that notion, I grabbed up my bag of tools, heading for the sliding door to the dining room.

It was time to get to work. It'd be practice, for when I finally punished my girlie.

NOAH SPENT the next day feeling like something was missing. Something essential, like his first cup of coffee. Or breakfast. He had an empty spot in his day where Winter should have been.

He'd done his best to pay attention while he met with Bree to divide up witnesses for follow-up. She'd known what his problem was, though. Around lunch, she'd finally broached the subject.

"Are you going out for coffee again?" Bree made the question sound casual, but the look she gave him was pointed.

"What? No." Noah shook his head and looked back down at his computer.

"Are you sure? I saw Winter heading out. She had a bike helmet on and her laptop case. I just wondered if the two of you were meeting for coffee again."

He didn't want to talk about Winter, but he didn't want to offend Bree, either. It wasn't her fault he'd been an asshole and was on the outs with his best friend. He forced a smile and winked, for her benefit. "Maybe I was hoping to take my partner out to lunch."

She leaned back in the chair and crossed her arms. "Nice try. As if you didn't know my fiancée was coming to pick me up. I told you Shelby was swinging by around noon when you came in this morning."

Rather than admit he hadn't been paying attention when she'd mentioned it, Noah changed the subject. "Have you talked to Detective Bardo about the speeding ticket I flagged in the files? Happened about three days before the murder?"

Bree shuffled through the print copies of the incident reports in front of her, looking for the one he was referring to. Behind her, a tall, dark-skinned woman appeared in the doorway of the conference room. Shelby was the yin to Bree's yang, he could tell right away. Where Bree was curved, Shelby was sleek. Bree's skin was light brown. Shelby's was dark as night. Bree dressed for work in whatever happened to be closest when she opened her closet. Shelby looked like she modeled for Gucci in her spare time.

Shelby smiled at Noah and held a finger to her lips.

"I think it might have slipped out of the stack," he told Bree helpfully. "Did you check under the table?"

Bree rolled her chair back with a clatter, almost running over Shelby's toes. "Are you sure?" she asked, her voice muffled as Shelby silently pulled out a chair and slipped into it, at the head of the table. "There's a paper by your foot. Is that it?"

Noah leaned down and grabbed the paper. "Must've been mistaken," he said with a grin.

Bree sat up. When she saw Shelby, she let out a startled laugh.

"Ready for lunch?"

"You scared the shit out of me." Bree waved a hand in front of her face, like she was having palpitations. But her eyes lit with a warm glow as she scolded Shelby. "You know I hate it when you sneak up on me like that. You're like a fricking cat, even in heels."

Shelby glanced at Noah and gave him a sly wink. "She doesn't hate it that much."

"You want to come along, Dalton?"

Bree stood, straightening up her work area. He'd discovered she was a little OCD. His own spot at the table was covered with Danish crumbs and coffee rings, plus enough sticky notes to make a full pad of them.

"I'm good. Thanks for the invite, though."

He waved them out, glad of the chance to be alone for a while. Noah liked Bree, but his head was feeling cluttered and having other people around didn't help. He also couldn't focus on the case like he should be until he shoveled out some of that clutter.

Noah flipped a page in his notebook to get to the list he'd started. He had several lists in his notebook, but if this one needed a title, it would be "Worries about Winter." On the top was her visions. It was easier to call them migraines, but he had to stop dancing around the issue. The visions were a part of her.

She'd had them since she was a kid, she told him once, after she'd come out of her coma post-Preacher. She'd also lived in Harrisonburg at the time, and had stayed for a few months after the murders, with her grandparents in a rental house in the same town.

He pulled up Google Maps. There weren't a lot of doctors in or nearby a small town like that that would deal with brain function post head trauma, and he had an idea on how to get more background on Winter's exact injury. The trick would be finding the doctor or psychologist her grandparents had taken her to.

He didn't expect to find many, and there weren't. But when he expanded his search area, wondering if Winter's grandparents had taken her to a big-city specialist, the number became hard to manage. He deliberated for a good ten minutes, but finally decided the best way to do this was by calling Beth McAuliffe himself.

"Dr. Robert Ladwig," Beth told him after getting over her surprise at his call. "He's the psychologist we took Winter to."

"I'll let my sister know." Noah would have felt just as miserable lying to his own grandma in that moment, but he'd needed a valid-sounding reason to call that wouldn't provoke any probing questions. An imaginary niece had been his excuse. "I meant to ask you at Christmas and forgot. Thank you, by the way, for the invite. I'm sorry we had to leave so soon."

"Oh, that's okay. We'll be sure to invite you back for Easter," Beth promised. "Do you like ham as much as you like meatloaf?"

Noah laughed. It was no secret that he'd steal Beth away from Grampa Jack for her meatloaf alone. "I'd eat chocolate-covered shoe leather if it came out of your kitchen, ma'am."

Her delighted laugh lasted a few seconds. "Tell Winter to call me, will you, Noah. Why didn't you just ask her about her doctor? I thought you'd be working the case that brought you back to town. Were you assigned to a different one?"

Winter hadn't told her grandma that she'd transferred departments.

"No," he answered truthfully. "We weren't assigned together this time."

"That's too bad," Beth replied, her tone a little coy. "I know Winter enjoys spending time with you."

He wrapped up the conversation quickly after that. Gramma Beth was getting ideas about them. It wasn't that he had a problem with it. It was the guilt he felt over the current state of their friendship, and the fact that he'd just told Beth a bald-faced lie to get information Winter wouldn't want him to have.

Wouldn't do any good to grapple with his conscience right now.

Noah looked Ladwig up on Facebook and LinkedIn. The guy was younger than he'd imagined. Good-looking, with dark hair and intelligent gray eyes but probably no older than his mid-forties. He got great reviews from patients, which struck Noah as odd since Winter made it clear she hadn't liked him.

Ladwig's office was in the greater Richmond area, which would make things easier. The Preacher case would be taking up the majority of his time, but the doctor's office was in Lakeside, which wasn't far from the FBI offices. He could make time to see the guy, find out what he could indirectly about Winter's condition.

He called and spoke with a receptionist. Giving his name as Brady Lomond, he explained his cover story. He told her he'd experienced a concussion in his teen years, playing football. He was recommended to Dr. Ladwig after he'd begun experiencing some strange symptoms recently, including odd dreams that seemed to come true.

The woman took his number and said she'd give it to the scheduler, her tone carefully neutral. But less than five minutes later, when his phone rang, it was the doctor himself calling. Noah hung up after the brief, oddly intense conversation with an appointment in Ladwig's office for the following day.

He was looking forward to it. Not only because he might get some answers about Winter, but because something about Dr. Ladwig was making his own intuition stand up and take notice.

12

"Thanks for meeting with me."

"No problem, *boss*." Winter's tone was sharp with annoyance. The implication that she'd had no choice in the matter was clear.

Aiden acknowledged her inference with a small smile.

"I hope you've been settling in all right. I decided to give you a day or two to acclimate."

"I didn't need them," Winter replied flatly, leaning back in the leather chair across from his desk. "I'm not here to win friends and influence people."

He kept a close eye on the happenings in his own department, and he'd heard murmurs about Winter already. Mostly curious ones, wondering for the reasons behind her transfer and why she hadn't been assigned to any teams yet. Others were already steering wide of her. Her keep-away attitude had a few people convinced she was a bitch.

"Can I assume you've called me in here to finally hold up your end of the bargain?"

Aiden slid a thumb drive across his desk. "Here's all of the information we have. Victims. Profile. Extra things I've added on over the years. Familiarize yourself with it, but that information doesn't leave this office."

"Why?" Her eyes were clear and direct on his. They were also suspicious.

"Because. I told you that you could work on this case, but I want to stay apprised of any moves you plan to make. You garnered the reputation of somewhat of a loose cannon in the VCU."

"Will you just stop?" Winter grabbed the thumb drive and shoved it in the breast pocket of her blazer. "You may have gotten me here, but you're my boss in name only. Don't pull this bullshit condescending front, acting like I'm some new hire off the street."

She pushed to her feet, laying her hands on his desk and leaning forward until they were eye level. "I'm still Winter. I'm the messed-up kid you've been looking out for since she was barely a teenager. I thought that I was also your friend. What I never intended to be was a member of your staff. I'm here because you blackmailed me into it. I never promised to play by your rules."

Winter turned and left. He'd expected her to slam his office door until the mini blinds rattled, but she'd just closed the door with an ominous click.

He spun his chair around and looked out his office window at the wet, gray parking lot outside. Only when his back was to the door, did he let himself smile. She wasn't a kid anymore, that was for sure. Winter wasn't even the same person she'd been twelve months ago. Everything she'd gone through—the trouble in college that had brought her back on to his radar, the cases she'd seen so far as an agent—it had all been steadily whittling away at who exactly Winter was.

She was developing some very interesting sharp edges.

Aiden's smile fell away.

She could struggle all she wanted. Those new sharp edges wouldn't cut her out of the net she was wrapped in now.

WINTER LEFT AIDEN'S OFFICE, ignoring curious looks from other members of the unit. She didn't know anyone's names. She wouldn't be here long enough to learn anyone's name. The thumb drive in her pocket felt like it was burning a hole in her shirt as she walked briskly past her own desk and out of the office.

Instead of heading for the elevator or the restrooms, she turned right. She knew a guy in computer forensics, and she needed some help.

Doug Jepson sat at his computer looking like a linebacker pretending to be a computer nerd. He was tall, dark, and built like a brick house, with shoulders so wide he probably had to turn sideways to get through doorways. He looked like Terry Cruz. He also wore thick glasses and spoke softly around women, blushing pretty much constantly.

Noah had told her not long ago that Doug had a crush on her. Winter hoped not. He was cute and sweet, but she already had enough men in her life.

She knocked on the top of the short divider that separated his cubby from an empty one. "Hey, hero."

He looked up and moved his chair too fast to face her, almost knocking over a half-empty bottle of Coke on his desk. "Winter. How's it going? I meant to thank you."

"For what?" She grinned at him. "You're the guy whose skill saved our asses last month with the Presley heists. I'm not here about that, though. I have a tech question."

He took off his glasses and set them on his desk. "Thank you for talking to my boss. I got a raise out of it, so I owe you. But whatever it is that you need help with," he went on, grinning, "did you try turning it off and back on first?"

"IT humor. Nice."

She sat down on the edge of the desk beside him and pulled out the thumb drive, glad that the other cubby was currently empty. "No, I have a different kind of question." Setting the drive down beside Doug's keyboard, she lowered her voice. "I'm not supposed to let this leave here. Is there a discreet way that I might be able to liberate the information on it so that I can follow a direct order from SSA Parrish to not let that drive leave this building?"

His eyes widened as he looked up in surprise. "Um…"

"Just a yes or no nod will do." She kept her tone low and friendly, conscious of any possibility of being overheard. Inside, she was worried that she'd overstepped, and Doug would go to Aiden.

Doug looked at her silently for a moment, his expression wavering between disappointment and resignation. He gave a brief nod. A few minutes later, the info had been copied through a cloaked program and Doug was handing her back two USB drives.

"Thanks a lot." The words were breezy, but the look she gave him was grateful.

"No problem. Just don't make a habit of it."

He didn't smile at her again, just put his glasses on and turned back to his screen, a deliberate cut. Obviously, Doug had read into the fact that she wasn't asking him for a favor as a friend. She was out to get something, and she didn't mind using him to do it.

She didn't blame him for the cold shoulder. Whether or not it made her feel shitty, that was exactly what she'd just done. Used him.

As she headed back to the BAU offices, she hoped that she hadn't just squashed a possible friendship. Finding The

Preacher first, though, was the most important thing. Every-thing—*everything*—else had to take second priority. If she had to take advantage of any relationships she'd made along the way, so be it. Relationships were fleeting.

Winter stared straight ahead on her way back to her desk, ignoring the look from Aiden she intercepted on her way. He was watching from his office. She didn't react to the scrutiny, even though her palms were sweaty. She rolled her chair in front of her computer, moving quickly. Knowing that he could likely access her computer at any time, she pulled the original thumb drive out of her pocket and put it in the USB port.

She spent the next twenty minutes skimming over the information on the file. Then, she went over and read again, deeper. Keeping in mind everything she knew about the killer. Creating a fuller picture. Aiden, Noah, the murmurs of other unit members, everything else was forgotten as she lost herself creating the most complete outline of The Preacher to date.

The FBI profile was sketchy, as she'd been told to expect, but there was enough there to solidify some of the empty spaces in the shadowy figure of The Preacher. He was esti-mated to have begun his killings sometime in 1970, a man who killed without conscience, or apparent rhyme or reason.

It was a shock to realize that he'd been working—targeting and killing—since the days of Charles Manson, John Wayne Gacy, the Zodiac Killer, Son of Sam, The Hill-side Strangler, Jim Jones. The 1970s were a scary decade to be alive.

Ted Bundy was apprehended in 1975 and later escaped to kill again. He managed to murder somewhere between thirty-six and a hundred women before he was caught. The Preacher's body count was unknown. Sixty-four victims had been attributed to him in the last five decades. Fifty-eight more unsolved murders were listed as possibly linked.

And while Bundy was sitting in his electric chair in 1989, The Preacher was continuing to kill. Undetected by police because his methods were so varied and his victims so disparate, no one had even thought to attribute them to one man.

Until the Black family.

A feeling of unreality came over her as she read the file. In cold, analytical language, her family tragedy had been parsed into reports, statistics, and theories. One document, a single-spaced, two-page list of known or suspected victims, hadn't been updated since its creation in 2007. The four entries at the bottom of the last page caught her attention.

Bill Black, male, aged 44. Deceased. Cause of death, cranial trauma from medium-velocity GSW.

Jeanette Black, female, aged 42. Deceased. Cause of death, homicidal cut throat.

Justin Black, male, aged 6. Missing. Condition unknown.

Winter Black, female, aged 13. Blunt force cranial trauma. Currently hospitalized, with score of seven on Glascow Coma Scale (GCS) at last update. Prognosis unknown.

It was jarring to see everything laid out in sterile terms. Medical terms. Emotionally unattached. The brief descriptions on paper were far from adequate when it came to the bloody, terrifying scene she witnessed and experienced.

She didn't remember the coma—it was just a blank spot, even years later—but she remembered being grateful that night when pain exploded behind her head and dragged her into blackness. She hadn't wanted to deal with the awful reality of what she'd seen, and at thirteen, had wanted to die beside her family. In that quick second, she'd assumed her brother was dead too. That the killer would have dispatched him first, so he could focus on the grisly project ahead.

Living was unthinkable in that moment, and she'd been grateful to the killer for not sparing her.

But she hadn't died. And, it seemed, neither had her brother. If he was still alive, she had to find him. To do that, she'd have to catch The Preacher.

Winter took a deep breath and shook herself loose from the grip of the past. The office was silent, and she glanced at her watch. It was already after eight. She stood cautiously, muscles protesting her hours of focused stillness.

Aiden was still in his office. She felt his eyes on her before she looked up and saw him watching her. Even from a distance, his cold blue stare was intent on her. She stifled an instinctive shudder.

Trust no one.

Oh, she wouldn't.

She pulled out the thumb drive he'd given her and left her cubicle, winding her way through the office to his. Aiden's door was open, paperwork spread out on his desk.

"Did you stay late for me?"

"No." His tone was flat, unconcerned, but he was lying.

She reached out and set the drive on his desk. "I feel like maybe you were waiting around to make sure I returned this."

Aiden made no move to pick it up. "Any insights yet?"

Plenty. None that she was going to share with him, though.

"I'm still processing. Heading home to get some sleep."

"Do you need a ride? It's cold, and I noticed you've been biking."

She gave him a tight smile. "No. I can take care of myself, thanks."

"I never doubted it," she heard him murmur as she turned to leave.

She grabbed her jacket and headed out. The halls were

quiet, and there was no one at the elevator. Winter's nerves were strung tense as violin strings, and she was glad Aiden hadn't followed her out. She had a lot to process—she hadn't lied about that—and would have rather taken the stairs than subject herself to the uncomfortable ride in the elevator with him.

She strapped on the helmet she'd left dangling from the handlebars of her ten-speed, trying to ignore the fact that she felt like a kid grounded from driving. Pedaling home, though, her muscles loosening and warming with the exertion, she felt better. Winter hadn't been running regularly lately, and she thought best when she dealt with stress through physical activity.

The burn in her underused muscles faded into the background as her brain focused on puzzles, profiles, and next steps. Everything in her wanted to talk things over with Noah. He'd gotten closer to her than anyone had managed to in a long time. Closer, even, than Aiden had ever gotten. But he'd made his position clear. He wanted her out of the case, and far away. He wouldn't share information.

So, distance. She could accept that.

But she had to know what they'd uncovered in D.C. Not just reports, but firsthand information—everything he knew about the Delosreyes murder. He wouldn't share it, and the realization was a bitter one. He didn't know her as well as she'd thought he did.

Her heart jumped in her chest, bringing her surroundings into focus as she veered right to avoid a braking car. She pedaled hard, focusing on getting through the busy intersection ahead. Winter had forgotten how much drivers sucked when it came to coexisting with bicyclists, and a slip in her vigilance could easily land her useless and in traction in a hospital room somewhere.

She'd call Bree, she decided, after she navigated the traffic junction and settled into a fairly level straight away. Noah wouldn't budge on this, but she might be able to talk Bree around into feeding her information.

Winter ignored the pang in her conscience. She was going to do this by any means necessary, she reminded herself, and trust no one in the process.

13

Noah parked his truck in front of a building in Richmond that looked more like a credit union than a doctor's office. Neat beige brick, with a sign out front that read "Connections Psychology and Counseling."

It looked no different from any other doc's office, but that didn't keep him from having an uneasy feeling about the whole thing. He turned off the ignition. He could be just nervous about prying into Winter's past without her knowledge or permission. But that didn't feel right. There had been something about the doctor's voice when he'd called Noah back that had rung a distant warning.

But he had an appointment at nine, and there was no time now to question his plan.

The inside of the office was decorated in soothing pale greens and earth tones, with lots of plants and soft music. It was an environment that invited patients to relax, even though the lobby chairs were empty of any other patients. Even the receptionist was calming, a middle-aged, motherly woman with soft brown eyes and a quiet voice.

"Mr. Lomond," she said, smiling up at him from behind

the counter. "Welcome. I have a few forms for you to fill out while you wait for Dr. Ladwig."

"Thanks, ma'am." He smiled back, forcing himself to get into character. He was Brady Lomond. Former football player. Good guy, not real bright. Having brain issues possibly caused by a concussion as a teenager. "It was good of the doctor to see me so quick."

Noah took the clipboard she handed him and sat down beside a quietly gurgling fish tank. An angelfish eyed him obliquely as he looked down at the paperwork. This would be interesting. He winged it, creating a fake medical history, fabricating personal background and insurance information as he went. He'd barely made it through the first page before the door from the offices to the lobby opened.

"Mr. Lomond?"

A tall, thin man in his mid-forties stepped into the seating area. He looked like a doctor should, with a white lab coat over a muted plaid shirt and plain tie, khaki pants, and polished, expensive loafers. He had a reassuring, friendly face and close-cropped brown hair, flecked with gray at the temples. His eyes were hazel, muted behind discreet tortoise-shell glasses, but the intensity of his stare caught Noah off guard.

The impression faded as Dr. Ladwig smiled, showing a slightly crooked front tooth and a deep dimple at one side of his mouth. "Come on back." His voice was even and professional. "I've been looking forward to meeting you since we spoke on the phone."

"If I can just get your insurance card—" the receptionist began.

"Later, Sue."

The receptionist blushed and subsided, giving Noah a curious look. "Sure. I'll just catch you on your way out."

The doctor led him to an office at the back of the building. Noah had never been to a counselor, so he wasn't sure what to expect, but the room pretty much fit what he would have imagined. Dark colors, shaded windows, low lamps. He could have been in a wealthy guy's home office instead of a modern doctor's clinic. Walnut bookshelves lined the walls, with texts on psychology and brain function tucked next to thrillers by popular authors like James Patterson and Clive Cussler.

There was a desk and a computer, but they were off to one side of the room. The focal point was a conversational grouping of cozy-looking chairs. And the stereotypical therapist's couch, of course. It wasn't an old-fashioned chaise, but a big, squashy-looking leather piece. The perfect football watching couch, Noah thought.

"Have a seat," Ladwig invited.

The couch was as comfortable as it looked, sinking and giving beneath his weight. Everything in the room, the doctor included, was designed to put a patient at ease and have him spill his deepest secrets. Brady Lomond would be no exception, but Noah Dalton had to keep his head clear.

Ladwig settled in the chair across from him, leaning forward with what looked like repressed excitement, his elbows on his knees.

"So, tell me about yourself, Brady. Do you mind if I call you Brady? You said on the phone that you're experiencing some unique occurrences?"

"Yes, sir," Noah said, his voice bashful and hesitant. "Sounds a little weird when I tell it out loud, though."

"Trust me." Ladwig laughed easily, the sound warm and confiding. "Nothing you could tell me would be anything I haven't heard before in my line of work."

"Well, when I was a kid, I used to play football."

"Good," Ladwig encouraged. "I could see that. You have

the build of a football player. I knew you were a former football player right off."

Actually, Noah had never played. He'd been too busy helping out on his grandparents' ranch. The doc was like a carnival fortune teller, "predicting" things you already knew. But Noah smiled back at the doctor, aiming for a pleased and proud expression at the doctor's "insight."

"Took my team to the division finals my senior year." Noah grinned through his lies before taking on a sober expression. "That last game, I took a hard hit. A defensive lineman collided with me, and that's the last thing I remember. Lights out. After that, boom. I woke up in the hospital three months later."

Ladwig's eyes sharpened, though his professional facade didn't slip. "Wow, that's some story. What kind of cranial trauma did you suffer? What was your exact diagnosis?"

Noah shrugged, remembering that Brady Lomond wasn't a bright guy. "I dunno. A hard knock to the head? All's I remember is they were glad I came out of the coma. I'd gotten all skinny and stuff. Atrophy or something like that."

Ladwig nodded with a tinge of impatience. "How about other symptoms? Any funny things you noticed right away?"

Noah pretended to think. "Besides being all scrawny? Well, noises were real loud and everything looked extra bright. I had a lot of headaches."

"What about the 'weird' stuff?" Ladwig used air quotes. He was literally on the edge of his seat, waiting for Noah to answer. Noah thought about what Winter had told him.

"It was nothing I could put my finger on at first," Noah cautioned. Ladwig nodded, silently urging him along. "I could see *better*, if that makes any sense. Lots of little things, details, I started noticing."

"Good! That's the kind of thing I'd like to hear about."

I bet you would, Noah thought. The man was way too

excited about the whole conversation. It was creepy. This must've been why Winter hadn't liked him. He was too…something.

"You ever heard of things like that before with people that came out of comas?"

"Oh, yes," Ladwig enthused. "Though not many. Not that you're unusual." Ladwig's laugh rang false. "As a matter of fact, I had one patient who came out of a coma the same length as yours with many unusual symptoms."

"Like what?" Noah didn't have to feign curiosity.

Ladwig answered carefully, aiming for a balance between putting "Brady" at ease and not giving suggestions.

"This patient received a blow to the head that knocked her out for three months. When she came around, she noticed her observational skills were enhanced. She took in more than the rest of the world, when it came to looking at things. Smells, colors, textures, tiny details…it was overwhelming at first, but really an amazing gift. With my help," he added, a little smug, "the patient was able to filter out some of the new, visual 'noise' she was taking in, allowing her to use her gift properly."

"And your patient," Noah asked. "Did she have any other weird symptoms? Like, kind of…visions, maybe?"

"Is that what you're experiencing?" Ladwig leaned over even farther, putting himself in immediate danger of falling off his chair.

"Maybe." Noah kept his voice vague, inviting further confidences from the doctor. "Like, sometimes a dream or something will just come out of nowhere. Even during the day."

"Do you get sharp headaches?" Ladwig produced a notepad and an expensive-looking pen. "Nosebleeds?"

"Is that what your other patient had?" Noah knew from Winter herself that her visions hadn't started until college.

This doctor had stopped treating her years before. Why did he know about the headaches and nosebleeds?

Ladwig nodded, distracted, still looking down at his notepad. Noah could see the top of his head, where the doctor's hair was beginning to thin at the crown.

"Oh, yes. She sometimes feels completely debilitated. Her visions are very powerful."

His vague sense of unease with the doctor intensified. There was no way the guy could—or should—know about Winter's visions.

"You mean *were* very powerful?"

Ladwig's pen stopped moving. He looked up at Noah for a moment, his face curiously blank. "I'm sorry," he replied after a quick moment. "What did I say?"

The guy was weird. Noah pasted on his aw-shucks "Brady" smile.

"You were sayin' something about the patient you had a long time ago?"

Ladwig's face cleared, his professional mask sliding back into place with an almost audible click. "Yes. She had visions."

"What caused 'em, doc?"

It was Noah's turn to falter. He wondered if he'd laid on the hayseed accent a little too thick when the doctor cocked his head, studying him intently.

"Unfortunately, I'm not sure. Her family discontinued treatment and moved away. California, I think. Now, tell me more about your headaches, Brady."

Ladwig had no reason to add the lie about Winter's family moving to California. That rang a louder alarm bell. To his experience, the average person didn't lie about things they didn't consider important. But before he could pin the doctor down on the falsehood, his phone vibrated in his pocket. Noah reached for it automatically, ignoring the doctor's disapproving look.

He stood up in a rush, startling Dr. Ladwig. He had to go.

The text from Bree had been brief and to the point.

He got another one.

ROBERT LADWIG WATCHED Brady disappear through the doorway with a narrow look. It could have been the meds making him paranoid, but Rob was proud of his skills. He could read people with great accuracy, and he had a feeling that Brady Lomond was more than he appeared.

He went to his chair behind his carved mahogany desk. It was an exact copy of the one he had in his office at home, built to replicate one he'd seen in a picture of Sigmund Freud. If his soon-to-be-ex-wife, Hannah, hadn't sold it yet for coke money, he thought with a pang of irritation.

Going over his notes on Lomond again, he frowned. He'd been so sure, when he'd talked to Brady Lomond on the phone that he'd found another Winter. He hated getting his hopes up, but he'd been searching for a case like hers since her grandparents had discontinued treatment. He felt the familiar surge of rage. He'd been so close with her. So close, until her grandparents had turned her against him and taken her out of his reach.

He felt a pang of unease.

He'd told Lomond that his patient had relocated across the country, not to a different part of the state. As a brilliant psychologist, he could ask himself why and trust himself to be honest. But he couldn't think of a good reason for the lie. He'd just said it.

And Lomond, Rob thought. Had Lomond been more interested than he should have been about his old patient?

Rob Ladwig shoved to his feet and ran a hand through his thinning hair. Pacing the Persian carpet that lined the floor of his office, he took calming breaths.

In through the nose. Out through the mouth. Clear your mind.

He was probably linking Brady Lomond with Winter Black in his mind because their cases had sounded so similar. He'd fallen into the trap of getting his expectations too high, and then being disappointed when the reality didn't live up to the hype he'd created. Something he always cautioned his patients against.

Or, Rob reminded himself, his meds were making him paranoid again. He didn't like the idea, but it was always a possibility with untested drugs. Why else would he be suspicious of a redneck who'd probably concussed his last brain cell to death as a teenager?

Still.

Rob picked up the papers Lomond had left behind and took them to his desk.

It wouldn't hurt to do some digging. He'd have peace of mind, anyway.

14

This murder had taken place a month to the day after the first killing.

Bree held a handkerchief tightly over her mouth. The last crime scene almost had her breaking her own personal rule about puking during an investigation. This time, she'd brought one of her grandma's embroidered linen squares, sprinkled with a couple of drops of ginger essential oil that Shelby had promised would help with any nausea.

It hadn't been a stretch of the imagination to anticipate a crime scene as bad as the last one. And she didn't mind looking like the heroine of a Victorian novel by carrying the lacy cloth if it meant she wouldn't puke at a crime scene. She hadn't, however, thought that the second crime scene could be worse than the first.

The victim, Audrey Hawkins, a thirty-six-year-old interior designer from Roanoke, Virginia, was left splayed out on her bed in much the same way Detective Delosreyes had been. Like Delosreyes, The Preacher had mutilated the body almost beyond recognition. He'd also written cryptic messages and Bible verses in blood on the walls, though not as prolifically this time. That was where the similarities ended.

Audrey's body had already been taken away, but they'd seen the crime scene pictures. Any sign of Audrey's identity as a female had been removed. Her breasts, her lips, her hair, and most disturbingly, her eyes. To Bree, it looked like The Preacher had either escalated sharply or held some kind of personal grudge toward the victim.

"Did they find them before they took her?" Bree asked Noah, her voice hushed in the empty room.

He didn't look away from Audrey and was visibly shaken at the carnage. "Find what?"

"Her eyes."

Noah shook his head grimly.

She suppressed a shudder, realizing that The Preacher must have them. Was there no end to this man's depravity? She stifled the urge to curse as a couple of gowned crime scene techs came into the room.

"Have you seen enough?" the nearest tech asked. "We need to finish up."

Noah gave the room another look, his body tight with unsuppressed tension. Finally, he nodded.

Bree wasn't sorry to leave the bedroom behind, but back at the local police station, it was almost worse.

The woman's husband, Wesley Hawkins, sat at a metal table across from the Roanoke PD detective in charge. He was a weedy-looking guy, small and thin, dressed head to toe in black. The meticulously curled black mustache he wore, along with a pair of black Buddy Holly glasses and expensive black combat boots, marked him as a hipster. Bree wondered if his wife had been too.

The Roanoke detective, a solidly built woman who'd introduced herself as Monica Dunn, was questioning the husband. Noah and Bree didn't interrupt but stood in the corner of the small room, quietly observing the interview.

Wesley Hawkins looked shell-shocked, answering Detective Dunn's questions in a dull, flat monotone.

"Tell me your story again." Dunn's voice sounded probing and suspicious, and she held Wesley pinned with a hard stare. "Where were you yesterday?"

Bree wanted to speak up. The detective had been briefed on the reason for FBI involvement before they showed up. There was little doubt that the murder had been committed by The Preacher. This poor man had found his wife's body less than ten hours before. Why was Dunn now treating the victim's husband like this?

She could feel Noah stiffen beside her. He was probably biting his tongue too. They'd rushed straight out from Richmond, arriving late in the afternoon of the same day the murder had taken place. They'd been careful to make it clear that local LEOs were handling the investigation, assuring Dunn that they were only there as support and assist. The locals would run their own investigation, and the agents would run theirs.

Wesley Hawkins looked angry for a moment at Dunn's tone, stirring himself enough to answer.

"I'm an art director for LMV, a global ad agency." His eyes flicked over the three of them, coming back to Bree. Probably because she looked like the most sympathetic. She wasn't the best at hiding her feelings.

"I was working on a pitch with my team yesterday," he went on, his watery gray eyes behind their black-framed lenses fixed on her like a lifeline. Pleading for understanding.

She nodded, just slightly, to encourage him, and a little of the tension in his face eased.

"I had to go over wireframes. We were working on a pitch for Kellogg on Monday." He shook his head as if to clear it. "Tomorrow, and we were nowhere near ready because—"

"Tell me again," the detective interrupted, yanking Hawkins's attention back to her. "If you were just *working*, why didn't you discover your wife's body until almost three o'clock this morning?"

Wesley paled at the reminder of what had been done to his wife and flinched visibly. "We went out for drinks." The words were miserable. Guilt-ridden. "The creative director took us all out to celebrate."

"And why didn't you ask your wife to go? Did you even try to contact her before you left? Was there a reason you didn't want her to go with you?"

Bree opened her mouth to intervene, but Noah beat her to it. He cleared his throat sharply, drawing the detective's eyes to him. He didn't say anything, just gave Dunn a look that asked why the hell she was torturing the guy.

Detective Dunn glared back before shoving to her feet, a belligerent scowl on her face.

Bree rolled her eyes. Ooh. A pissing contest. That was *exactly* what seasoned professionals always did in front of traumatized family members of victims.

"Noah," Bree murmured. "Chill. You too, Detective Dunn."

Bree wanted to scream at her that they were all there to do the same job. Just because they had special agent tacked in front of their names, rather than detective, didn't mean they were going to yank the case. Instead, she crossed her arms and stared the woman down, until Wesley spoke up from the couch.

He'd been oblivious to the whole exchange and answered Dunn's question without looking up from a space on the metal tabletop in front of him. His voice sounded loud in the tense room.

"I didn't even think to ask Audrey," Wesley said thickly. "We've been married for fourteen years now. I have my work. She has—had—hers..." His voice dissolved and his face crumpled as loss set in.

"You weren't cheating on her?"

Wesley didn't react to the question.

"I should have asked her to go with me," he said instead, tears running down his cheeks as he stared at the floor. Dunn had broken him.

Vibrating with fury, Noah stepped in.

"Detective Dunn. Hallway. Now."

Monica Dunn smiled at him in challenge, and Bree realized in disgust that she hadn't been pushing Wesley Hawkins because she thought he had anything to do with Audrey's murder. She'd been doing it to get a rise out of the big, bad FBI agents, who she figured were going to take over her case.

Bree moved to the table and sat beside Wesley. He didn't react. She put a hand on his. It had probably been the first human contact he'd felt since he found his wife.

"Listen," Bree said. His cold fingers twitched under hers. "I know it may seem cruel, questioning you like this. But we have to be sure that we're getting all of the information we can to catch the monster who did this."

Wesley nodded. He looked up, finally. "How can she act like she thinks I'd do something like this?"

Bree wanted to tell him it was because Dunn was clearly a stone-cold bitch, but she kept the words to herself.

"Detective Dunn may not seem compassionate to you right now, but she's going to do everything she can to help. Can I get you a cup of coffee? Water? Have you eaten anything today?"

He shook his head dully. "I couldn't."

"All right. Let me know if you change your mind. As long as it's just the two of us here, can I ask you a few questions?"

"Why not," Wesley answered, dropping his head back against the wall. "This is all a nightmare. You can't make it any worse. Audrey is gone."

A spasm of emotion crossed his face.

"I'm not going to ask what you saw when you found your wife. I think you've been through enough questioning on that. But I want you to think about when you got home last night. Did you notice anything odd before you came into the house? Even the smallest thing, out of place, can help in an investigation like this."

He was silent for a moment, and the two of them heard Noah's voice on the other side of the door, low and rumbling. Implacable. Detective Dunn's voice was shrill and defensive, but they couldn't make out the words.

"I don't," Wesley finally replied. "I wish I did, but I was a little drunk. I came in the house—"

"You used your key?" Bree interrupted gently. "It wasn't unlocked?"

"Yes. I do remember that, only because I had trouble digging them out of my pocket. I unlocked the door and came in."

"Do you have a security system?"

"I do." He blinked. Straightened. "I didn't have to turn it off."

Bree felt a little pulse of excitement. "Does your wife leave it on when she's home alone?"

"Always," Wesley said, showing some fire in his eyes for the first time. "She always leaves it on. When she was in college, she was alone in her apartment one night, and a guy with a gun broke in. Took her jewelry and scared the hell out of her. She used to be scared to be home alone, back when we were dating. It got better over the years, but *never*, in all the time we've been together has she not set the security alarm when she was going to be home alone."

❄

"WE'D BE a lot further along if the Roanoke PD would assign a different detective to the case," Noah growled.

"Not the first time you've said that," Bree reminded him dryly as she hurried to keep pace with his long strides that ate up the sidewalk ahead of them. "If you could stop antagonizing her for three seconds, maybe we'd get brought in on this stuff sooner."

"I can't help it," Noah admitted. They'd spoken to the Hawkins's neighbors on the other side, and they were approaching the neighbor's house through the north. "She's got the type of personality that practically demands hassling."

From the end of the driveway, the neighbor's house looked very similar to the Hawkins's house. It was large and contemporary, with lots of glass and boxy angles.

"Wesley said his wife had done the interior design here," Bree said.

"Not my style." Noah shrugged as they made their way up the pathway that led to an imposing front door. "But it's interesting."

It was late on their third day in Roanoke, and the sky had already been dark for two hours. Bree knocked briskly on the door. Through the illuminated window, she could see a well-dressed blonde moving toward the front entrance.

She pulled the door open, the light overhead illuminating a sharp-featured face. Botoxed and meticulously made-up, Lisa Mayer could have been anywhere from thirty to sixty years old.

"Come in," she offered breathlessly, in a young-sounding falsetto. "You must be the agents who called earlier."

She led them through a yawning entryway done in stark contrasts of red and black. Metal and wood combined to give the place an industrial feel. It wasn't homey, and neither was Mrs. Mayer.

"Can I get you both anything to drink? Perrier? Chardonnay?"

Lisa's smile was bright and brittle, and there was greedy curiosity in her eyes. Bree pasted an impersonal smile on her face. It always bothered her, this dark glee some people showed when a crime hit close to home but didn't affect them directly. From the looks of her, Lisa would thrive on the murder of her neighbor and personal interior designer for months.

"Thank you, no. We'll try not to take up too much of your time."

Lisa waved one tanned hand in the air. "No worries at all. You're here about poor Audrey. She did this room, you know. Just last summer." Lisa dabbed a crumpled tissue under one dry eye.

The living room had a heavy, modern feel, with hard furniture in bright, primary colors that stood at counterpoint to the corrugated steel that lined the walls. Not to her taste, Bree thought, but it looked expensive. Noah was looking around like he didn't get it.

"Can you tell us if you've remembered anything that might be helpful since Detective Dunn's officers spoke to you?" Bree asked.

Lisa pursed her lips. "No, I'm afraid not. So, you haven't caught the man who did it?"

"Not yet, ma'am," Noah drawled, turning on the Texan charm.

Lisa's eyes glimmered with lust, and Bree stifled the urge to wrinkle her nose. The woman was gross. Before she could extricate them from the situation, a noise near the doorway caught her attention.

"Mama, I'm thirsty."

Lisa jumped up, looking suddenly embarrassed. Her cheeks flushed. She rushed to the high arch that led to a staircase, where a little boy in jeans and a striped, long-sleeved t-shirt stood. He looked like a small nine-year-old, and only had one sock on.

"Shia, sweetie, Mummy told you if you needed anything to ask Carmen."

"Carmen's busy," he replied in a flat voice. "She's talking to her boyfriend on her cell phone." A lock of blond hair stood up on the back of Shia's head, making him look like Dennis the Menace, but his small face was serious. "Are you the FBI people?"

Noah—who was good with kids, Bree had noticed—smiled at the boy. "We are. You're a smart kid."

"I know. Can I see your badges, please?" Shia asked, taking a step forward and ignoring his fluttering, red-faced mom. "I watch *Forensic Files* and *Criminal Minds* and *The First 48*, and I know you're supposed to show them if I ask."

Obliging him, Noah took out his badge and handed it over for the boy's inspection.

He nodded. "Good."

Bree wasn't a kid person, but she liked this one. He acted like a small grown-up, and she'd rather deal with him than his vapid mother. She also had a cousin on the autism spectrum, and Shia reminded her of Jay with his single-minded focus.

He was still looking at the badge when he said, "I can give you my witness statement now."

Lisa tittered. "No, sweetie, go play. This is adult business."

Noah and Shia ignored her. Bree gave Lisa a small smile. "It's all right, Mrs. Mayer. We'll take his statement."

Lisa's shoulders slumped a little in relief, and she looked more human. More like a mom who was glad her child wouldn't throw a fit in front of visitors, and less like a trophy wife with a figure that had never even considered childbirth.

Shia climbed up on the couch next to Noah and folded his hands in his lap neatly. "The suspect accessed the victim's house through a hole in the fence. He parked his truck on the service lane in the back of the woods that line these properties."

Noah's eyes shot to Bree's. She closed her mouth, aware that she'd been gaping. Behind them, Lisa gasped.

"Did you see the man, Shia?" Noah kept his voice calm, matter of fact, as he made notes.

"I did, but not well." Shia scrunched up his face, thinking. "His truck, I saw pretty good. It was green and red and had some writing on the side, but I couldn't read it through the trees. I don't know anything about trucks, so I can't tell you what kind it was. Old, I guess."

Lisa broke in, sounding less gleeful and more scared. "When did you see this, honey? Why didn't you tell me?"

The killer had brushed closer to her than she'd thought, and suddenly, the novelty was wearing off.

Shia gave her a mildly disgusted look. "You wouldn't have believed me. I tried to talk to Detective Dunn, but she wouldn't listen either. I was going to call the tip line, but I heard you talking to the FBI agents this morning, so I just waited."

"Do we have your permission to record this interview, Mrs. Mayer?" Noah asked.

Lisa nodded, biting her lip.

"What else can you tell us, Shia? What do you remember about the man you saw? Hair color, approximate height, identifying features?"

"He looked like Santa," Shia said. "Which I think is supposed to be a joke, because his truck is red and green. I don't know anything about jokes, though. He had white hair and a white beard and glasses. He was old, like his truck."

"Shia has an eidetic memory," Lisa said, her voice shaky. "And he doesn't lie."

Bree blew out a slow breath, trying to calm her racing heart. They had their first eyewitness, and he was a nine-year-old autistic kid.

Detective Dunn was going to shit a brick.

15

Winter sat on the curb in the cold parking lot, dampness creeping through the fabric of the seat of her pants. She'd been pretending to fix the chain on her bike for twenty uncomfortable minutes, waving off the occasional helpful co-worker, when Bree pulled up in her little hatchback.

It wasn't until Bree spotted her and changed direction, heading her way, that Winter breathed a sigh of relief. She quickly retightened the loosened chain. It was a breezy forty-nine degrees. The sun was shining, but they were in the middle of a cold front that had it feeling more like up north than down south.

"Having trouble?" Bree called out cheerfully.

She'd debated over whether to get in touch with Noah. They'd been close. She could apologize. Maybe that would prompt him to help her out. Ultimately, though, she'd decided she wasn't going to use Noah like that.

"Not anymore," Winter replied, giving the pedals an experimental spin to make sure the chain held.

Bree, she didn't know as well. She could work with Bree.

She flipped the bike right side up and fell into step beside the shorter woman.

"How's it going?" Winter asked. "I haven't seen anyone from VC in a while."

Bree looked at her, tucking her hands into her armpits. She wore a light jacket, more suitable for spring. "Going okay, I suppose. How's life treating you in the BAU?"

Working with Aiden, who insisted on shadowing her? Sitting at her desk under the curious eye of several other people every day? Excruciating.

"It's been interesting seeing how the other side lives."

"Is it true that they have a better vending machine?"

Winter laughed, despite herself. "I don't know. I've been too busy working to find out. I heard there was another murder."

Bree nodded, her smile falling away. "Yeah. It's not like anything else I've ever seen in my career, that's for sure."

"I'm sure. Taking a peek into The Preacher's mind is no picnic, even though I haven't seen any of his current work firsthand. I wish I could, just to see if I'd have different insights." She wasn't going to point out that Bree hadn't known any of the victims she'd seen so far.

Bree slowed. "I hope you don't hold it against Noah that you weren't assigned, and he was."

Winter tried to shake off the knee-jerk anger. "No. He's got a job to do. He can't control Max's decisions on placement."

"Do you really get to look inside his head?" Bree asked curiously. "The Preacher, I mean. Not Max. No offense, but I thought you were barred from the case, top-down."

Bree was nibbling at the hook and Winter had barely put on the bait.

She stopped completely, turning her back to the cold. "I'm unbarred, actually," she admitted. "Unofficially. I've known

SSA Parrish for a long time. He's doing me a favor. I'm only working on The Preacher right now."

"I guess maybe they just wanted you out of the field," Bree mused. "Makes sense. They still get your expertise, but you're not on the front, so to speak."

"No, Ramirez doesn't know. Honestly, Parrish bribed me with this so I'd take the transfer. Working with Noah, you might be able to see how that wouldn't be cool with him. You know how he is."

"Yeah." Bree grinned, and Winter felt a twinge of something too much like jealousy to examine closely. "I know how Noah is. Hey, we've gotten the reports from the BAU, but..."

"But you want to know if I have any insights that haven't been shared on the reports?"

"Yeah." Bree ducked her head sheepishly, her wild, spiraling dark curls bouncing in the wind. "It sounds like corporate espionage when you put it like that, but Noah trusts your gut on The Preacher."

"Hey, I'm focusing on behavioral analysis investigation techniques now, but my limited experience is with the traditional footwork approach. I'm still getting used to that, and I want to make sure we're in sync. We should be working together to catch him. We're on the same team, right? Why shouldn't we be working together?"

Winter tucked her bike in the rack outside, not bothering to padlock it. If someone stole it from the front of the FBI building, they deserved it. They started walking again, an agent in a hurry cutting in front of them on his way through the doors.

"You want to meet for a beer later?" Winter asked, a little uncomfortable with Bree's thoughtful silence. She didn't want Bree examining the request too closely. "Completely informally and not for information sharing reasons?"

Bree seemed to come to some internal conclusion and nodded.

"Yeah. That sounds good. I'll text you when I get things wrapped up for the night, and we can drive together. I hope you don't mind if we take my transportation instead of yours." She chuckled, taking off her knit hat and running a smoothing hand over her hair.

"Sure," Winter agreed. "Just do me a favor. Keep this on the down-low? I don't want Parrish getting in trouble with ADD Ramirez. He's circumventing a direct order."

"No problem." Bree hit the button on the elevator. "Parrish is smooth, and handsome, and debonair...but he also has that low-key crazy thing going for him. I do *not* want to be on his bad side."

WINTER WASN'T a bar-hopper by nature and didn't socialize a lot, so she let Bree pick the place. The Blue Room was crowded.

"Mai-tais," Bree declared to the bartender. "It's too damned cold out there for us Virginians to be dealing with this. We need something tropical to take our minds off the weather." She claimed a couple of bar stools and asked the waitress to let them know when a quieter two-top was ready.

Winter sipped at the fruity concoction. The lime and rum provided a stronger kick than she'd expected from the fru-fru name. Bree's dark brown eyes glowed with enjoyment as she raised her glass and her voice, attempting to be heard over the crowd of mostly college kids. "Cheers."

"Ditto," Winter replied, clinking her glass against Bree's. The rum slid a slow, sweet burn down her throat, and she cautioned herself to go slow. She set her drink on a napkin on the bar in front of her but had to grab it again when a laughing kid in a VCU sweatshirt bumped into their table. At the front of the room, on a makeshift stage, a band of black-dressed girls started tuning guitars with a wail.

"Doesn't it make you feel old to go to places like this?"

Bree laughed out loud. "You don't pull any punches, do you? I like that in a person."

Embarrassed, Winter flushed. "I didn't mean it like that. I meant it makes *me* feel old to come here, and you're a couple of years older…"

"Oh, don't ruin it and get coy now. I'm forty-five." Bree grinned, tucking a lock of hair behind her ear. "I know I don't look old, but I'm not exactly young, either. I've got twenty years on you, right?"

Winter grinned too. "Something like that. You wear it well."

"Have you met my fiancée, Shelby? Hell, she's fifty and doesn't look a day over twenty sometimes. It's downright intimidating dating a model."

They fell into a comfortable conversation for a while and ordered another round.

"Got your table ready, Agent Stafford." The perky blonde waitress grinned. "You want to grab those drinks to go?"

She led them away from a Courtney Love cover that managed to butcher the song worse than the original, to a table that was surprisingly quiet. It was tucked back in a small hallway that Winter had assumed led to the bathrooms and kitchen. There were a few other people there, having conversations they could actually hear over the thrumming baseline just outside.

"Only the regulars know about the quiet tables," the waitress told Winter before turning to Bree. "You want your usual?"

"Yep. The appetizer trio and a Coke."

"Make it two, please. And a glass of water." Winter felt a

little lightheaded. She hadn't been sleeping well and had been forgetting meals altogether. The late hours and two-hour-roundtrip bike commutes weren't helping.

Bree seemed to be noticing the same thing. "You doing okay lately? You look a little scrawny and peaked. Not that you had much color before, but you're worse now. Like, transparent."

Winter blinked. "Speaking of not pulling punches."

Bree smiled, but it was tinged with concern. "Don't work yourself to death, Winter. He's not worth it. Give it your best but put yourself first. Good advice from an old-timer like me," she acknowledged wryly before taking another small sip. "Easier said than done, I know, given your connection."

The waitress brought their food. When she left, Bree pulled out a manila envelope. She slid it across the table to Winter. "Very clandestine, no?" She faked a French accent and a furtive manner.

Before Winter could open it, Bree shook her head in the negative. "The pictures aren't pretty. Save them for later so you can at least get some calories in yourself first."

Winter didn't care about mozzarella sticks dipped in ranch dressing or greasy, deep-fried pickles. The thought already made her stomach want to turn.

Her fingers itched to undo the clasp on the envelope, but she tucked it away in her bag instead and pulled out an identical envelope. FBI standard issue, apparently.

"I brought you a present too."

Winter had filled it with the printouts that she'd pulled off the thumb drive Aiden had given her. She printed them from home the night before, figuring that even if she was caught accessing the info from home, Aiden really couldn't say much.

He was blackmailing her, essentially. And she always had the option to quit.

She didn't include the sketch she'd made of The Preacher.

"As long as we're switching to shoptalk," Bree commented, tucking her own envelope away, "did you hear about the big break? Our pint-sized witness?"

"I did. The story traveled around fast."

"It was glorious." Bree popped a fried pickle into her mouth. "I watched this nine-year-old kid take down the Roanoke detective in a debate on police procedure when dealing with minors. Little dude knew his rights and wasn't about to let her push him around."

"So, his story checked out?"

"Absolutely." She looked grim for a moment. "I'm just glad the kid wasn't spotted. Apparently, he likes to sneak out of the house and play cops and robbers by himself in the woods. His mom thought he was in his room all afternoon."

"He was too close." It was chilling. The kid was lucky The Preacher hadn't seen him. Goose bumps raised on her arms as another thought occurred to her. Had her brother still been alive in captivity at nine years old? She pushed away the thought, along with the half-eaten platter of food. "Is he protected? The boy?"

Bree's gaze softened. "Of course."

"Good."

"It may not be in the reports yet, because Roanoke is holding up their official verification of the kid's witness statement, but the guy looked like Santa Claus."

"Santa Claus?"

The Preacher's face flashed into her head. His soft, Southern-accented voice whispering sibilant sounds inside her mind that made no sense. His white hair and beard, beatific smile, and dead, black eyes.

"I know," Bree went on. "That narrows it down to approximately ten percent of the old white guy population. I feel like we're playing Guess Who, flipping down cards. What's next? A mall Santa lineup for a child witness? A defense attorney would have a field day with something like that."

Winter didn't reply.

She didn't know what was going to come next, but there was a slight, nagging pain behind her eyes—one that had been there for days—that told her she might not have to wait long to find out.

16

Aiden watched Winter, feeling an unaccountable pang of guilt.

She was hunched over her computer, her shoulders rounded, her back curved. She wore a black, long-sleeved t-shirt. Even from his place behind his desk, he could make out the knobby ridge of her spine. She'd quit dressing for the job, leaving off the blazer, trading jeans for the dress pants she normally wore. It was like her professional shell was melting away under the fire of stress and obsession.

She'd always been slim and fair-skinned, but her face was paler than usual. Her cheekbones were more pronounced, her dark blue eyes shadowed with gray smudges of fatigue. She hadn't been eating or sleeping, he could tell. Even her hair, usually gleaming like black steel in the thick braid she wore it in, looked lank. Diminished.

The Winter who had made a habit of popping by his place with Chinese food and sarcastic banter to cheer him up during his recuperation was gone. This Winter burned with an intensity of purpose that would likely consume her whole.

He pushed away from his desk and left his office, heading for her cubicle.

"Break time," he pronounced.

She jumped skittishly, and her fingers flew over the keyboard, minimizing whatever window she had pulled up on the screen.

"I don't need a break." She looked up at him, exhausted but defiant.

"Fine. Meeting, then."

He walked away, heading toward the small conference room he used for team status updates. She'd follow, he told himself. He was the boss. In the last several weeks, he was confident that she'd come to understand and accept that.

Still, Aiden was relieved when Winter followed him in with her laptop and sat down at the small table. He picked up the office extension and asked one of their interns to get some bagels and coffee and bring them in.

"Is it your turn to feed me now?" Winter asked with a ghost of her old humor.

"Someone has to," he replied harshly. "What the fuck are you doing to yourself?"

She sank back into the chair, humor gone, arms folded. "I thought this was what you wanted."

It was. But not at this cost.

"You look half-dead." His tone was harder than he'd intended. "You don't show up for work half the time, so I have to assume you're pursuing things on your own. That ends now."

"If you don't like the way I work," Winter offered, her eyes glittering, "you could always fire me."

It was a standoff. He wanted to grind his teeth. He thought he'd had her where he wanted her. No, he *did* have her where he wanted her, but he couldn't physically force her to take care of herself.

Looking at the waifish figure in front of him, he felt like a monster. He didn't appreciate guilt. It wasn't an emotion that he'd ever had to battle with before.

"You and I are working together from here on out," Aiden decided out loud.

Her face shuttered instantly. "I don't need a babysitter."

"Yes. Yes, you fucking do need a babysitter."

"Don't pretend you're doing this for me. That your motives are virgin-pure."

Winter was shooting in the dark, but the bullets were coming close. Fortunately, she was young. Impulsive. He had more practice developing a shell and ruthless self-control. He focused on what mattered, no matter what it took to get there. Manipulating others to get the results he needed was a talent and a skill that he'd begun to cultivate in the last few years, and he was good at it.

He smiled. Slowly.

"Quit if you need to, but today would be a bad day for that. We have another possible victim."

Angry color bled into her cheeks as she stood and planted her hands on the table.

"Then why wouldn't you say that instead of playing these Machiavellian games, *Parrish?* You enjoy pulling puppet strings so much, you're going to keep doing it. Forget about the unlucky women who could die while you're getting off on your power games, right?"

He ignored that, but it stung a little. Winter would be a force to be reckoned with in a few years. The thought brought a strange stirring of pride.

"Sit down." He kept his tone mild. "If you're done with your temper tantrum, I'll tell you what I've come up with. I know where he's going to hit next."

The steel in Winter's blue glare could have sparked fire to wet kindling, but she sat back down in her chair. "Where?"

"Murder number three. Ocean View, New Jersey. Gabby Dean."

He waited, giving her a significant look. She opened up her notebook to a fresh page and jotted a few words down. Satisfied that she was with him now, he went on.

"Gabby was a student at Rowan University. Twenty-three years old. Lived alone in a small apartment near campus. She was found by a study partner who came to pick her up for a class."

Winter didn't look up. "And the MO is the same."

"Surprisingly different. If not for the set of numbers on the wall and the fact that we're watching for him, we might have missed it. On the ceiling in blood, where the vic would have been able to see it, he wrote 31:30. This time, a cross on the victim's forehead, almost like a benediction. Cause of death, throat cut, but no genital mutilation."

Winter had stopped writing and was staring off into the middle distance. "She was pretty. Vivacious. Charming."

"Yes. The sorority girl type. Physically fit and attractive, with a regular, predictable running and exercise routine. How did you know?"

"Charm is deceptive, and beauty is fleeting; but a woman who fears the Lord is to be praised."

"Proverbs 31," Aiden agreed with a short nod.

"The ultimate blueprint for the perfect woman. What did he do to her, if it wasn't something sexual?"

Aiden hesitated for a moment, and then turned his own computer around so she could see the image pulled up on the screen. He watched Winter's face. There was no reaction, and that, more than anything, made him want to question everything he'd done up to this point.

"You see what's been done to her?" he pushed, almost angrily. Where was her disgust? The emotional connection?

Winter just looked up at him, her eyes flat. "Yes. She's

been flayed. Like the adage, beauty is only skin deep. So, he removed her skin to show the ugliness on the inside."

Aiden wanted to yell at her. Shake her out of this dispassionate zombie mode. Ask her when she'd gone so cold. But he screwed the lid down on his own unwelcome conscience and drew a deep breath.

This was his fault, not hers.

He turned the laptop away and closed the screen.

"You said you know where he's going to hit next?"

There was no mistaking the gleam of anticipation in her eyes, and he regretted telling her. It was too late. He couldn't change his mind now without weakening his position.

"Yes." Aiden pulled a printout out of a folder and turned it around. It showed Richmond and the surrounding areas. He'd marked the locations of the murders in red ink.

"You told me that the killer had a Southern accent." It had been skimpy information at best. He knew she had more info in that brain of hers but had a feeling he'd need to work at her to get it out.

"We've been looking at priests, religious figures, and church members who have an obvious obsession with scripture and the idea of a perfect woman. Hence the nickname, The Preacher. But I think I've figured out his killing pattern. Watch."

He pointed to Washington, D.C., where Officer Delosreyes had been killed first. Then, Roanoke, Virginia, to the south of Richmond. Ocean View, New Jersey, to the east.

"It's the Holy Trinity." For a moment, her face was animated at the discovery. Winter lifted her own hand to her forehead, her chest, her left shoulder, and her right. "The Father, the Son, the Holy Spirit. Is he Baptist?"

Aiden grinned, and let himself enjoy the shared moment. It was discoveries like this that reminded him why he'd joined the FBI to begin with. The satisfying click of a conclusion made when you snapped it into the rest of the puzzle and just knew it was the right one.

"I think so, if my theory holds. I've got a couple of people working on the old cases, grouping them geographically and checking to see if this has been his MO all along. And look what's west of Richmond, within that radius."

"Harrisonburg." Her face lifted, lit with anticipation. Shit. Time to backtrack. "He's going to hit in Harrisonburg."

"It's a big maybe. But we stay here."

"Of course," Winter murmured, looking down again. "Tucked up nice and safe behind our desks in the BAU."

"And that's where we should be. We're BAU. Not VC."

"You're BAU."

"And so," he concluded, his voice silky, "are you. Remember that."

"Are we done here?" Winter asked, her tone remote and face distant.

"No. I have a theory on when he'll hit again."

"Spill it," Winter invited, life coming back into her pretty features.

Aiden narrowed his eyes. "I don't think so."

She'd go rushing off to Harrisonburg, and there would be no holding her back. He wasn't a profiler for nothing. He could see that the obsession had tipped over far enough that she wasn't worried about the consequences.

Winter was only focused on her one consuming goal. Getting to The Preacher.

"Fine." She gave him a deceptively casual smile. "Holding back information for personal gain fits your profile…the BAU has taught me a few things. I can figure out the rest."

She stood up, gathering her things.

He'd lost control of the situation.

Aiden picked up his Montblanc pen, running it through his fingers lightly. It had been a gift from ADD Ramirez on the day his promotion to the SSA of the BAU had been officially announced.

"We'll meet again this afternoon. End of day."

"Sorry." Winter shook her head in mock-regret. "I'm leaving soon for a doctor's appointment. Girl stuff. For a very personal, embarrassing reason that's most definitely off-limits to Aiden Parrish, my supervisor. Ramirez, HIPAA, and Human Resources will all tell you that you can't question me about it or dig too deep without getting punched in the teeth with a lawsuit. And, gosh..." she batted her lashes at him, "wouldn't that be a black eye on your record."

She gave him a cool, triumphant glance on her way out. He wouldn't be surprised if she'd booked an appointment already, just to give herself the alibi.

He could easily picture the smirk on her face as Winter's voice quieted the hum and bustle of his hardworking, effective, completely controlled department.

"You have to work within the strictures of the system, Parrish," she called out. "The FBI frowns on going rogue."

Aiden flinched as the snap of his breaking pen echoed sharply in the small room.

17

Winter held back the fierce grin that threatened to split her face. She didn't stop in her office, just stuffed her computer in its laptop case and slung it over her shoulder with her messenger bag. She grabbed her leather coat and insulated steel water bottle and left everything else. If she forgot anything, it would probably just get boxed up by HR and sent to her house after she was fired.

God, that had felt good.

The last vestiges of that hero worship she'd always felt for Aiden Parrish had burned away in that little conference room. She'd finally let herself see him for what he was.

She rounded the wall of her cubicle at a fast clip and headed toward the exit. She wasn't worried about Aiden catching up to her. Finding a reason to keep her here. He couldn't. He wasn't some infallible epitome of the perfect FBI agent, all-seeing and all-powerful.

He was just the first FBI agent she had ever known. His was the first face she'd seen when she'd come out of her coma. He'd been in her room. Watching over her.

She wasn't afraid of Aiden. Aiden had been trying to

show her from the beginning that he was just a man. A broken, manipulative, scared, controlling man who had no power to stop her. She could handle him.

Winter hit the elevator button for the main floor.

It was *time* that she worried about most. Every second ticked closer to the end of an innocent, faceless woman's life. The Preacher would steal her from her family. From her friends. From her destiny. Possibly from her children or husband.

Would the next victim have a child? A thirteen-year-old girl? A six-year-old boy?

It wouldn't matter, she promised herself. Because there wouldn't *be* a next victim.

Winter crossed the lobby, digging in her purse for her keys. It wasn't until she saw her bike that she remembered.

Shit. She wasn't driving anymore.

Energy hummed through her body. Urgency, pushing and clawing at her to act. She had to get home. Her bike would take too long. So would a taxi. She pulled out her phone and tapped the screen feverishly. Bus schedules. Private plane.

The quickest possible option would be to drive the Civic to Harrisonburg. She just had to hope she didn't go into a seizure on the way, crashing her car and killing herself and anyone too close.

What the hell. She'd just aim for the closest tree if she felt one coming on.

Decision made, she just had to get to her car.

When the door opened behind her and Noah stepped out, she didn't hesitate. "I need a ride."

Noah blinked twice, his moss-green eyes widening when he saw her. She realized it was the first time they'd been face-to-face in over a month, and they'd both changed dramatically.

Noah's dark brown hair had been clipped short, almost

military style, sometime recently. When they'd worked together last, he'd let it grow out long enough to curl around his collar a little. Like Mel Gibson in the *Lethal Weapon* movies, even though he had more of a Danny Glover personality.

Instead, she was reminded that her kind, funny, easygoing friend and sometimes-partner was a former Marine. He wasn't a cuddly teddy bear before he met her. He was a trained soldier, an MP, and then a cop. His familiar face, rough with a day's worth of stubble, looked hard. One side of his mouth was creased with tension. Normally, there was a dimple there instead.

"Where to? What's wrong?"

Of course, Noah would pick up on her tension. He was practically an empath when it came to guessing how other people were feeling. Especially her.

She let her face relax into an embarrassed smile.

"Sorry, I didn't mean to bark at you. I was just stressing about a doctor's appointment later. I have to stop at home first and forgot I rode my bike. How are you doing?"

His guarded expression softened a little but didn't disappear.

"Fine. I was in a hurry myself. I have a p…a thing."

Liar. He was going to Ocean View, New Jersey.

Bree had sent her a text this morning.

Leaving town for a few days.

The one simple line had cued Winter in that something was up…and allowed Winter to find out about The Preacher's most recent murder before Aiden ever called her in to tell her about it.

Winter had gotten a few random texts like that in the last few weeks. And she'd sent a couple of her own, too, just to keep the collegial *quid pro quo* going. But she was steps ahead of everyone, and she had to keep it that way.

"You're not stopping home first, are you?"

"Yeah, I can drop you there. Sorry I can't take you to your appointment." He was already thinking about something else, his voice distant. He hit the button to Beulah, his giant Ford.

Then, he caught himself and shot a quick glance at Winter, adding, "You know, because I have one too. An appointment."

She almost rolled her eyes and asked him why he had to grab a go-bag for a supposed doctor's appointment, but she held her tongue. The old Noah wouldn't have lied to her. Probably because he sucked at it. But the new Winter had no problem lying to him, so she guessed it evened out.

"No worries," she said instead. "I'll set up a Lyft pickup while you drive me home."

She matched his fast steps as he closed the distance to his truck. He moved in a hurry, like he was late, and she didn't want him to miss his flight. He and Bree could go to Ocean View, with her blessing.

The farther from Harrisonburg they were, the better.

THERE WAS no automatic feeling of nostalgia for Winter, passing by the city limits signs to head into the town she'd grown up in. Hell, it hadn't been that long since Winter had been to Harrisonburg. Less than a year. She and Noah had worked their first solo FBI case there.

No nostalgia, or warm and fuzzy feelings, even as she passed the elementary school she'd gone to as a kid. Tension had been knotting her neck muscles for the second half of the two-hour trip. In the last ten minutes, that tension had escalated into solid apprehension.

Winter drove past the hotel where she and Noah had stayed the previous fall. You weren't supposed to judge a book by its cover, but the peeling avocado-green paint on the outside of the squat, cinderblock walls was pretty indicative of what the inside looked like.

It was in one of those second-floor hotel rooms that she'd discovered a hidden camera, mounted behind an ugly 1980s-era painting over the TV. She'd also had a picture slipped under the door. It had been the first one she'd received from The Preacher, taken of her brother, Justin. He'd worn the SpongeBob PJs she'd last seen him in.

She'd always assumed that it was by chance that The Preacher had found her in Harrisonburg. She'd imagined that he'd occasionally take trips down memory lane and stumbled across her by accident. It hadn't made any sense then, and it didn't make any sense now. Especially since everything in his profile leaned away from him being the type of guy who needed to revisit his crime scenes. Aiden believed the opposite: that he had an out of sight/out of mind mentality. When his victim was dead, mission accomplished. He had no further need for contact.

She passed the houses of childhood friends, grade school teachers…did The Preacher live next door to one of them? Participate in neighborhood potlucks? Did he pass for normal in the real world?

Monsters too often were able to blend in.

Winter slowed the Civic as she approached her old street. The streetlights were just coming on as she turned right. She should have been somewhere else. Getting a hotel room for the foreseeable. Maybe a room at the original place she'd stayed last fall. The desk clerk would remember her, though, and she was a gossip.

Her presence wouldn't stay secret for long, especially with how high-profile they'd become in town, working their last case. But maybe that wasn't a bad thing. She could draw him out.

The houses on her childhood street were older, two-story, single-family homes. There were bikes in driveways and treehouses in backyards. It had been a good place to grow up, and she'd forgotten that.

She slowed the car to a crawl as she reached the circular turnaround at the end of the street. The last streetlight was out at the end, leaving the curve of the sidewalk in unrelieved shadow. The loop she made with her car now had been one she'd made thousands of times as a kid on a ten-speed. A purple, hand-me-down Huffy with pink tires. She'd gotten it from a cousin, and when she'd been eleven years old, she'd painted it silver with a can of spray paint she'd bought with babysitting money.

She stopped in front of her old house. Peeling paint. Boarded windows. The same For Sale sign in the yard that she'd seen last time she was in town.

Winter knew it wouldn't sell. No one in their right mind would want to live there, unless they had a fascination with serial killers. It had been the scene of a double homicide, attempted murder, and kidnapping.

The Preacher had been back to this house. In the second-floor master bedroom, where her parents had been murdered, he'd left her another picture of Justin in the long burned out ashes of the fireplace.

Winter didn't shift the car into park. She needed to go through the house again, but not now. Down the street, kids played basketball in the gathering twilight. The yells and trash talk sounded blessedly normal and chipped away a little at the icy feeling that had come over her.

Did those kids dare each other to walk up to the porch on Halloween? Touch the front door? Hold their breath and pedal faster when they passed it? Did some of the older kids in the area use it as a make-out spot? Scaring their dates into cuddling up next to them, with gory stories about the family that had been killed there?

She couldn't blame kids. They were still young enough to have an immortality complex that extended to their families and friends, keeping them cozy in their illusion of safety. They had no idea of the evil that existed in the world, rubbed elbows with them every day.

A movement on the shadowy sidewalk had her grabbing reflexively for her gun.

A young mother pushed a toddler in a stroller through the cool evening air. She stared Winter down suspiciously as she passed. She held her phone conspicuously in one hand, implying she'd call the police, given the smallest provocation. Winter smiled and gave the woman a little nonthreatening wave as she pulled away from the curb.

Maybe teenagers didn't break into her old house to neck. Not under that neighbor's watch, anyway.

Even putting distance between herself and the house didn't do anything to set Winter's mind at ease. She had to go through it again. Open herself up to anything that she might experience, painful or not.

The Preacher was in town, and he was going to kill again if she didn't catch him first.

Still, goose bumps rippled over her skin, and her stomach felt faintly queasy.

Walking through the house wasn't going to be any easier the second time than it had been the first.

18

Gabby Dean. She'd been pretty before The Preacher had chosen her.

Noah's stomach turned, even though the picture was the smiling, happy girl that Gabby had once been. Not the life-less pile of flesh The Preacher had left behind. His stomach turned because the waste was sickening. Who knew what the girl could have done with her life? From all indications, she was a good girl. She was working on her master's degree in nursing, for shit's sake.

Fury. Regret. Guilt.

It all twisted up inside Noah as he studied the heart-shaped face framed by auburn hair that waved smoothly to her shoulders. Gabby grinned sweetly out at him from a glossy color photo provided by one of her friends.

"You doing okay over there?" Bree's voice cut through his reverie, sounding loud in the close confines.

They'd been given a breakout room to themselves, cour-tesy of the local LEOs. Their reception hadn't been warm, but at least it had been professional and cordial. Judging by the windowless room they'd been given at the back of the building, Ocean View preferred to pretend that the agents weren't there, rather than engage in open hostility.

"I'm fine. How about you?"

"I could do without seeing any more crime scene photos for a while. You want to take a break? Put this on hold for a half hour and grab some dinner?"

"Can't believe I'm saying this, but I don't think I could eat."

"That's not the Noah I've come to know. You're a freaking bottomless pit."

Noah made the effort to disengage from his funk and grinned at Bree.

"Aw, you noticed."

She snorted and gathered up the files that the detective had given them, tapping the edges against the table until they made a small, neat pile.

"I might be a bottomless pit, but at least I'm not OCD."

Bree shrugged good-naturedly. "It's my cross to bear. True genius comes with side-effects."

Wasn't that the case? He pictured Winter's face. More gaunt than thin these days…there were demons that drove her, that was for sure.

It was Noah's turn to choose the restaurant, so they went for New Jersey Italian at a little bistro near the station.

"I still say you're too damned quiet tonight." Bree glanced over the top of the reading glasses she'd pulled out to look at the menu. "Spill it, and I'll let you get the veal parmigiana *and* half of my spaghetti marinara."

He didn't hesitate. "I gave Winter a ride to her apartment before I left Richmond today."

The smile melted into concern. "Did you guys get a chance to talk on the way? Patch things up at all?"

Noah narrowed his eyes at Bree. He'd done his best to make his concern for Winter sound completely platonic. Either his best hadn't been good enough, or Bree was the genius she claimed to be. She was good at reading between the lines.

"We kind of talked. Well, not really. I lied to her." He winced and shoved a hand through his hair. "Told her I had a doctor's appointment."

Bree stilled, the wine menu suspended in her hand. "You didn't tell her about the most recent murder?"

"No. She needs to stay out of it. It's not her case."

A waiter appeared at the side of their table, pen and paper in hand.

"Give us a minute, could you?" Bree asked, setting the laminated wine list down on the table in front of her. When he'd gone, she pinned Noah with a look again. "Tell me honestly," she demanded. "Why don't you want Winter involved in this? Is it because you're afraid she'll get hurt? Afraid that she'll put herself in a dangerous position? Or are you on the side of the higher-ups, and believe she's a liability?"

He flushed a little. "I like you, Agent Stafford. But that doesn't mean I have to answer every personal question you get it in your head to ask."

"You're going to want to answer these ones, Noah. Trust me."

Blowing out a long breath, he leaned back in the chair, considering his options. The hell with it. "I told her I'd do this for her," he blurted. "It should be enough. She should trust *me*."

Bree's face softened for a second, and he relaxed a little. She was a romantic. She was on his side.

But just as quickly, her expression shifted to exasperation.

"Does Agent Black strike you as the type who needs a white knight? Or wants one, for that matter?"

Winter had told him roughly the same thing when he'd tried to explain his reasoning at the outset. He wasn't any happier to hear it now. "See? You don't get it either. It must be a female thing." When Bree just stared at him, he tried again. "She's obsessed. She's not going to be thinking objectively. She—"

Bree held up a hand. "Maybe." She sighed and gripped her glass with both hands. "But she's a big girl. She got hired on for her merits, not her traumatic history. She's FBI now and deserves her chance to be in on this takedown, as equally as anyone else."

"Hold on." Noah stilled, crossing his arms. "I didn't realize you were so firmly in Winter's camp. You guys hardly know each other."

It was Bree's turn to squirm. "We've hung out a little."

He raised an eyebrow. "You never mentioned it."

Bree heaved a breath. "Fine. I met with her a few weeks ago. We agreed to keep each other updated on any details that might slip out of the official reports in this case. Parrish has given her rein to work on The Preacher case from the BAU."

His arms dropped to his sides. "Wait, you've been feeding Winter information? Does Parrish know?"

"I assumed that she would have gone to you if you two hadn't been on the outs," Bree prevaricated, looking uncomfortable as she twisted in her seat. "Parrish doesn't know. She's protecting him from getting in trouble with Ramirez. Winter had a solid argument. We should all be working together on this. I don't know that she and I have provided each other with anything really useful, but we're keeping the lines of communication open."

Noah felt a pulse of anger but squashed it. Winter was not only working around the edict, manipulating Bree, she was protecting that cold bastard, Parrish. Parrish didn't need any protection. Winter needing to take care of the asshole was as ludicrous as a gazelle needing to take care of a cheetah.

He and Bree didn't know each other well. They liked working together so far and complimented each other's styles in a lot of ways, but the co-worker relationship hadn't really gotten any deeper than that. The case took up too much of their attention to leave any time for work-related bonding.

That didn't mean he wasn't furious with Parrish. The asshole had been working angles since the beginning, and he'd probably seen the situation as a perfect carrot to use to get Winter under his thumb. The guy was a self-centered dick.

"Why's Parrish letting her work on this?" Bree asked thoughtfully. It looked like she, too, was questioning the logistics of that. "Does he have some kind of personal stake in this?"

"Knowing Parrish like I do, he wouldn't make a move if he *didn't* have a personal stake in something."

"Could he have thought the VC would use Winter as bait?"

It was a good question. "I don't see him as being that selfless."

Bree shrugged. "I don't know the guy as well as you all do. I mean, we worked together for a couple years in VC but never on the same thing."

She went on, but Noah stopped hearing her as a thought occurred to him.

"Do you have the file with the pictures of the victim?" he interrupted.

She raised her eyebrows at the abrupt question. The waiter came around again to try for their order, but Noah gave him an apologetic look as Bree dug into her bag for the right folder. "Five minutes," he promised the kid.

Bree slid the file across the table. It was freshly labeled with a neatly typed adhesive strip that read "victim profiles."

"Do you keep a label maker in your car?" he asked. She flushed a little, and he shook his head, letting out a laugh. "Genius side-effect? That's just anal."

But his half-smile fell away as he opened up the manila folder and spread out the pictures of the victims. Not the crime scene photos, but the photos of living, breathing women taken at various times before their deaths.

"Shit," he murmured under his breath.

"What is it?"

"He's killing her."

Bree stared at him. "Killing who?"

"Winter." A cold feeling settled in his belly as he turned the pictures toward Bree. "Do you see it?"

She studied the pictures, her dark eyes flicking back and forth between the prints and then widening. "I feel so stupid. With the second victim's eyes missing...the bodies so unrecognizable..."

"The Preacher came out of retirement *for* Winter. He's going to kill her."

Bree's voice shook a little. "The hair on Tala Delosreyes. Thick, black, pulled back in a braid. Audrey Hawkins, deep blue eyes. Gabby Dean. Their builds are similar enough that they could have played stunt doubles for each other. That long, athletic type..." Her voice trailed off, and she looked up at him. "You think Winter is the target."

"Remember how we talked about the murders all being within a two-hour radius of Richmond?" Excitement and dread tangled in his gut. "Picture the hit locations like a compass rose. North, South, East. Richmond is the center. What's West?"

Even as he asked the question, he knew the answer.

"Where were Winter's parents killed?" Bree asked. She was on the same track.

"Harrisonburg. Two hours away from Richmond. Roughly west."

The waiter popped back up with a hopeful expression when Bree and Noah got to their feet.

"Sorry, man." Noah dug out his wallet and handed the surprised kid a twenty. "We're not eating after all."

Bree had already picked up her phone to text Max and tell him about the change of plans. "We going to drive?" she asked Noah as they left the restaurant, expertly navigating puddles in the parking lot without looking away from the phone screen.

"Might as well," Noah replied. "I'll drive if you can extend the rental reservation too. Harrisonburg is a four-hour drive from here, but it'll take that long just to arrange any other kind of transportation."

"Noah."

He stopped, turning around.

Bree had halted just behind him, a look of trepidation on her face, her phone forgotten in her hand. "Why was Winter going home this afternoon? You left the office about one, right?"

"She said she had an appointment."

"Like *your* appointment?" The question was gentle but pointed.

He was already shaking his head before his answer left his mouth. "She wouldn't lie to me, and she wouldn't know about the possible Harrisonburg connection. If anything, wouldn't she try to get here? To Ocean View?"

But he remembered her face. Drawn. Intense. Of course,

she would lie to him.

He knew her, and catching The Preacher was the most important thing in her universe right now. If it was a doctor's appointment, what was it for? Would she be thinking about scheduling an annual physical right now? Not likely. Unless it was something worse. Something to do with her migraines.

Or, she could have lied.

Bree started walking again but more quickly.

"Say she is obsessed. Say she manipulated me to get inside information. Even if she didn't, and she's just working with whatever the BAU has come up with, couldn't she have put the Richmond circle pattern together herself, just like we did? She's brilliant. She could have beat us to it."

Noah yanked open the door to the silver Prius they'd rented for their stay.

"Maybe," was all he'd allow. The thought that she'd be heading for Harrisonburg wasn't a good one. Nothing was good with Winter right now.

Minutes later, they were on the road, heading west.

"Do me a favor," Noah said to Bree. "If Winter tries to get any more information out of you, consider misleading her. I know I sound like a chauvinist now, but she needs to be kept safe. Both from herself and from The Preacher. I don't care how much that pisses her off. Her safety is most important right now, not her feelings."

Bree surprised him by immediately agreeing.

"There's no question she's a target. Whether Winter likes it or not, I agree with you. And I'm afraid he's speeding up his timeline. One month between Delosreyes and Hawkins. Three weeks between Hawkins and Dean. What's next? Two weeks? One? It's already been two days since Dean was killed."

Or maybe, Noah thought grimly, Winter would speed up

The Preacher's timeline for him. If he found Winter in Harrisonburg, there would be no need to wait for another perfect victim.

Noah prayed they were wrong, and Winter wouldn't be there for him to find.

19

The hotel hadn't been updated since Winter had last stayed there. She'd been put in a different room, but everything was the same, from the musty, stained beige carpeting, to the pastel-splashed cheap wallpaper. She'd checked for cameras the night before and found none. Then, she'd tried to sleep for a few hours, without much success.

Coffee.

But first, she had a question for the manager.

Winter pushed open the door to the lobby. The overhead bell that had dinged last time to announce visitors had quit working sometime in the last couple of months. She moved farther into the dingy office, carpeted in a tired floral pattern, hearing the excited murmur of conversation coming from the back room.

She could sit and wait, though the rickety, Naugahyde-covered chair to her right looked as though it would fall apart if she sneezed at it.

Alma Krueger, who ran the place as far as Winter could tell, was probably burning up the phone lines. Someone had to let people know that one of the FBI agents who had investigated the old burial grounds in Linville had rented one of her rooms.

Or maybe someone else had put together who she was, and information was flowing into Alma's ear, instead of out. Anyone who had known her as a kid could have seen spooky Winter Black, back in town again.

She'd run into old acquaintances last time she'd been to Harrisonburg. Sam Boxley, nee Benton. Her childhood BFF-turned-frenemy had been directly involved in the case she and Noah had worked on. The local police knew she was the daughter of Bill and Jeanette Black—murdered in their beds back in the 2000s. Sam's husband, Tom, was an officer with the Harrisonburg PD.

Samantha and Tom Benton probably had their hands full with their own lives these days. They'd been trying to adopt a child when she'd seen them last. If anyone was talking about Winter, it was Alma. There were people who could sit on a juicy tidbit of news like that without sharing it with someone else. Alma Krueger wasn't one of them.

Winter hadn't made any effort to keep her identity a secret, and if it got out now, who cared, she decided. The sooner the word got out, the better.

Bring on the endgame.

She was reaching out to tap the little silver bell on the counter when the murmuring voice in the back got abruptly louder.

"I tell you, Elva, I bet she's here about that old case. It's just like the last episode of that new show on the TV." Alma rounded the corner, her face flushed with excitement, her helmet of gray curls shellacked into submission around her rounded, avid face. "I talked to Bernadine, and she thinks... oh!" Alma dropped the phone, throwing a pudgy hand to her chest. "Land sakes, I didn't know anyone was out here. 'Bout scare me to death, why don't you?"

"Sorry." Winter smiled, doing her best to make it seem genuine. "I just had a quick question for you before I head out for the day."

"Go ahead, dear." Alma's face lit with interest. "What can I do to help you?"

Before Winter could speak, Alma held up one hand and shot her a warning look. "If you ask me about anybody who knows anything, though, I'm not telling you. The last person I sent you to ended up *dead,* God rest Elbert's sweet, loving soul."

Winter winced at the reminder but nodded. It was a valid concern. Alma had been trying to get into Elbert Wilkin's pants for years, and the irascible old man had been murdered shortly after Winter's arrival.

Alma's phone was still on the floor. "Aren't you going to grab that?" Winter nodded at the bulky, '90s-model cordless that emitted squawking shrieks.

It wasn't broken. It was Alma's sister on the other end, demanding to know if Alma was dead.

The elderly woman huffed and fluttered her hands. "Of course, of course." She scooped it up, not bothering to let Elva know that she was alive and tucked it in the pocket of the smock-like apron she wore.

"Now. What can I do for you, Special Agent Black?"

"Just Winter," she corrected. "I'm not here on official business."

Alma snorted. "Sure you're not. Everyone who stays with us at the Kreuger Motor Inn comes back for the lovely atmosphere."

The statement surprised a quick laugh from Winter. "Honestly, I just had a question for you. Last time I was here, I thought someone had maybe been in my room."

Alma puffed up indignantly. "If you're suggesting that I would steal your things, young lady—"

"No, not at all! Is there anyone else who works for you? Housekeeping staff? Maintenance? Some things had been moved around, and I was just curious about it." She grinned. "FBI agents are naturally curious. Heck, maybe it was my imagination. Sometimes I think my brain invents things if there's nothing else to investigate."

Alma gave her a look that clearly said Winter was crazy.

"I don't have much help here, taking care of the place," she finally admitted. "My sister's neighbor's daughter, Sue, comes in and cleans up after the guests. As a matter of fact," she added, narrowing her gaze on Winter, "Sue said that there was some drywall dust behind the TV in one of the rooms a few months ago. If that was you, I'll have to ask you to pay for any damage to my wall."

"That wasn't me," Winter replied serenely. "Is there anyone else who comes in to help Sue out?"

"No. We don't get a lot of business, and she needs the money."

"What about maintenance?"

"No. We had a man that came in to do that for us." Alma sighed, sounding sad.

Winter tensed, keeping the slight, interested smile on her face. "Does he still come around?"

Now, Alma looked downright wistful. "No. After years of being the most reliable handyman you could ask for, he quit showing up one day."

The hair raised on the back of Winter's neck. "Oh? How long ago?"

"A few months. But it wasn't Barney who touched your things. He's such a sweet man," the older woman enthused.

Winter's stomach iced as she connected the dots. Could it be?

Staring at the woman, she realized that Barney could have very well been The Preacher. In fact, her intuition practically screamed that her theory was true. Alma must have had a crush on the serial killer. The Preacher who had done handyman work for her for years but quit coming around after he'd made contact with Winter months ago.

"Barney?" The name almost scalded her tongue. "What was Barney's last name?"

Alma jammed her hands on her hips, giving Winter the stink eye. "Now, look here. Barney wouldn't go through your things any more than I would. He was such a gentleman. Always told me what a fine woman I was."

"His last name?"

Alma looked surprised at the sudden steel in Winter's voice. "Fife," she squeaked.

Winter blinked. "Seriously?"

Alma chuckled, appearing to relax a little. "I know. Sounded like a fake name to me, too, and a bad one at that. But I've known Barney for years. He'd no more lie to me than my own sister. Plus, Barney had his own key, but I trusted that he would *never* go into occupied rooms. If you thought any of your things were moved, you must've been mistaken."

Even as the woman was talking, Winter's mind whirred with questions. Possibilities. Concerns.

"Do you have his social security number on file? Copy of his driver's license? Did he drive a green and red truck?"

"He did, but—" The phone in Alma's pocket squawked, interrupting. "Oh! If you'll excuse me."

Without waiting for an answer, she pulled out the handset. "Shut up, Elva. Couldn't you hear any of that?" she hissed in what she probably thought was a whisper. She disappeared around the corner and Winter heard her say, "I was talking to *her!* The spooky law girl!"

Conversation over.

Barney Fife. What the hell.

Winter's own phone rang in her purse, the ringtone a twangy country song she'd downloaded and assigned to Noah's number. She dropped the idea of faking a warrant to get into Alma's employment records as she dug her phone out of her bag and left the lobby. The Preacher's real name was not Barney Fife.

Outside, the air was bright and fresh with the smell of wet dirt from the rain the night before. The morning sky was a vivid blue and birds twittered. It wasn't spring yet, but Mother Nature was thinking about it. Winter hit the talk button.

"Morning, Noah. What's going on?"

"Not a lot. Just checking on you." His voice was deep and rumbling, tired sounding, like he'd just woken up.

"You're checking up on me? After such a long radio silence? Odd. I'm fine."

"How'd your appointment go yesterday?"

Winter headed for her Civic. She recognized a probing question when she heard one, and Noah hadn't contacted her out of the blue like this in weeks.

"Super fun and exciting. Annual pap smears always are. You want details?"

He made a choking noise, and she grinned, even as a pang of wistfulness shook her unexpectedly.

She missed him. The goof.

"How was your appointment? Did you have a pap smear too?"

"Seriously, can you just stop saying 'pap smear?'" Noah demanded, sounding pained. "Hey, I've gotta go. I'm actually getting ready to head out. I just wanted to check in with you real quick."

"Well…thanks? You still in Ocean View?"

He paused for a moment, clearly startled that she knew.

Good. She wanted him off-balance.

"Yeah," he finally said. "I'm not telling you anything though, so don't ask."

"Wasn't planning on it. Different departments now, right? Not my circus, not my monkeys."

That might have been laying it on a little thick. She wrenched on the door handle to the Civic a little harder than she meant to. The rusting spring inside creaked.

"Where are you going?" Noah demanded. "Was that your car door?"

Winter cursed under her breath. "Work. You know, where we go and do things and get paid?"

"I thought you weren't driving."

She held a hand over the phone speaker. "Thanks, Jake," she said to the empty interior of her car.

"Who's Jake?"

"Jesus, Noah," she burst out. "Why the third degree? It's not any of your business, but Jake is the Uber guy who's been driving me to work. He lives in the next apartment complex over from us, and I've seen him every morning for weeks. He's twenty years old, blond/blue, six foot three, and moved to Richmond from San Diego three years ago, for college reasons. We're practically best friends now."

"I thought you said yesterday that you use Lyft."

She blew out an exasperated breath, and then grinned reluctantly. He was good.

"Bye, Noah. Thanks for the morning interrogation."

"Sorry." The one word sounded genuinely regretful, and she pulled her car door closed with a quiet click. "I'm just worried about you," he added.

The words poked a hole in her conscience. Guilt leaked out. She struggled to shove it back.

"I miss you, Noah."

She hadn't meant to say that out loud.

It had apparently surprised Noah too. There was silence

on the other end, and then his voice, rich and warm like coffee. "Miss you, too, Winter. Take care of yourself."

He hung up.

What if she was wrong? What if The Preacher was really in Ocean View still, and *Noah* was the one in danger? The thought took her breath away. She never should have let him get as close as he had.

It took her a minute of using anger to gather the shards of her armor around herself again, find the single-minded focus she'd managed to gain, but Winter finally started the car. It was time to get back to work.

The countdown clock had been reset the last time The Preacher had killed. Whether it dinged in a week, or two weeks, or a matter of hours, she had no time to waste on self-pity. Noah was where he needed to be, and Winter was where *she* needed to be.

It was time.

Even the nosy, stroller-pushing mother who lived on her old cul-de-sac now wouldn't think Winter was up to anything this morning, she decided as she headed out of the parking lot. It was a lovely day, bright and sunny. She needed coffee, and luckily, there was a Starbucks nearby.

Anyone seeing a car parked out in front of the old Black house and a young woman in jeans and a sweatshirt going in with a coffee would think she belonged there. She could pass for a realtor or prospective home buyer.

Instead, she was going to be inside, deliberately trying to provoke a painful vision of blood and death.

MY HANDS JITTERED on the steering wheel, my knobby knuckles still aching from all the work I'd been doing lately. In the old days, I could keep up. Now, not so much.

All those tiny little cuts I'd had to make on my girlie…

I loved workin' for the Lord, but it was hard craft for an old man's arthritic hands. Winter had looked almost cleansed when I was done, though, I thought with a smile. I'd exorcized every last sinful sign of the bitch.

She'd brought punishment on herself, tarting up like she had, prancing around town in those little running shorts. Flashing those long, white legs for anyone to see. I didn't mean to do it so soon, but she made me. Taunted me into it.

She'd been tricky about it, sure. She'd dyed her hair a harlot's red. And even though her eyes had been brown, she hadn't fooled me. I saw Winter looking out, smug and evil.

Until I'd started to kill her. The memory of the fear I'd seen in her eyes after I ran my blade under her chin made my pecker hard all over again, right there in the truck.

Even though it hadn't felt up to movin' around that day for my girlie, I remembered in disgust. Fucking prostate.

The light turned red up ahead, surprising me. I'd been woolgathering again and hadn't even seen it turn yellow. I slammed on the brakes, almost running into the car in front of my truck.

Bessie Lou managed to stop and rocked forward, creaking on her rusty old chassis. In front of me, in a little blue hatchback, the girl in the driver's seat couldn't have been more than seventeen. She looked at me in the rearview and glared.

I wasn't ashamed to admit, I got angry, and I glared right back, inching Bessie closer until I nudged the little bitch's car. The Jezebel had the nerve to raise her middle finger up to me.

My fingers itched and trembled with the need to teach her about a woman's place. If God wanted women to drive, or use crude hand motions, he'd have given them the intelligence he handed out to menfolk as he sent 'em out the pearly gates.

The light turned green, and I pulled forward with the car in front of me, hanging right up on to her back bumper. The girl kept looking back at me, her mouth moving as she spewed what was probably foul language. From the distance, her eyes looked brown.

But they could have been blue. Deep, quiet blue.

I shook myself loose of that thought and backed off her bumper.

Winter was dead, wasn't she?

I'd killed her in New Jersey.

My head was starting to hurt a little, and I rubbed my forehead. No, that wasn't right. The girl in New Jersey hadn't really looked like Winter at all once I'd cornered her in her apartment.

My girlie was a tricky one. She'd fooled me with the police officer.

She'd looked out the eyes of the fat gal in the big, expensive house.

Another red light.

I slammed on my brakes again, and they made a grinding noise, taking longer than necessary to stop the truck. Least this time there was no one in front of me, or I'd have hit them for sure.

The girl in the car in front of me was gone. I hadn't seen her get away from me. In a daze of confusion, my heart beating hard, I watched a little black Honda Civic cross the intersection in front of me. Behind the wheel, her black hair shining in the morning sun and her face all pale like porcelain, I saw my girlie. Winter.

She didn't look at me, just drove past, like in slow motion. Then, the car was gone, and I was left feeling a little queasy.

I'd been seeing—and killing—Winter Black every damn where.

Hadn't I?

How many Winters would I have to kill before she really died?

20

It was nearing eleven when Aiden finally stopped watching the door and accepted the fact that Winter was not coming into the office.

He left the room then, fury vibrating through him, and went to her cubicle. The thumb drive he'd given her sat conspicuously beside her keyboard, but her computer was gone.

So was her water bottle. Her jacket. He pulled open the drawers of her desk. Empty, as if the office had been recently cleaned out for a new occupant. Or as if the old occupant had never truly planned on staying.

He texted her for the fifth time. His hands shook with impotent anger.

CALL ME NOW.

Winter had been right the day before. The leverage he'd held over her had been made on the assumption he knew who she was. Again, his illustrious profiling skills had played out for shit.

Winter wasn't a fragile person who'd never fully healed from the traumatic wounds she'd received as a child, he told himself as he headed back to his office. Instead, she'd started showing signs of being as hard and purposeful as a battle-scarred Valkyrie on a mission of vengeance.

And now, he'd handed her the keys to the investigation, and practically fucking dared her to slip her leash. What was the saying? When people show you who they are, believe them.

He hadn't believed Winter.

Grabbing his spare set of keys from his desk, he decided it was time to drive. He still favored his stiff leg and had been taking a hired car to work in the mornings since he'd come back. He couldn't waste the time on travel planning, though. He had to get to Harrisonburg. Thankfully, his Mercedes was still in the parking lot, since he hadn't bothered moving it after his accident.

Pushing his bad leg, and ignoring the burn in the under-used muscles, SSA Parrish headed for the door.

CLOSING HER EYES, Winter took inventory.

No headache. Clear mind. There was fear, but so far, it was staying banked at an acceptable level. She was as good as she was going to get.

She got out of the car, glad to see that the street was empty. It was a school day and a work day for the middle-class, two-parent households that made up the block residents. A cool breeze tickled the back of her neck as she walked up the sidewalk that was achingly familiar and strange, all at the same time.

The square with the signature of five-year-old Winter etched in it was still there, but one of the adjoining concrete blocks had been pushed up by the maple tree that had decided to grow wild, to the left of the little sidewalk.

The front porch still creaked, but with a louder, groaning undertone now. Soon, if it wasn't maintained, it wouldn't be structurally safe anymore.

The door was locked this time.

She stepped back, glancing at the empty street. Setting her green and white coffee cup on the peeling white railing, she turned and raised her foot, slamming her booted heel just above the handle. She felt like Chuck Norris when the wood splintered away, and the door swung wide.

Grabbing her mocha again, she headed inside, taking a deep breath and opening herself to any kind of vibes. It sounded new-agey, but Winter wasn't sure how to go about summoning a vision. She'd try whatever.

She'd had no expectations, so the overwhelming feeling of sadness that swamped her—almost bringing her to her knees—was shocking. Winter carefully moved out of the small foyer, to the flight of stairs that ran upward in front of her.

Disoriented, she closed her eyes against the drowning tide of emotion and sank down on the step. A dried leaf had found its way in and crackled drily as she dislodged it from the stair tread.

She tried to focus on the warmth and smooth surface of the cup of coffee she had in her hands, and not the scalding tears that washed down her cheeks. It was frightening. She had no control over the reaction.

Focusing on her breathing, orienting herself to her surroundings, she pulled her way out of the emotional sand trap, hand over hand.

She could smell the dusty, unstirred air in the house. Behind her closed lids, she could see a faint glow to her right, where the plywood didn't reach all the way to the top of the window casement, and the sun pushed its way in. She could imagine the dust motes, disturbed by her presence, swirling and dipping in the stagnant air.

The tears stopped, and the vicious press of grief lightened.

Cautiously, she opened her eyes.

Inventory.

No headache. Clear mind. Fear: under control. Sadness: manageable.

"What the hell was that?" she whispered into the silent rooms.

She could add more items to that list, Winter thought as she stood up on legs that trembled faintly. Apprehension. Trepidation. Anxiety and foreboding.

Before another wave of...whatever...could hit her, Winter climbed the stairs, leaving her coffee cup on the step. Every movement upward ratcheted that anxiety up higher. Her skin seemed to crawl and shiver, like an opera singer had hit a high note and she was the glass about to shatter.

At the top of the stairs, the window to her left showed that the sun was still shining. Birds were still fluttering. A dog barked down the street. It was a reminder that normal shit was still happening outside, even if it was as still and oppressive as a crypt in this house.

Straight in front of her, the door to her parents' bedroom hung partially open.

Her feet felt heavy, and she recognized as she moved toward the room that she was consciously blocking out anything right now that might hurt. Like the sadness that had engulfed her earlier.

Walking into the master bedroom, she took a breath. The air was fresher here, thanks to a branch that had fallen and broken through a pane of glass. A quick glance around showed that nothing had been disturbed since she'd been there last. Footprints in the dust could have been hers from her previous visit. They were scuffed and indistinct.

To her surprise and relief, she noticed that the dust was completely undisturbed near where the bed had been. In the sunshine, it turned into a grayish, opalescent film that lay thick over the brown stains in the hardwood.

Okay. It was time. She took in another gulp of the cool, wet-smelling air that wended its way through the room from the broken glass of the window.

Open up to it, Winter told herself silently.

With a rushing noise like the beating wings of a thousand bats, darkness swept down on her, clawing her to the floor.

"Turn here."

It was Bree's turn to drive, and she glanced over at Noah. Her brown eyes were bright with curiosity and the thrill of the hunt. They were close. The Preacher was in town, and they both could feel it.

"I thought we were going to the Harrisonburg police station."

"We are. I just want to see something."

He directed her to the Krueger Motor Inn.

"Nice place," she snorted, pulling up in the parking lot in front of the decrepit-looking hotel. "But I don't think I want to swap out our reservation at the Motel 6 for this."

The parking lot held only a couple of cars. It was after check-out, almost one, but he had a feeling it wouldn't look much busier around peak hotel hours.

He couldn't shake the feeling after he'd spoken to Winter this morning that she was a lot closer than Richmond. Like The Preacher, he could feel that she was here. He didn't like it. He thought about going into the office, talking to Alma

Krueger. But picturing her avid, wrinkled face—and the way she had of undressing him with her eyes—he chickened out.

"If you turn out of here and go left, there's a Starbucks just down the street."

"Now you're talking." Bree's hands were smooth and capable on the wheel as she pulled a rapid U-turn at the back of the lot.

In the drive-through, he still couldn't get Winter out of his head. She liked iced mochas, he knew. Skim milk, no whip. Sometimes, she'd get a hot one, but he'd never seen her order anything but mochas.

"Ground control to Major Tom," Bree said, waving one slim hand in front of his face. "To the sheriff's office?"

"No. Turn here. To the right."

"Some notice would be nice," Bree mumbled, whipping a tight turn and rolling her eyes. "Like, more than none. Anything particular we're looking for on this nondescript residential street, Agent Dalton?"

"That." His tone was grim. "That's Winter's Honda Civic."

"Fuck." The curse word was hushed, drawn out. Bree picked up the pace, pulled around and parked behind it at the end of the street. "Is this her old house?"

He was already out of the car, moving toward the house and didn't answer. The door was closed but pushed open easily. It had been broken in, and only lightly pushed closed so that it didn't draw the attention of neighbors.

A white and green cup rested on one of the lowest stairs. She'd gone with a hot mocha today, he thought inanely.

Bree huffed to a stop beside him. "That's hers?"

"Yeah."

"You sure?" She reached out, laid her fingertips against the side. "It's cold. Could be from this morning or a week ago."

He moved quickly up the steps at a run. In the upstairs hallway, fresh smudges marked the dusty floor.

The door they led to was closed.

He jiggled the handle.

"Winter!" he roared, hearing Bree climbing the stairs. "Stay back," he yelled at her, pulling out his service weapon.

The door slammed against the interior wall after one solid kick, hard enough to wedge the door handle into the drywall. In the center of the room, crumpled facedown on the grimy floor in a puddle of bright sunshine, was Winter.

"Jesus Christ, Noah, is she dead?"

He holstered his gun and dropped into a crouch.

The pool of blood that surrounded her head had dried to a thickish, viscous mess. It was unpleasantly sticky under his hand when he braced himself beside Winter to take her pulse.

He held his breath, feeling sick with regret. Remorse.

Rage.

Until, under his fingers, he felt it. A pulse, fluttery and faint like the insubstantial brush of a moth's wings. He let his breath out on what sounded like a sob, too relieved to care what Bree thought.

"911?" Bree asked shortly, taking in the surroundings in focused, trained movements. She was looking for signs of a struggle. Blood on the walls. Scripture or crosses. The Preacher's calling cards.

"No. It wasn't him. I know what this is. She'll be okay."

Judging by the size of the blood spill, this vision made the previous ones look benign. The blood alone showed she'd suffered more of a hemorrhage than a nosebleed.

He rolled Winter over and slapped lightly at her cheeks, calling her name. She didn't show so much as a flicker of a reaction. Behind him, Bree stood in watchful, worried silence.

"It's this house. Let's get her out of here," Noah ordered. He scooped Winter up in his arms. She was all bones, it felt like. She had a tall, leanly muscled build, normally, but she'd definitely lost weight in the past weeks. She was hardly heavier than a ten-year-old kid.

"I'll explain once we get her out of here," he told Bree, meeting her eyes. She was apprehensive. Confused and frightened, though you never would have been able to tell from the expression on her smooth face. There was no FBI SOP manual that would cover a situation like this.

They left the house, the fresh air outside a balm after the sick, clammy atmosphere inside Winter's childhood home. He'd made it to the top of the steps, when a black Mercedes roared down the street, rocking to a stop in the middle of the turnout. The door flew open, and Parrish climbed stiffly out, favoring one leg.

The normally immaculate profiler looked disheveled. His tie was gone, wrinkled dress shirt unbuttoned at the neck. His hair was rumpled and his face stubbled, hollowed cheeks tight with pain.

"Is she alive?" he barked out, the fear in his voice obvious.

"Yeah." There would be plenty of time for animosity and finger pointing later. "She's not coming out of this one like normal, though."

Noah moved carefully down the steps, trying not to jostle Winter, meeting Aiden at the bottom. When Aiden called her name, she stirred a little, and Noah had to stifle a flick of jealousy. Not the time.

She opened her eyes with a quickness that startled a gasp out of Bree.

With blazing hot eyes, looking almost feral, Winter glanced around wildly, struggling in his arms. "Let me go," she screamed, her throat working to force out the words. She started in with her fists, and Noah flinched when she caught him just under his left eye.

"Winter. Knock it off." He didn't yell it, but he said it loud. He let her feet slip to the ground and pulled her into a bear hug.

Whether it was the commanding tone or the resonance of his voice, or maybe the restraint of his arms, something snapped, and Winter went boneless in his grip. He had to adjust his hold, so she didn't collapse completely.

"Sweetheart, hush. You're okay, darlin'," he whispered against her hair.

"You're all dead," she moaned, wrapping her fingers tightly in his shirt. The forlorn words sounded broken.

Aiden and Bree watched silently as Noah rubbed Winter's back and let her cry.

21

B lackness. Cold. Death.

Bloody, gory images of crosses and viscera and sinew and bone. Gleeful pictures of violence overlaid by what sounded like the shrieks of a thousand demons.

Winter wanted to put her hands over her ears, just to block out the memory of the sound.

Underneath was a sibilant hiss, like the sound of a record when the song was over, and the needle was left spinning in the dead space at the center.

Kill them all. Exorcize their Godless souls from their bodies.

"Winter, dammit, look at me. Don't drift off on me again!"

The voice was loud. Louder than the malevolent whisper, and she grabbed on to it like a lifeline.

Pulled away from the thought of her little brother, too young to even walk to the end of the block without one of their parents, taken by a human being capable of that kind of savage brutality.

Her eyelids drifted lower, even as sadness rushed up in an overwhelming wave and her eyes filled with tears. The same sadness that had swamped her when she'd opened herself up inside the house the first time.

Little starbursts of sensation sparkled across the sides of her face, and her lashes flickered open. Noah's scowl wavered into focus, and the darkness receded. His eyes locked with hers. Deep green, like grass in the shadows, with little flecks of gold near the irises that she'd never noticed.

Familiar, compelling, they brought her fully back to the light.

"Winter." He stopped slapping at her cheeks. "You back with me?"

The darkness still tickled at the edges of her consciousness, but she nodded.

"Good. Sit down." Noah eased her down to the curb. His shoulders blocked out the sunlight, leaving his face in darkness, like an overexposed photo. She sank to the ground, her knees twinging in pain. Her joints hurt and her stomach ached.

She bent over her knees, fighting a wave of dizziness, and rested her head in her hands. She heard Noah's boots scuffing against the pavement as he moved away. Her headache was gone, but she felt unbalanced. Unsteady. She tried to focus on her breathing.

Her uneven heartbeat steadied itself while Winter struggled to orient herself with the real world. She could hear birds again. A woodpecker tapped a staccato against the trunk of a tree somewhere off in the near distance. The sun warmed the top of her head with an afternoon glow.

When she'd arrived, it had still been morning.

How long had she been gone?

"Drink this." Noah's voice sounded like honey poured over concrete. She looked up, and he handed her a lukewarm can of Pepsi.

"You know I like Coke." Her voice sounded raspy, and her

throat hurt. She took a sip and grimaced at the flat, syrupy taste.

Noah chuckled, some of the tension easing out of his face. "Hell, sweetheart. I'll buy you a case of Coke. Just don't scare me like that again, all right?"

She didn't laugh.

Winter hoped never to scare herself, or anyone else, like that again.

"How did you find me?"

"Psychic link?" His tone was flippant, but his face was sober. He was analyzing her with that cop look he had. Taking her apart, piece by piece, with the formidable intellect he hid behind his affable attitude.

"Stop staring at me, you jerk. Or at least take a picture. It'll last longer."

It felt juvenile to say that, considering the terror she still felt at what she'd seen in the house. She could still feel the presence of the evil she'd brushed against, looming large behind her. She didn't want to turn and look. Didn't have to. The experience was burned into her mind.

Noah gave her a wry smile. "There's the Winter we all know and love."

The soft sound of someone clearing their throat came from nearby, and Winter realized with a mild shock that they weren't alone. Bree held out a small packet of wet wipes, and Aiden stood in watchful stillness a few feet away.

"The gang's all here," she muttered, taking the package from Bree. "Are you all psychic?"

"Just those two." Bree gave her a careful look. "You might want to use a mirror on that cleanup job. You've got…" She gestured toward her face vaguely, her voice trailing off. "Do you mind?"

Winter looked down at the wipe. It was flecked and stained already with more blood than she'd expected. She reached up to touch her face. The skin was tight around her lips and mouth, and the side of her face felt rough, her hair tangled and matted. She grimaced and nodded.

"May I?" Bree pulled out several of the wipes, and without waiting for an answer, gently started cleaning the blood from Winter's face. Her touch was brisk, but kind at the same time. It was embarrassing, but her embarrassment just brought her back fully into the real world. The dark shadows in her mind faded into the background a little bit more.

When Bree had finished, clucking with approval like a mother hen, Noah was beside her with a crumpled grocery bag to take the stained cloths.

"You okay to walk?"

The question had come from Bree. Bree helped her up, as both men took a step forward, and abruptly, Winter felt claustrophobic.

"I'm fine." The words came out harsher than she'd intended. She was grateful for their concern. But she didn't want it. The need to run pulsed heavily in her chest.

She slipped out of Bree's grasp, intending to move out of the center of the trio, but Aiden blocked her way. Leaner than Noah, with more of an elegant strength, Aiden smiled without humor. His blue eyes were dark with an expression she couldn't read.

Superimposed for just a moment over his aristocratic-looking features, she could see another face. Blue eyes stared blankly, leached of their sharp intelligence. The skin of the face was white and lifeless. The neck, above a red-stained collar gaped in an obscene grin.

She glanced at Bree. Bree was worse.

Gone were her pretty, round-cheeked, sensitive features. Instead of dark coffee-colored skin stretched smoothly over a fine-boned structure, the bones themselves were visible. A grinning skull was in its place, the bone nicked in places from some kind of sharp surgical instrument. Her beauty had been stolen, and evil had left its mark.

Winter stifled a roll of nausea in her belly and looked toward Noah, automatically and subconsciously for comfort. Noah's handsome, rough-hewn face had been burned. The skin was blackened and curled in places, the eyes bloodshot and—

She couldn't look any more. Her head spun as she closed her eyes against the malevolent images. She had to get away. The longer she stayed, the closer The Preacher would come to them, and he was death incarnate.

Cold rippled over her skin, and her breathing felt labored.

When she looked back to Aiden, his face was normal again. She wanted to sob in relief.

"Move it, Parrish," she ground out. "I'd hate to get blood on your designer suit."

Aiden didn't budge. He spoke, instead, his voice silky and controlled. "Get in the car. You can clean up at the hotel."

His car? Not a chance.

"And get blood all over your nice leather seats? No."

She edged around him, heading for her Civic.

"Winter." There was a warning in Noah's tone.

"Guys." Bree was kind, but firm. "I'll drive her. Where are you staying, Aiden?"

Their voices faded and Winter stumbled a bit. Then, Bree's hand was at her elbow, warm and steady, steering her toward the passenger's side.

Bree opened the door for her as if she were a child. Winter was pathetically grateful to have someone take over for her. Her limbs felt like they were weighted with lead bullets. Heavy and awkward. The instinct to escape was still strong, but sudden fatigue thundered over her like a tsunami.

She'd be a danger on the road, and it was galling to admit it, but driving anywhere would be suicide.

Winter's lids were heavy like they were filled with sand, and she fought to keep them open. Bree slid into the driver's seat and pulled it forward briskly, adjusting it for her short legs. Without asking for permission, she dug around in Winter's messenger bag where it rested between the seats and expertly fished out the car keys.

"Buckle up."

Her tone was friendly, but there was still caution there.

Winter didn't blame her. The whole experience had to be disconcerting for her.

She let her lids drop the rest of the way and leaned her head back against the seat, trying to focus on the now and not the future. They rode in silence for a little while. Winter didn't know where they were going and was too tired to care.

"So, you got the sight, huh?"

The question was matter of fact, but the content of it startled her.

She forced her eyes open. "What do you mean?"

Bree glanced away from the road ahead and smiled at her. "It's cool. My grandma and my mom had it. I think I'm too practical. It skipped a generation."

Winter shook her head in automatic denial, but Bree pressed on.

"You might not remember if your mom was," Bree commented carefully, "but is your grandma sensitive?"

Gramma Beth? The thought distracted her enough that she gave serious consideration to it. Gramma Beth, with her sweet, pretty face and vintage-style dresses. Always perfectly turned out, a wizard in the kitchen, with a clever, biting wit. Grampa Jack, big and quiet and good-natured, had always seemed like the strong one when she was a child, but as an adult, Winter had come to the realization that her grandma ruled the roost with a firm, neatly manicured grip.

Gramma Beth, who had shown up in one of her dreams a few months ago, essentially saving her life.

Gramma Beth, who had accepted Winter's calling and had started watching police procedure TV shows. They'd discussed one of Winter's cases, and she'd shown a keen interest and good instincts for actual investigative theories.

Still. The sight? That was a word that came from Steven King novels. It reminded her of *The Shining*. Fiction.

Bree didn't get it.

"I'm not sensitive," Winter finally replied. She might as well share the story with Bree. Everyone else had heard it by this point.

"I was the one who found my parents. I came home from a friend's house that night. We never kept the doors locked. I came in the house, went upstairs to go to bed. Their door was cracked open, just enough for me to see..."

Bree didn't look away from the road, just nodded. Winter felt her sympathy, but the fact that she didn't speak made it easier to go on.

"My dad had a bullet hole in his forehead. He didn't suffer. My mom...she got the same treatment as the rest of The Preacher's victims." She closed her eyes again against the memory. "The Preacher had been there. I didn't realize he still was, until I turned around and he was behind me. He hit me with something. Knocked me out. I don't remember anything after that until I woke up in the hospital a couple of months later."

"Your coma," Bree murmured, hitting the turn signal. "And...your brother?"

The shaft of pain at the thought of little gap-toothed Justin had dulled over time, but it still hurt. Like having your heart carved out with a butter knife.

"He was gone."

Bree grimaced. "'I'm sorry' is too inadequate. I can't imagine. But I have a younger brother," she said simply. "He's not a little brother anymore. He's at least a foot taller than me and has a wife and three kids, but…I can't imagine."

She made a right-hand turn, and Winter saw a hotel ahead. The Motel 6, by the highway.

"Listen," she said to Bree, urgency tickling at her nerves again. "I appreciate that you all have a job to do, too, but you need to leave."

Bree's eyes were calm and velvety brown. The expression in them was resolute.

Even as she was shaking her head, Winter pushed on. They were almost to the hotel. "I need you three to leave," she insisted. "I know you're working the case, but please. Make them go. Manufacture a lead or something and get them the hell out of here. Parrish and Dalton."

"Sorry, sweetie. We're in this together."

Bree did sound sorry, but Winter's temper simmered. She wasn't listening.

"I don't have the shine, or whatever the fuck you think I have. I'm not psychic. My brain is messed up because I had a closed head injury and spent a couple of months lying unconscious in a hospital bed. But you have to trust me when I tell you that it's not safe for you all here."

Bree pulled into a parking spot. Beside them, Aiden parked his Mercedes. On the other side, Noah was parking.

She felt boxed in. Trapped.

"Dammit, Bree, please." The words were desperate, and Bree probably thought she was unhinged, but Winter didn't care.

Bree turned the key in the ignition, and the car engine died with a soft sputter.

"Listen to me." She turned in her seat, locked eyes with Winter. Reaching out, she grabbed Winter's hands.

Winter wanted to pull away from the connection. It was

uncomfortable. She and Bree were co-workers. It felt like awkward boundaries were being crossed, but Bree held her panicked gaze with a soothing, steady one.

"Listen to me," she repeated, her hands warm on Winter's, the palms slightly calloused. "We are in this together."

Winter heard the car door of the Mercedes slam. Noah stood like a monolith on the sidewalk in front of the Civic. Her heart fluttered in panicky, shaky beats. She felt penned in.

Winter opened her mouth to protest, but Bree cut her off firmly.

"I said *we*. You're not officially assigned to this case. Neither is Parrish. But all of us have been working at cross-purposes, convinced that we're the only ones who can take The Preacher down. It's time to combine our efforts so that we actually can. He's here. We're here. We need to quit wasting our fucking time playing games and put our heads together before he kills again."

Slowly, Winter's frantic heartbeat evened out. Bree squeezed her hands gently one more time and released them.

They got out of the car and headed for the entrance to the shabby hotel. Bree and Noah flanked her. Aiden was a brooding presence from behind.

The fatigue ebbed away with the decision Winter had made. She'd work with them. For now. Bree was right. It might take all four of them to track The Preacher down.

But she'd cut them out at the end.

Winter would be the one to kill him.

22

Wynona Baines hated her name.

It made her sound like some old lady, big-haired country singer. It wasn't her fault that her dad was obsessed with Wynona Judd and her mom hadn't insisted on Parker as a first name. Her dad had won that argument thirteen years ago, and Parker had become her middle name.

Parker sounded like a cool girl. Someone who could navigate eighth grade with no problems and would never dream of tripping over her own big feet in the hallway, dropping her books right in front of Jake Popper, the cutest guy in school.

Parker would be a blonde, smart, popular girl who had it all together. Not a skinny, black-haired, awkward girl with a pimple on her chin that looked like Mount Vesuvius, even though she'd covered it up with some of her mom's foundation that morning.

"Wynnie, did you check with your parents about Friday night?" Becca, short and pudgy with brown eyes and overgrown bangs, looked up at her like a puppy. Becca lived down the street, and they'd been friends since they could walk.

"Parker," Wynona automatically corrected, lifting her chin. "I'm going by Parker now."

She tried to correct Becca every time, even suggesting Becca go by her full name—Rebecca Montague, which sounded way more sophisticated—but Becca never seemed to remember. She was kind of childish, still. Probably because she was only twelve and a half.

But Wynnie and Becca sounded like little kid names. And at nearly thirteen, nothing was worse than being labeled a little kid.

"Yep," she answered. "I'm good to go. I just have to make sure my chores are done, and I get a B or better on my history test."

"Cool," Becca breathed, relieved. "You'll ace it for sure. You're smart. And I can help you with your chores if you want. I don't mind doing dishes."

Becca linked arms with Wynona, making her remember why they were friends. Becca was so earnest all the time. That had been one of her vocab words in Lit and Comp last week, but it fit her friend perfectly. *Showing sincere and intense conviction.*

They were BFFs, even if Becca was a little immature.

They walked the rest of the way to Becca's house, reminiscing about Barry Klippington throwing up in the lunchroom that morning. Sucked to be him, but he was always pulling Wynona's hair in pre-algebra, so she couldn't summon up much sympathy. Barfing Barry, though…that name was going to stick with him. She winced in sympathy.

The birds were chirping, and the sky was so blue, it almost hurt to look at it. It felt like spring, and she and Becca were both in a good mood when Wynona left her at her front door.

"See you in the morning!" she yelled, waving, and headed down the sidewalk. Her own house was just one street over. About ten houses away, and around the corner.

She was thinking about how Barry was kind of cute, when he wasn't being annoying and losing his lunch in front of the whole school, when a voice behind her caught her attention.

"Winter?"

Wynona turned around, confused. It was spring, not winter.

An old man with a friendly smile was a few houses behind her. He waved at her like he knew her, and a little trickle of unease dripped down the back of her neck, like one cold raindrop. Giving the stranger a small smile, she turned around and kept walking.

Her red Converse sneaker caught on a crack in the sidewalk, and her heart stumbled as she almost tripped.

"Hey, girlie. Can you help me out?"

She wanted to run. But why? He was a harmless old dude. Not very tall, with white hair and glasses, like her Grandpa Baines. She slowed and turned around reluctantly.

Looking at him again should have made her feel less freaked out. He was closer now, just two houses behind her. But he was *old*. Like seventy. He had red cheeks and a cherry nose, like the picture of Santa in one of her little brother's Christmas books. Plus, it was the middle of the afternoon in the bright sunshine. Bad things didn't happen in the middle of the day. Did they?

But his eyes were black. Dark and creepy. Something about them made her skin crawl, like when she and Becca had stayed up late on Halloween and watched *The Conjuring*.

His eyes were like the doll, Annabelle's. Goose bumps rose up on her arms.

"Sorry," she said, trying to sound sorry. "I've got to get

home and do my homework. I'm late, and my mom's going to yell at me."

She turned around again and ignored him when he mumbled something else that she didn't hear. It sounded like "winter" again.

Hair raising on the back of her neck, she walked faster, getting ready to cross the last street before her block. She felt stupid, but she had the same creeped-out feeling she sometimes got when she pulled the chain on the light that hung in their basement, after she finished taking care of laundry, her least favorite chore.

She felt like she had to run up the dark steps to the main floor fast, or a monster would grab her ankles through the gaps in the stair steps.

But monsters weren't real. They were just in movies.

Still, Wynona wished there was someone else around. A grown-up. Even Becca.

She stepped into the road, ready to run whether that made her look like a loser or not, when he grabbed her. She tried to scream, but a hard, knobby hand clamped down over her nose and mouth, cutting off her air.

Fear flooded her, and she thought she might barf. She thought about Barry for some reason and felt bad for him all over again. She struggled, trying to focus. Trying to get away. But the old guy was strong, with thick arms, and she couldn't breathe. She was getting dizzy.

She'd been wrong, she thought, her brain getting fuzzy as the old man dragged her to a gross, rusty old pickup truck that was parked by the curb. All those times she'd felt dumb for running up the basement stairs as a little kid, scared.

The inside of the pickup smelled like dirty socks. Tears leaked down her cheeks, and her stomach pitched while the old man wrapped a dirty bandanna around her mouth. He pinned her down with his gross, old man body while he tied her wrists and ankles up with rope.

Wynona Parker Baines learned something very important in that instant.

Monsters were real.

NOAH LEANED BACK in the uncomfortable hotel room chair. It was a hard and unforgiving spot for a guy his size, especially since he'd been sitting in it for the last six hours. He glanced at Aiden. The guy was almost as tall as he was, but he didn't seem to be affected. Aiden sat ramrod straight, studying the laptop screen in front of him with the same intensity he'd shown at five o'clock when they'd all finally hashed things out and had gotten to work.

He was probably too prissy to admit that his ass was asleep, Noah thought darkly. The guy probably never even used the word ass. Too plebian.

Bree looked tired, but even at eleven o'clock at night, she still seemed alert as her fingers flew over the keys of her own laptop.

There wasn't enough room for two to work comfortably at the small round table in Noah's room, and three was downright cramped. Behind them, Winter was stretched out on the bed with her own computer, propped against a pile of pillows.

He studied her for a moment. She seemed to have bounced back a little, especially after getting a slice of meat lover's pizza down, even though he'd had to practically force-feed her. Now, her face was shadowed, and beneath her blue eyes, the skin was dark-tinted. Still, she radiated fierce concentration.

He worried about her. He'd tried to convince them all

that she needed to get checked out at the hospital, but he'd been outvoted. Noah rubbed at the crick in the back of his neck. They hadn't listened to him, he remembered grimly. The other three had been focused on the case to the exclusion of everything else.

It would serve her right if she worked herself to death. He shoved to his feet restlessly and grabbed his phone, unhooking it from the charger. He checked the voicemail display, even though he knew if the Harrisonburg chief of police had called, he'd have heard it ring.

The first thing the four of them had done as an actual team was to put out an APB for The Preacher. Finally combining all of the information they had, they'd contacted Gary, chief of the Harrisonburg police, who they'd worked with before. He and one of his officers knew Winter, and that added a personal stake in seeing The Preacher caught.

Plus, the killer was in their territory now. Noah had to trust that the Harrisonburg police were motivated and would work as hard to find him as his own team would, even though *he* wanted to be the one to take him down.

White knight, he reminded himself. Winter had been right. She didn't need him to do it for her, and more, she didn't *want* him to. However, when they found the bastard, he'd be protecting her every step of the way, whether she liked it or not.

Noah was still supremely pissed that Winter had never told him about the other times the sadistic fuckwad had contacted her. He probably wouldn't get over the betrayal of that for a while. He'd been right there with her the first time it had happened, only one tacky hotel room away. He should have pushed her harder back then to tell him what was wrong. He'd had a hunch that there was something, but he'd let her get around him.

But at least he didn't feel like she was holding back

anymore. Everyone's cards were on the table now. Except maybe Parrish's. Who knew what that asshole was thinking. He was an FBI bigwig. Head of his own department. He probably had something to gain from helping, otherwise he'd still be in his office back in Richmond, busy being a control freak there.

Noah set his phone down on the nightstand and pulled out his own well-worn deck of cards. They felt soft and worn in his hands. He was going to need to get a new pack soon, he thought as he unwound the rubber band that held the dog-eared deck together.

It was an odd habit, but an old one. Ever since he'd been a teenager, learning Poker at his granddaddy's knee, it had helped him think.

Before he'd shuffled once, Noah's phone sang out the John Denver tune *Country Roads.* He stuffed the deck back in the breast pocket of his shirt and grabbed for it as the King of Hearts fluttered to the floor.

It was the chief.

"Dalton. What's going on?"

He felt everyone else in the room still, eyes on him as he listened. His palms began to tingle and the aches and annoyances that had seemed so pressing a second ago burned away in the next instant.

Thrumming with new energy, he grunted and disconnected.

"Time to roll, posse."

Noah grinned savagely at Bree and Winter. Aiden was already on his feet, unrolling the sleeves of his dress shirt and buttoning his prissy cuffs.

"The Preacher's crawled out of his hole again. If we move fast, we might be able to catch him before he goes back in."

23

Wynona was still numb.

She'd just had a bad dream, she told herself.

Even though she'd been saying that for the last two hours, she still didn't believe it. But she didn't want to poke at the thought. It was too raw. She'd pushed something in her mind way, *way* down, where she couldn't hear it squirming around, but she still knew it was there.

She was scared that it was going to jump out at her—like a *monster*, no, no, don't think about that—and she had the sick feeling that pushing it down would work about as well as slapping a Band-Aid on for a severed arm.

Somehow, she'd gone from walking home from school with Becca, talking about Barry, to sitting here at the Harrisonburg Police Station, way past when she'd have been told to go to bed because it was a school night.

Bad dream, she repeated silently.

Her mom sat beside her on one side, clutching Wynona's hand tightly. Her eyes were bloodshot, and she looked pale and weird. She wasn't wearing her usual makeup that she always put on before she'd let anyone see her. Her skin was blotchy from crying, and old acne scars made the surface look bumpy.

She looked away from her mom, toward the can of Pepsi on the table, picking reflexively at the zit on her own chin. She had to use her left hand, because of the thick white bandage the chief had wrapped around the pointer finger on her right one.

Her mom's acne scars made her feel sad. She didn't want to feel sad.

Wynona gritted her teeth. Why hadn't her mom bothered to do her makeup? Why'd she have to show up here looking like that, in front of people?

She couldn't look at her dad, either. He wasn't holding her hand, but she could feel him at the table next to her. Big and mad. He didn't lose his temper a lot—usually only when the satellite TV wasn't working and he couldn't watch football—but when he did get mad enough, he seemed different. Mean. Like a grizzly bear instead of his usual teddy bear demeanor.

He wasn't mad at her, but it didn't seem to matter. If she looked at him, she felt scared anyway. Guilty. He wouldn't look at her, though, and hadn't since...since she'd gotten home. Her brain shied away from the memory of how she'd gotten there.

Her mom made a noise next to her, like a pathetic little moan. Wynona wanted to scream. Her mom grabbed another tissue out of the box in front of her. It was her second one. She'd already used up the first box, just in the time since her dad had driven their old minivan to the police station and they'd been rushed back into this room.

They'd wanted to take her to a doctor, she remembered, nausea twisting in her tummy. She didn't remember anything about the few minutes after they'd told her that.

Her mind just...skipped when she tried to think about it. Like a scratched DVD.

She'd gotten home. Her parents had been super worried, asking all kinds of questions. The next thing she'd remembered, she'd been in the car, sitting in the back seat. The radio was playing country music, but her dad wasn't singing like he usually did when he drove.

Garth Brooks crooned about thunder rolling while Daddy's deep bass voice stayed silent, and her mom cried. Big, racking tears that shook her whole body. Her arms had squeezed around Wynona tight. Too tight. It hurt. Made it hard to breathe. Meanwhile, Daddy had driven so fast, the Dodge's half-bald tires had squealed at every corner.

She got scared just thinking about it again, and her hands clenched around the warming can of pop. She wished her mom would shut up. The crying was getting on her nerves.

Guilty. Scared. Sad.

Wynona's emotions went around and around, swooping like a Ferris wheel stuck on high speed, until she felt dizzy and wanted to throw up again. Had she already done that? Her mouth tasted sour, but she couldn't remember.

The door to the room swung open, screeching on its hinges.

Mom stopped crying, and her dad shifted in his chair, suddenly alert.

Wynona looked up, afraid the kind and sad-eyed Chief Gary had come back to ask more questions she couldn't— wouldn't?—answer.

The chief walked through the door first, followed by four regular-looking people, one in a suit. Two girls and two guys, like her parents' age. Big deal, except for one of the girls, who was looking at Wynona with dark, super intense eyes.

She caught Wynona's attention because she didn't look all cold and hard, like the brown-haired, rich-looking suit guy.

She wasn't sad, like the short black lady and the huge man who towered behind her.

This lady looked pissed off, actually.

But that didn't make Wynona feel guilty, like her dad's anger had. Because she looked like she *understood.* Understood what, Wynona didn't know. But the bad thing she was avoiding, the deep cut that hurt like the worst toothache ever when she poked at it...this lady had been cut like that too.

She didn't question the knowledge. Didn't listen to the words the FBI agents were saying. Even the little tickle of excitement at the fact that she was going to meet real FBI agents—because she recognized FBI when she saw them and loved *Criminal Minds*—didn't penetrate. She just stood up and moved toward the lady without thinking.

She looked so cool, like Wynona wanted to be. She had black jeans on, tucked into black combat boots, and a loose blue shirt on that looked like it belonged to somebody bigger than her. But the shirt didn't make her look like a dork. It hung to her thighs just like it was supposed to fit that way, and she wore a black, beat-up leather coat over the top of it. She was gorgeous, like a too-skinny model, and her hair was black.

Wynona almost snorted. That was all they had in common. Long black hair that fell around her shoulders in carelessly perfect waves, like a shampoo commercial. Wynona's teeth were too big for her head, even though her dad said she'd grow out of that and her pudgy baby fat. Her own eyes were just plain, boring blue, and too far apart.

But, she could admit without bragging, they both had awesome black hair.

The thought cheered her up, and without thinking, she smiled and grabbed the woman's hand when she held it out. She almost got embarrassed when everyone in the room suddenly stopped talking all at once to stare at them.

She realized her mom was crying—*again*—and her dad had been standing up, yelling at the chief. Dad's face was all red, and a vein had popped out on his forehead. Was he about to get arrested?

She winced, wanting to sink into the floor and die.

But the awesome FBI agent didn't look like she cared. Her voice was calm and quiet, but powerful. Her fingers were smooth and cool, where they held Wynona's cold, clammy ones, and she didn't seem to care that Wynona's hands were a little sweaty.

"We'll be back," she promised their audience like it was the most natural thing in the world. "Wynona and I are going to go someplace quiet and talk for a little bit."

The other FBI agents looked at her, nodding like she was the boss, and made a wall between Wynona and the rest of the people in the room. As they walked out into the hallway, police officers watching them from their desks outside, the FBI agent pulled the door closed behind them.

Wynona was glad. Her dad had started screaming about victim rights and about how she was a child.

"I'm Special Agent Black. You want a Coke?"

Special Agent Black. Even the FBI agent's name was cool. She did *not* want to look like a dork right now, on top of everything else.

Wynona shook her head. "They gave me a Pepsi. I didn't drink it."

"I don't blame you." Agent Black wrinkled her nose. "I'm a Coke fan, myself."

That gave Wynona a warm little glow.

"Me too." She tried to sound casual. "Pepsi tastes like cough syrup."

Agent Black wrinkled her nose. "My friend in there thinks Coke tastes like battery acid." She lowered her voice conspiratorially. "Like he ever drank battery acid to compare it to."

They shared a grin and Wynona giggled.

The agent let go of her hand when they got to the vending machine, digging quarters out of the black canvas messenger bag she wore slung across her shoulder. Wynona had seen one like that at the mall. She was going to ask for it for her birthday next month, she decided, and who cared if no one at school wore messenger bags anymore.

They were just kids. Their opinions didn't matter.

Agent Black grabbed the Cokes and started poking her head into open doors along the dingy hallway until she found what looked like an empty breakroom. There was a fridge and a coffee maker and a couple of rickety tables in the middle. Dirty coffee mugs were lined up by the sink and a couple of squashy-looking chairs covered with cracked leather squatted in one corner.

"This okay?"

Wynona nodded. Agent Black could have been being just been polite, but Wynona had the feeling that if she'd said no, they would have kept looking for another room. She cracked the tab on her Coke and took a cautious sip. The familiar taste and fizzy bubbles made her stomach feel better almost right away.

They settled into the chairs, and Agent Black opened her own Coke and took a long drink.

"Better than Pepsi?" she asked Wynona with a smile.

Wynona couldn't smile back, though. She realized with a sick feeling that, as casually awesome as this lady was, she still wanted what everyone back in that other room wanted. To talk about the *thing* Wynona wasn't going to talk about.

But Agent Black seemed to understand.

"We haven't been introduced." She held out one of those

slim, cool hands again for Wynona to shake. Just like a fellow adult. "I'm Winter. Do you go by Winnie or anything?"

"No. I've been thinking about Parker. It's my middle name. You can call me whatever, though. I haven't decided—"

Wynona let her fingers fall out of the agent's hold. Darkness tinged the edges of her vision as she sucked in a breath. "You're her. The one he wants to kill. His girlie."

Winter's face went grim. She showed no surprise.

"I'm her," she confirmed, getting up to close the door of the breakroom, flicking the lock.

A stab of fear went through Wynona, and she carefully set her Coke down on the coffee table in front of her.

"I'm the one he wants." Winter's voice was soft as she sat back down in her chair. "And it's my fault he got *you*. I've been tracking him for months. Years, really."

"It's not your fault."

She was still scared and sick-feeling, and she didn't know why, but Wynona wanted to make the older woman feel better. Her dark blue eyes were still mad, but sad now too. Because of Wynona.

Guilt.

"I should have run faster."

Agent Black was already shaking her head no before Wynona had even finished her sentence.

"Listen, I want to hear about how you ran. You're a badass kid, and I bet after a couple months, or even a few years, you'll realize that. I knew without even hearing your story. But first, let me tell you something. Whatever bad things happened to you—no matter how bad—this was *not* your fault."

She held up a hand when Wynona would have argued.

"They're not. He's a sick fucker—sorry—and you were just an innocent victim in the wrong place at the wrong time."

The swear word made her feel a tiny bit better. An FBI agent was talking to her, a thirteen-year-old, like a grown-up. Then Winter held up a lock of her shiny black hair.

"You were targeted because of this. We have the same hair. Long, pretty, and inky black. Mine looked just like yours when I was younger. That's all. The Preacher wanted me, and you have the same hair, so close enough. There was *nothing* you could have done to stop him."

"The Preacher?" Wynona shuddered, trying not to think of a white beard and black eyes hiding behind wire-framed glasses. "What a creepy name."

"He's more than creepy. Monsters are real, and The Preacher isn't a man anymore if he ever even was. He's a killer. A monster."

Wynona knew that, firsthand. The monster had *touched* her. In places that little kids were told were private. Stranger danger.

Monsters were real.

The smell of sweaty socks and the sour taste of the dirty rag he'd stuffed in her mouth.

The hard, mean hands.

With that, the floodgates opened. Through tears and snot and sometimes straight-up ugly crying, Wynona told Winter everything. About Becca, and Barry throwing up at school. About the harmless old man and about the monster that had whispered exactly how he was going to punish her while he drove down the road fast, away from Harrisonburg.

About the nasty way he'd grabbed her through her jeans when he'd stopped for gas and how she'd almost thrown up but didn't want to because she'd have choked on it and died, and she still wanted to live.

And then, about how she'd gotten out of the shitty truck. Wedged her hands up under the door handle and almost completely ripped off one of her fingernails in the process.

About how she'd fallen onto the pavement outside, hitting her shoulder against the concrete lip of the gas pump. Gotten to her feet somehow, which was hard when your hands were tied.

And how, sobbing, she'd climbed into the open back door of a crew cab pickup truck parked at the next pump and scrunched down on the floor. Her heart had beat like a rabbit's, and she might have passed out. When she woke up, the truck was moving, and she was afraid she'd been with the monster, but it was just a young Hispanic guy who looked like he was barely out of high school. He had been as scared as she was when he realized he'd closed her in the back of his work truck without noticing.

He'd pulled over and untied her, careful not to touch her more than he had to. He'd guessed that someone else already had.

In messed-up English, his warm brown eyes wet with tears and sympathy, he'd told her he wasn't in the country legally and couldn't take her to the police. He'd dropped her off at home and made sure she got safely in the front door.

She didn't even know his name, but he'd saved her.

Then, Wynona had cried some more while Winter quietly thanked her, promising things would get better now, and saying how The Preacher was dirty and evil. What he'd done to her was like an infected cut. You had to let out the poison, and it hurt, but she'd feel better for it. She'd waited patiently while Wynona got herself under control, handing her tissues when she needed them.

Wynona had been as weepy as her mom. Who she suddenly wanted to see, weepy or not.

Winter agreed to take her back to the other room and helped her up out of the chair. Wynona felt better, but she was so, *so* weak, and she really wanted to take a hot shower now and see her parents.

"Hold on." Winter unlocked the breakroom door but paused to take a little silver case out of her bag. "The title on here's not right, and I probably won't be with the FBI much longer," Winter said, pulling a business card out of the case.

She took out a pen and scribbled a phone number on the back and an email below it. "But here's my cell. Call it. Email me, *especially* if you think you're bothering me and it's not important. I only check it once a day, but I'll answer you."

Winter looked at her, locking eyes as Wynona took the little paper rectangle.

"I mean it," she added, her voice intense. "The 'victim' thing? No one's going to understand. They're going to love you and try to protect you by not talking about it. My grandparents did for a lot of years. My grandpa still does. But you need another survivor to really understand. Even Becca won't 'get it' like I will. You're not a victim. You're a *survivor*, just like me."

Wynona met Winter's eyes directly. "I'll keep in touch."

The breathless promise was a solemn one, and she would have spit in her palm and sealed it with a handshake if the FBI agent had asked her. Wynona *wanted* to keep in touch with Agent Black. Winter. It was like she had a connection now with this impossibly cool person who wanted to be friends with *her*, Wynona Baines. They were like sisters now.

She grabbed a last tissue from the box on the table before she could change her mind, and wrote down her own email, handing it over. "You can email me too. If you want, I mean."

Winter clinched that feeling of friendship when she took the tissue Wynona held out. She folded it into a neat square, tucking it in her wallet like it really mattered. She reached out again, this time knocking Wynona lightly on the shoulder with one fist.

Her gorgeous, serious face creased in a grin as she tucked the wallet back in her bag.

"Count on it. I'll be emailing you if I don't hear from you first. Even if it's just to find out if you've asked Barry Klippington out yet."

Wynona's grin fell away.

Winter winked. "And don't worry about The Preacher. Pretty soon, he's never going to hurt anyone again."

24

That stupid little bitch.

I kicked out at my La-Z-Boy chair, I was so mad still, and forgot I had my house slippers on. Almost broke my toe, it felt like.

Gentlemen don't swear, I reminded myself, almost hearing my momma's voice in my head. I was hearing her more and more lately. I didn't believe in spirits and devil things, but it was starting to feel like she was trying to haunt me after all these years of being dead.

I slumped down in my chair, ignoring my throbbing foot, and turned on the TV.

If God was just, the little girl had gotten hit by a car or taken by a child molester when she'd tried to hitchhike back to Harrisonburg. It was going on four in the morning by the time I'd finally given up looking for her. She'd vanished, right out of my truck.

Now, I was home. Holed up in my house. I planned on sleeping for a spell and heading back to Harrisonburg in the morning. If she'd made it home, I'd just grab her again. It might take a few days, but I could be patient. I leaned my head back on the headrest and closed my eyes.

I must've dozed, because a quiet voice woke me a while later.

She's out of your reach.

I woke up, mid-snore, snuffling and choking on my own air.

Ten years ago, whispered a sly voice, *you wouldn't have forgotten to lock the door. You wouldn't have gone to a gas station in broad daylight and just thrown a blanket over your catch to hide her from prying eyes. You'd have knocked her out, hog-tied her right there in the road, tossed her in the back of your pickup with a tarp over the top* and *made sure your gas tank was full before you did it.*

I didn't like the voice.

At first, it sounded like my daddy, but he'd have never been so harsh to me. He'd always told me I was special, just like him. Momma had been the mean one who made me do chores before I went outside and would take my dinner away if I sass-mouthed her. Daddy popped her in the mouth but good when he'd caught her doing that.

You wouldn't have made any mistakes and Winter would be dead. I'd have killed her and drunk her blood by now.

Was the voice my daddy?

He hadn't been a vampire, though. He was a preacher. Vampires were devil creatures.

"My girlie is a slick one." My words sounded loud and belligerent, even over the blaring television, and I jumped. I hadn't intended on speaking the words, and the sound of my own voice startled me.

You should have fucked her and killed her when she was young. Now, she's going to fuck you and kill you.

My daddy would never use such foul language. And even

if he did, he'd never suggest a weak woman could best his boy.

"That's not true." My hand shook as I reached for my glass of Jim Beam. "I don't know who you are, but don't say such things."

A canned audience laughed at a trio of perky, idiotic morning news hosts as my eyes darted around the living room, looking for the source of the soft, hissing words.

Winter has escaped you. Three times now. The littlest one was just a GIRL.

The voice boomed on the last word, from a whisper to a roar that seemed likely to shake the house down. The glass of liquor dropped from my fingers to the dirty green carpet beside my chair. It landed on its side, spilling out alcohol that spread in a dark stain on the rug.

"I kilt the first two." My voice sounded thin and whiny, even to my own ears. "I punished 'em good."

The voice dropped back down in a whisper again, so low that I almost couldn't hear it over the commercial man hawking special pillows on the TV.

She's going to kill you, you know. The harlot whore of Babylon slut bitch is going to send your wrinkled old ass straight to Hell. You're going to die, Preacher.

"The hell she is," I yelled, struggling to put the footrest down. Fear rose up in a black wave, feeling like it was choking the air out of my chest. Little purple dots danced around in my vision.

I was old, but I wasn't dead.

I was a predator on the sinful women of the world. God's chosen, given the power and the smarts to cleanse the female filth. But fear still trembled in my hands.

Go to Richmond. Now. Get her before she gets you.

I stopped looking for the voice when I realized it had been coming out of my own mouth. My temples throbbed as

I sucked in deep breaths. One after the other, till I got my balance back.

Turning the TV off, I left the empty glass on the floor. I didn't need to clean it up. The whole damned house could burn down, and it wouldn't matter now.

I shuffled to the bedroom to pack. Tiredness dragged at me, but sleep would have to wait.

I had to get my girlie before she got me.

There would be no going back to finish what I'd started with Little Winter, to make her pay for running off on me like that. Like the voice had said…she was out of my reach. I had to move forward now. I had to go to Richmond.

My lips moved in what I thought was a mumbled prayer, and I headed down the cellar steps to gather up my best tools. Some, I hadn't used since I'd carved up a pretty hippie girl in the seventies. I whispered as I touched a shiny metal scalpel.

Clean and purifying.

I laid it reverently in my canvas bag of work tools, still murmuring to myself. I didn't hear the words, but they trailed after me as I headed back up the crooked stairs.

Get her now. This is your last chance. You mess up this time, boy, and I'll just have to do it myself.

WINTER WAS LOSING HER MIND.

It had only been two days, but two days was too many to be under house arrest. She was technically home alone, barricaded into her apartment, but there was always an agent parked outside in an unmarked car.

Usually Noah. He'd taken to showing up without texting first or calling about some case-related question she knew damned well he already had the answer to. Like she couldn't see him sitting in his big-ass red truck through her kitchen window.

They were playing the waiting game.

Every law enforcement agent or officer within a hundred-mile radius had been provided with a copy of Winter's sketch of The Preacher. Bree was working with Parrish and a couple of his BAU team members to identify him, and possibly track down his whereabouts. Meanwhile, Noah hovered protectively over her, and her grandparents were being watched too—without their knowledge—in case he tried to get to her through them.

Winter wanted to try for another vision, but the last one had scared the hell out of her. Not the content—which was bad enough—but the aftereffects. She hadn't physically recovered from that yet. Her joints still ached mildly, like her body was getting over a bad bout of the flu, and shimmering migraine lights illuminated the edges of everything she looked at.

Plus, she still couldn't face Noah without seeing that blackened and deformed death mask that rested grotesquely over his face.

It wasn't worth the risk. The Preacher was already close.

Though she hadn't had another vision, and she hesitated to label it as "sensing" because she'd never believed in people who claimed psychic powers, Winter could feel him out there. Mostly at night. The Preacher was like a shadow, hanging malevolently just out of sight.

Her phone buzzed with a text.

You good?

Noah.

At this point, she'd passed beyond being irritated with him and was heading toward reluctant tolerance. She started to text back a snarky comment when the phone rang in her hand. Her heart immediately froze—The

Preacher?—but plunged when she saw her grandparents' area code.

She jabbed at the green phone icon on her screen, her fingers trembling. "Winter Black."

There was a pause, and someone took a breath.

Before they could say anything, she blurted, "Gramma Beth?" Grampa Jack had been in poor health—

A low chuckle interrupted her churning thoughts. Her hand clenched on the phone, dread walking up her spine like a spider on a web.

"Preacher? Who the fuck is this?" she demanded.

"My, my," came a warm, rich voice. "First, you think I'm your grandma, and then a murderer? You must lead such an unusual life as an FBI agent, Winter. I must say, I've never had anyone mistake me for a notorious serial killer."

It could be him. Bluffing. Her sketch of him had been all over the news. She'd been thankful her number was unlisted and hadn't been leaked to the media. But that meant that whoever was on the line shouldn't have her number, either. And this man didn't sound old *or* Southern.

"I asked," Winter pronounced deliberately, minimizing the call screen and tapping the record app on her phone, "who the fuck is this?"

The chuckle ended abruptly as if the caller was no longer amused. "My apologies, Winter. I was mistaken in my memory of you. You weren't so outspoken as a child. This is Dr. Ladwig."

Ladwig.

It was disorienting to hear that name from her past.

"I'm sure you're surprised to hear from me, my dear."

He'd always called her that as a little girl, like he was some old man, instead of a thirty-year-old just a few years out of shrink school.

He'd always say, "Hello, my dear," when she'd been

dropped off in his too-fancy office and subjected to tests that she hated but could never remember why once her grandparents picked her up. Thankfully, when they'd moved, she'd talked them into letting her drop the appointments.

The endearment scared her back then, for some reason, and apparently had the power to piss her off as an adult.

"I'm sure you're wondering why I'm calling. I have to say I still think of you often."

"How did you get this number?"

Only a few people had it, and she was FBI. Sure, she'd been quoted in newspapers and appeared in filmed media briefings, but thanks to the IT department, you couldn't just Google 'Winter Black' and find her cell number.

"That's not important," Ladwig replied smoothly. "I was hoping to find out how you're progressing these days. Any visions? Have your other symptoms gotten worse?" The eagerness in his voice was off-putting, to say the least.

She was tempted to hang up, but dammit, she had to know how he'd found her...and how he'd known about her visions. Those hadn't started happening until years after her time with Ladwig.

"Why are you calling now?"

"Kismet, my dear! I had a man in my office the other day with a case much like yours. Not *completely* like yours, of course."

There was that fake, avuncular chuckle again that made her molars grind. For a head doctor, he'd shown a distinct lack of care when it had come to the circumstances surrounding her injury.

"It was close enough that I'd hoped for a moment that I'd found another Winter," he went on, his voice losing some of its friendly edge. "I've been searching for another patient like you for years. He was so promising. Visions, painful headaches, head trauma in his early teens, the same age you experienced yours, nosebleeds…unfortunately, he was some-what of a mystery. Got up and left my office very suddenly. And, oddly, he filled out all his paperwork with made-up information, so I can't track him down."

Again, his reference to her visions threw her.

Winter narrowed her eyes as another thought occurred to her.

"What did the man look like?"

"The patient? HIPAA laws prevent me from—"

"Don't give me that bullshit. You either hacked or paid someone to hack a system and get my FBI-secured cell phone number. Tell me, or I turn you in for that right now. It's a hefty fine, and if someone were to leak your weird little story to the press—"

"Fine," Ladwig snapped. "He was Texan, a big guy. Dumb as a box of rocks."

That was Noah Fucking Dalton, all right, she thought, fury starting to boil. *Dumber* than a box of rocks.

Ladwig immediately lost any ability to affect her nerves. She was done with him.

"You will erase my number from your phone."

"Now, my dear—"

"Call me your dear one more time, and I will file a PPO and start a tell-all blog tomorrow. If I see your face anywhere near mine or that of my family, acquaintances, or local grocery store clerks—and be aware, I have excellent *vision*—I will have you arrested and paint you publicly as a stalky creeper, obsessed with a former thirteen-year-old patient. I'm afraid your reputation would be a little tarnished, and as I remember, your practice was relatively successful."

There was a moment of stunned silence.

"You wouldn't."

"Don't fucking test me, you stalking creeper son of a—"

She heard the quiet click of a desk phone receiver being

replaced as Dr. Robert Ladwig hung up the phone without saying another word.

This was going to require her attention, she realized, her anger at Noah flaring hotter. The man sounded unhinged. He *was* unhinged. For years, he'd called regularly to "check on" her, up until she was fifteen years old. Three whole years. Her grandma had decided it would be easier to change their number than to keep putting him off.

Grampa Jack had always scoffed at psychiatrists and psychologists, saying most of them were crazier than their patients. If Ladwig was still fixated on her, he was certifiable, and she was inclined to agree with Gramps.

She picked up her phone and pulled up Noah's text.

Doing ok. Bored. You bringing dinner again tonight?

He responded in less than a minute.

Chinese?

Sounds good. You know what I like. (:

The smiley face was probably overkill, she thought, hitting send anyway. Flirty. But Dalton would just be more curious.

Curious. She snorted. Such a mild word to describe Noah.

He was also an invasive, prying, sneaky, nosy, insensitive asshole.

Curiosity killed the cat. He might not know it yet, but Noah just darted out into a ten-lane highway.

25

B eth McAuliffe let the lace-trimmed curtain over the kitchen window fall back into place. The police car parked outside their house hadn't budged since early that morning. She was tempted to go out and ask the officer inside if she'd like a cookie and some lemonade.

Or grab her by the collar and demand that this officer call *her* superior officer, and so on, all the way up to the President of the United States, if Beth deemed it necessary. She wasn't a forceful person by nature, but she needed to find out what was going on with her beloved grandbaby.

"She hasn't called yet?"

Jack always managed to read her mind.

Beth turned to her husband, sitting at the little dinette table in the kitchen. She smiled. He always looked like the Hulk when he perched on one of those aluminum and fake leather chairs. She'd had similar thoughts, ever since they bought the set together in 1952.

But "Big Jack" didn't look as out of place in that chair as he had even a few weeks ago. He'd lost more weight. The flesh on his cheeks sagged in parchment-thin folds, and he looked…old. Unhealthy. The doctor said it was just old age creeping up on him.

Beth knew better, but she pushed the thought away. She'd have to face it soon, but not now.

"No. Not yet. Nothing since her text last night, telling us she was doing fine, working that new desk job of hers."

Jack snorted and took a little bite of the thick ham sandwich she'd made for him. Even a year ago, the plate would be empty, and he'd be whining like a little boy for a third cookie and another glass of sweet tea.

She knew he'd only taken the bite because she'd pester him into it otherwise, and that made her sad. Jack's mind was still sharp.

He looked up at her, his blue eyes narrowed under shaggy brows. "She never was a good liar. I don't think she's working a desk job at all."

"Neither do I. I think we should drop in on her. See for ourselves how she's settled into the apartment."

Jack shook his head in warning.

"Now, Bethie, she's been there for months. She's an adult now. We can't overstep."

"I'd never dream of overstepping," she responded indignantly. "But I'm going, and you're coming with me."

She stalked across the kitchen, her heels clicking on the old linoleum she'd polished for the umpteenth time the day before, until it shone like a new copper penny. Jack grinned and winked at her as she sat down but didn't laugh at her like he used to, when he'd ruffle her feathers on purpose. She missed his big belly laugh that always seemed to shake any room he was in.

"You promised me a vacation this year," she reminded him. "To anywhere I want to go. You can't go back on that now."

"To Richmond?" He snorted again. "Some vacation. I

thought you had Bora Bora or Italy in mind when you made me promise that."

It had been Ireland that she'd had in mind, along with a tour of Wales and Scotland, but Beth didn't correct him. He pushed the hardly touched sandwich aside and took a sip of the tea she'd mixed up fresh for him that morning. She squashed the urge to pester.

"I have to see for myself that she's really okay," Beth admitted. "She might think we're a couple of brainless old farts with nothing better to do than bitch and play bridge—"

He snorted. "*You* bitch and play bridge. I make pithy observations on life and play poker."

"Hush, you idiot," she told him mildly, a small smile playing on her lips. "I'm serious. You saw the pictures on the news last night of the serial killer they launched a manhunt for. It's no coincidence that the police have been camped out on our doorstep for the last couple of days."

Jack nodded, resigned now. "You have to check on your chick."

"It'll do you good to get out."

"Maybe," he allowed, popping the lid open on his pill organizer and fishing out an oblong yellow one. "But you're driving. These things make me sleepy."

An hour later, their overnight bags packed and hotel reservation made, Beth stepped out into the sunshine and headed for the Fredericksburg PD car parked at the curb. The woman inside straightened up quickly and dog-eared the page on the novel she'd been reading. She set it on the seat beside her and rolled down her window.

"Everything okay, ma'am?"

"Of course," Beth replied, her tone bright. "I just wondered if you'd like a chocolate chip cookie."

"That'd be great. I was just thinking about lunch, but

those smell a lot better than the egg salad sandwich I packed." The dark-haired woman, her nametag reading "Louise Felcher," took the small plate gratefully. "Thank you."

"Any sign of The Preacher?"

Louise had already fished out a cookie and taken a bite. Her eyes were half-closed in ecstasy but flew wide at Beth's casual question.

"Don't choke, dear," Beth fussed with a small smile, handing her a napkin.

Officer Felcher swallowed hard, her eyes watering. "No, ma'am," she coughed. "I heard The Preacher was in Richmond. What makes you ask that?"

Beth handed her the thermos of coffee she'd made as Louise coughed again, trying to clear her throat.

"That's a silly question, Officer Felcher, and we both know it." Beth waved a hand airily. "It doesn't matter. I just wanted to let you know that my husband and I will be taking an overnight trip, so you don't have to stay out here if you have better things to do. My granddaughter lives in Richmond. She's an FBI agent, you know." Beth smiled sweetly and tapped her temple. "Winter is a smart girl. Takes after her grandmother. She's smarter, though. I'm just a little old lady."

Louise nodded, finally composed, and her dark eyes twinkled. "Mrs. McAuliffe, I sincerely doubt you're an ordinary lady, young or old." She unscrewed the cap on the thermos and poured out some of the steaming liquid into an empty travel mug beside her, sniffing appreciatively. "Coffee. Bless you."

"Cops and coffee. It wasn't a stretch." Beth eyed the book Louise was reading. "Is that one good? I run to the store every time a new one of hers comes out."

Louise looked down at the Nora Roberts book in her lap

and gave an embarrassed chuckle. "Not bad. I'm glad I'm not the only one who likes a good happy ending."

"We all like happy endings, dear. And don't be ashamed." She patted Louise on the shoulder comfortingly. "If you didn't like happy endings, you wouldn't be a good police officer. Our spare key is on top of the doorframe. Feel free to come in and use our restroom if you'd like, and just set the dishes on the front stoop if you don't. I'll take care of them tomorrow."

Louise watched her with new respect. "If you're leaving soon, I might just head back to the office."

"I thought you'd say that," Beth replied. "Will my husband and I see you or one of your colleagues when we come back tomorrow afternoon?"

Louise laughed, a cheerful, tinkling sound that was at odds with her stocky frame and strong jawline. "You won't be able to get rid of me now that I've tasted your cookies, Mrs. McAuliffe."

"Do you play bridge, Louise?"

"No, but I'm a mean poker player."

"Then you'll have to meet my husband when we return. Enjoy the rest of your day, Officer Felcher."

"Safe trip, Mrs. McAuliffe. Give your granddaughter our regards."

Louise was still parked outside when Beth carefully backed their big, silver Buick down the driveway. Beside her, Jack was already dozing. She pulled out into the street, waving toward Officer Felcher as she drove by. Louise waved back and grinned.

Beth braked at the four-way stop down the block. Across from her, a white delivery van did the same. She waved him forward.

For some reason, a chill went through her as the van

slowly passed them, and she shuddered a little. The windows were darkened to the point where she couldn't see the driver.

"You okay?" Jack roused himself enough to ask.

"A goose walked over my grave, is all." She fixed her eyes on the van in the rearview mirror, but it drove past their home without braking. The police cruiser hadn't moved yet. Coincidence, she told herself.

"Damned geese," Jack muttered, closing his eyes again. "Devil birds. Just be glad it didn't shit on your grave while he was at it."

"Yes, dear," she murmured, too distracted to appreciate her husband's warped sense of humor.

She didn't want Winter to be the one to catch The Preacher—didn't want Winter within a million miles of him —but she was looking forward to the day when the monster was locked up.

Maybe when he was twisting in agony on the electric chair, the edgy anxiety and white-hot rage that had dogged her for the last twelve years would finally die too.

THE AIR FELT ELECTRIC, like a storm was getting ready to break.

Noah parked his truck in front of his apartment and grabbed the paper bags from the passenger seat beside him.

He was pretty sure the charged feeling in the air wasn't from the weather since the moon shone clear overhead and the night sky was cloudless. It had to be the waiting. They were doing everything they could—everyone who could be spared had been mobilized into action—but it still felt like The Preacher was calling the shots.

They hadn't turned up shit on him. He was a ghost.

He headed for Winter's door, a few down from his, his stomach already growling at the smell of food coming from the carryout bag. Kung Pao Chicken wouldn't take the kinks out of his neck from sitting hunched over his computer all day. Fortune cookies wouldn't ease the frustrated pulse that beat at the backs of his eyeballs. But tension headache or not, he was hungry.

He knocked only once before Winter's door swung open. "I thought I heard your truck. Come on in." She smiled, showing even white teeth.

Winter looked good today, he noted. She smelled fresh, like strawberries, when he moved past. Her hair was still wet from the shower, hanging down over her shoulders in damp, ropy strands. Her cheeks were flushed with color, and her eyes snapped blue sparks.

Wicked blue sparks. She was pissed. At him.

He set the bag down on the kitchen counter cautiously.

"Cabin fever getting to you?" He tried not to make eye contact as he grabbed two craft brews out of her fridge. "You seem a little on edge."

"Oh?" Her tone was sweet. "What would I have to be on edge about?" An undercurrent ran there, as sharp as a stiletto heel.

He popped the top off his bottle and took a bracing swig. "Out with it. What'd I do?"

Winter grabbed her own beer but made no move to open it. Her knuckles were pale where she gripped the bottleneck.

"Besides take advantage of our friendship? Sneaking around behind my back? Siccing a fucking lunatic doctor on me and telling him about my fortune-telling migraines?" This time, when she smiled, there was no missing the dangerous edge to it. "Other than that, you've done nothing, *friend*."

Dr. Ladwig. Noah swore.

"I'm sorry. I forgot all about that—"

Dammit, wrong choice of words. But he hadn't said a word to the doctor about the migraines.

"Forgot? Where do you get off, Dalton? My health is none of your business."

His own temper bubbled in response, but he pushed it back. She obviously didn't understand. If she had just gone to a doctor like he'd told her to, he wouldn't have *had* to go behind her back.

She wouldn't take care of herself. Someone had to.

He held tight to his own calm, not wanting to put a light to this particular pile of tinder right now. It wasn't a good time.

"Are we going to pull this food out and eat it while it's still warm? This restaurant is great, but I've heard bad things about their cold takeout."

She slammed her beer on the counter so hard that he was surprised the bottle didn't shatter. The sound grated his already exposed nerves. Fine. They'd fight. This might even be fun. He stopped fantasizing about hot and crunchy fried food and slippery hot noodles, and resigned himself to a lukewarm, greasy dinner.

Winter took two steps toward him, jabbing her finger into his chest with every angry word that poured out of her mouth.

"What gives you the right to pull something like this? To invade my privacy? Share details about my personal life?"

He smiled down at her upturned face, hot with anger. That smile just fueled the fire, but he didn't care.

"I never said a word about your visions. And, darlin', you can blame me all you want, but this is your own damned fault."

Gasoline to her open flame. And three…two…one…

He wasn't disappointed. The hectic color bled from her

cheeks, and she drew a deep breath to blast him. Her hands clenched into fists, and she brought one up, swinging straight for his face.

Winter was a formidable opponent when you were sparring with her. She'd taken him down in the gym, on the mat, and sometimes, she ran circles around him on the track. She was young, sure. Skinny to the edge of unhealthy right now. But she was no weak and wilting debutante.

He caught her fist an inch from his face.

Her only weakness was that when you goaded her, she lost her edge of control.

With an unyielding grip, he pulled her forward, into his space. He swept one arm around her back and held her still, so they were almost nose to nose.

"I care about you."

It wasn't a declaration of love. Neither one of them could handle that, and it wasn't the time. There was too much going on.

He could smell mint on her breath. She struggled against his hold like a feral cat, but as strong as Winter was, he was stronger.

His statement hadn't even registered, and he frowned fiercely in exasperation. This time, Noah spaced his words evenly and ratcheted up the volume, so she'd be sure to understand.

"I. Care. About. You. I'm not sorry I called Dr. Ladwig."

Her face was dark with fury, and he almost just let her go and damn the consequences. He could have apologized for what he'd done. But that would be a lie.

"You overbearing son of a bitch," she spat. "This time, you've gone too far."

So be it.

Noah released her arms. Braced for the blow. He could take it. Hell, who knew. Maybe he deserved it.

Instead of breaking his nose, Winter's eyes widened abruptly before they rolled back in her head. Before he could blink, she went boneless.

Thrown off guard, he barely managed to catch her on her way to the floor.

26

Winter was so wound up that she didn't even feel the vision coming. There was no headache to announce it. She was fired up and furious one second—Noah's smug face didn't even reflect *any* kind of remorse at the confrontation, and she hated being confined. In the next second, those angry green eyes were fading out.

This vision was different.

She went from fighting with her best friend in the kitchen to standing in the middle of a dark room in a bare instant.

The edges of the room were shadowy and indistinct. It felt small. Could have been a closet. She struggled to switch gears, fighting a sense of claustrophobia. To turn on her dispassionate observational skills, even while her chest still heaved with fury and a tinge of fear.

In front of her, beaming out from the darkness, a cherry-colored coat hung on a hanger. It glowed red, but not like anything that had been touched by darkness. It wasn't connected to a crime—at least not yet. It just hung in the center of her perception, the bright color a beacon of cheer and the cut of the coat signifying only that someone had good taste in outerwear. It looked so familiar that she reached out to touch the soft-looking, nubby-textured fabric.

Before her fingers could reach it, painlessly, the image evaporated.

She became aware of Noah's strong arms, still tightening around her as if she was in the process of falling, and sucked in a sharp breath.

"Winter?"

She was cradled in his arms, and he was looking down at her with concern, fear, and a touch of something else that she shied away from analyzing too closely.

"Sorry."

The word came out normal. Not a raspy whisper. Not a tortured moan of angst.

Just…normal.

Embarrassment flooded her, and she focused on getting her feet under her. She wasn't dizzy, so it only took a second.

"What was that?"

Noah released her but didn't move away, in case she went down again.

She let out a half-laugh, her anger forgotten.

"I have no idea. Am I bleeding?"

She swiped her hand under her nose without waiting for an answer. No blood.

"When's the last time you've eaten?" he demanded. "Go sit down."

It rankled, but she recognized that the bossy tone was just his way of showing his affection. Not unlike the way he'd gone to Dr. Ladwig. With his hand under her elbow, she made her careful way to the living room couch.

She sat down, but her head didn't spin. She was fine.

Noah was already back, chopsticks in one hand because he knew she preferred them, and a white cardboard container in the other. He shoved them at her and went back to the kitchen.

"Do you have water?" The question was steady, but she could still hear the concern. He'd said it himself. He cared about her. She felt tired, just thinking about it. Not drained, fatigued, or exhausted, but tired.

"Noah, I'm fine."

She heard the refrigerator open, and he came back a moment later with a cold bottle of filtered water, pushing it into her hand.

"I thought you liked Bree."

He'd taken the carton from her hand to open it since she apparently wasn't moving fast enough, but he stopped on a surprised laugh.

"What's that supposed to mean? Of course, I like Bree."

"I mean *like* like."

"Is this really what you want to talk about right now? I feel like you just regressed to middle school." He didn't make a move to get his own dinner, just sank down in the chair across from her to watch her closely.

"Just answer me." Anger tickled again, but it wasn't overwhelming. More like irritation.

"Bree is a lesbian. She's engaged," he added so patiently that Winter felt like an idiot. "She has a fiancée."

"I know," Winter huffed. "I just didn't know that you knew."

A smile that was laden with amused tolerance broke across his tired, stubble-shadowed face. "Winter, you know about my first marriage, right?"

She ducked her head to fish out a dumpling from her carton, hoping he wouldn't see her expression. Of course, she remembered his first wife. He talked about her openly, and with fondness. They'd married young. She'd divorced him and later married one of her best friends instead, another woman.

Noah had been the best man at her wedding. Winter suddenly wanted to be alone. To crawl into a small hole of shame.

"What's this about?" Noah asked, mercifully changing the subject. "Did you see something?"

"No, not really. I think you're right. I haven't eaten much today." She set the food down on the coffee table. She had no appetite now, either. "Listen, Noah, you should probably go."

His face darkened.

"No. I'm not mad anymore. Cabin fever and all that. I just want to be alone."

She felt like a specimen under a microscope while he studied her, making up his own mind whether she was really fine. After what felt like an hour, but was only a moment, he nodded reluctantly.

"Okay. But call me if you need me."

He got to his feet, and she followed him. Steady on her feet, she noted. No headache. A red coat? What the hell was that about? Why would she daydream about cute winter outerwear in the middle of a knockdown, drag-out fight?

Noah grabbed the bag off the counter.

"You want half of this? You should eat."

"You're stalling." She smiled at him, to take the sting away from the words, and pushed the bags toward him, along with the barely touched beer. "Thanks, Noah."

He nodded. "We're not done with our conversation, are we?"

"No, but it's not the right time."

He surprised her then, leaning over to kiss her on the cheek. It was a fleeting brush of lips, but its impact rocked her a little.

And then, with one of those sweet, brilliant smiles of his, he was gone.

Noah was just trying to help. She had to remember that and forgive him, like she'd forgive Gramma Beth for pestering her with caring texts, or Grampa Jack, for teasing her about getting married someday.

Somehow, even though she wasn't looking for it and didn't intend for it to happen, Noah had become just as important to her as family. And family was everything.

"I'M SURPRISED I haven't seen you in my office sooner."

Aiden resisted the urge to shift uncomfortably in his chair. Cassidy Ramirez, ADD of the Richmond FBI office, stared him down from across her desk. Her face was unlined and smooth, even though he knew she was at least fifteen years older than he was.

She was likely coming up on retirement, he reminded himself. Three years out from it. A career in the FBI was hard on the body. Hard on the mind. Lifers were rare, because if you did it right, the job burned you out to a husk by the time you hit fifty-seven, the mandatory retirement age.

His former partner watched him with alert brown eyes and an enigmatic smile playing about her lips. "How's The Preacher case going?"

"Fine."

The word was short and succinct. Both of them knew it was a lie.

"How can I help you, Aiden? I'll do whatever is within my abilities. You know that. Even though you're not the type to ask for help, and never have been."

He smiled back. Tightly. "I wanted to talk to you about the Black killings."

His former partner's smile slipped away. They'd both worked the Black case. Cassidy had been his mentor. He'd been brand new to the FBI, fresh out of Quantico. The Preacher had left his mark on both of them, albeit in different ways. They'd also slept together, ultimately dooming Ramirez's marriage, though neither one of them would ever acknowledge it.

"I've been digging into my old notes at home," she admitted, looking less like an associate deputy director, and more like the special agent she'd been more than ten years before. "I've been keeping close tabs on this for obvious reasons, but I'm afraid I haven't been able to come up with anything new that might help you."

Aiden had expected as much, but it was still disappointing. He'd grappled with coming to her to begin with. It showed weakness.

"Thanks for your time, Ramirez." He stood to go. "I've got a meeting."

"Bullshit." Her tone was amused. Exasperated. "Sit down, Parrish."

"Is that an order?" he asked stiffly.

She met his gaze evenly. "Don't make me turn it into one. I'd like to keep to our current level of mutual respect and animosity."

He grinned reluctantly and sat back down. "You're a good ADD, Cassidy. If I neglected to congratulate you on your promotion four years ago, let me do so now."

She rolled her eyes and laughed, an earthy, seductive sound that always took him off guard.

"Thanks. You're a hell of an SSA yourself. Congratulations."

She sobered and reached for a pencil from the container

on her desk. Running it through her fingers absently, a long-running habit, she pinned him with a look.

"As long as this mutual admiration society meeting is still in session, I'm going to give you some advice."

His shoulders stiffened, and his bad leg ached with sudden muscle tension.

"Relax." Her brown eyes twinkled with understanding. "It's just a little piece, take it or leave it."

He nodded for her to continue, focusing on keeping his expression blank.

"Don't make this a personal vendetta."

"Between us?" Her statement surprised him. He'd expected something different in the way of advice.

"The Preacher. I want to see him brought down as much as you do, but I don't view our time on that case in the same way."

"We failed." The words were flat. Emotionless. "He's killed three more women and traumatized another thirteen-year-old."

"Aiden." That one word was filled with a wealth of affection and exasperation, and he looked at her sharply. "You can't carry it around with you as a badge of failure."

"We failed, did we not?"

She flushed a little, her temper crackling. Cassidy always did have the most wonderful temper, he remembered, smiling a little. She credited her Latino roots.

"We did not," she countered. "We did everything we could, within the bounds of our jobs. He went into hiding. Sometimes our best isn't good enough." She raised an eyebrow pointedly. "It didn't slow our careers down any."

Aiden conceded the point but balked at her analysis.

"We had to have missed something. Security cameras, a witness…"

"No. You and I are among the best and brightest the FBI has seen since its humble beginnings."

It was said without a shade of self-consciousness. Because it was true.

She went on. "If we couldn't get The Preacher, with all of the resources available to us, that means he couldn't be gotten. Now, the Violent Crimes Unit has another chance and Tech is backing them. There have been major strides in law enforcement capabilities since the Black case. Plus, he's an *old man*. The Preacher is not some invincible being. He has to be slowing down. Step back. Let VC do their job, Aiden. They'll get him this time."

He was already shaking his head before she finished.

"They need me. Us."

"Aiden. You're obsessed."

He shoved to his feet and leaned over Cassidy's imposing mahogany desk. She shrank back automatically, but her dark eyes heated at the challenge.

"He needs to go down. We have to throw everything we've got at this."

"Obsession, Aiden." Cassidy's voice was soft. Intent. "In our line of work, one of the first things you learn is that obsession bleeds into fanaticism. From there, it's a short fall to extremist. You're losing control."

He straightened up slowly, furious with himself for losing his hard-fought power. But there wasn't fear or criticism in Cassidy's eyes. There was compassion.

He resented it.

Aiden opened his mouth to deliver a vicious takedown, but something she'd said suddenly clicked.

"Fuck." The word wasn't much more than a whisper, but Cassidy jerked as if he'd yelled it.

Extremist.

He headed to the door, cursing his healing leg muscles for slowing him down.

ADD Ramirez watched him bolt. She hurt for her one-time lover and former friend, but she'd done the best she could.

27

When she heard another knock at her front door, Winter was willing to give up on her recent vow to forgive Noah. But when she pulled open the door, her grandparents were standing on the sidewalk outside, beaming at her.

Her stomach sank a little. She loved them—adored them to pieces, which wasn't exactly in her nature—but dammit, she didn't have *time* for them right now. One look at Grampa Jack's tired face, though, and she ushered them in to sit down. He gave her a growling hug first, but he looked old and tired. Like a lion, with those bushy white eyebrows, but one past its prime.

Her throat tightened, but she squeezed out a smile for them both.

Gramma Beth shed her light spring jacket and sat down on the gray IKEA couch in the living room, fussing with her pale blue skirt. She didn't make eye contact, and Winter found that suspicious.

"Do you have any Bud Light?" Grampa Jack asked, already heading for the kitchen.

"Why would I have that?" Winter's voice was friendly but pointed. "It's not like I knew you were coming and had time to run to the store. You'll have to make do with Noah's craft beer."

"Told you, Bethie," she heard him laugh from the kitchen.

"All right. Out with it."

Gramma Beth finally looked up, her stylish calf-length dress as smooth and wrinkle-free as it had been when she sat down. "Noah?" She jumped on the crumb as fast as a starving mouse, eyes bright and alert. "Has he been around again?"

"Gramma. Stop prevaricating and spit it out." Winter sat down and pinned Beth with a hard look, trying to ignore the sweet and innocent act that had fooled her for so many years. "Why are you really here?"

Grampa Jack wandered back in from the kitchen. "Yeah, Bethie," he added with a wicked grin that showed off his pearly white dentures, "why are we here?"

If looks could kill, Gramps would have been writhing on the floor from an invisible nut punch. He winced, realizing simultaneously that he'd overstepped, and settled down next to his wife.

But not too close.

"We need a reason to visit our granddaughter?" Gramma Beth's voice was prim, but heavy with defensiveness.

She almost caved—she was dealing with her *grandma,* not a suspect—but Winter had to push on. The red coat glittered somehow ominously in her mind.

"When you've never seen reason to visit me anywhere before?" She gentled her tone and was glad she had when Gramma Beth's faded eyes filled with tears.

"*How could you?*" Beth burst out, surprising them both. "You've gone too far this time, Winter."

Even Jack seemed taken aback by his wife's outburst.

She'd gone from June Cleaver to Badass Bitch in a half a second.

Winter realized she'd never seen Gramma Beth lose her temper. Not like this.

It was terrifying. And she didn't know what had triggered it.

"Now, Bethie—"

Grampa Jack reached out a hand to lay on her arm, but she rounded on him. "Don't you 'Bethie' me, Jack McAuliffe. I'll deal with *you* another time."

His bushy eyebrows went up, startled at the threat in her tone. "What'd I do?" he blustered.

But when her eyes narrowed in menace, he held up a hand so quickly that Winter had to stifle a laugh.

"Never mind. Tell me another time." He pushed to his feet. "I'm going to see if Noah is around."

"You don't know which apartment—" Winter started to stand, wanting to follow him...and get out of the blast zone.

"I'll find it!"

With a last apologetic look and a helpless shrug, Grampa Jack took the coward's way out. Through the front door.

Winter wanted to laugh hysterically and scream in frustration, all at the same time. Or at least text Noah and tell him to rescue Gramps. But the flags of bright color high on her grandmother's smooth cheeks stopped her.

Sweet Beth McAuliffe was almost purple with rage, and the sight made her blood run cold.

"Jesus, Gramma—"

"Don't you take our Lord's name in vain, and *don't* you 'Gramma' me, young lady," Beth ordered, leaping to her feet. She started pacing the length of the small living room. Much like Winter herself did, when she was furious.

"I am sick and fucking tired of you two acting like I'm some fragile china doll."

Even as she said it, she *looked* like a china doll, Winter thought. Petite and pretty, in her perfectly matched vintage-style dress and pumps, her hair in perfect white waves. They bounced with her agitated movements. She and Winter couldn't have been more different in appearance...but it looked like they were truly the same, where it counted.

Her musings interrupted by a sudden realization, Winter's jaw dropped open.

"Did you just say the F-word?"

Gramma Beth flushed, but a bit of a brogue crept into her Catholic finishing school intonations. "My last name is Finnegan, remember? Elizabeth Mary Catherine Louise Finnegan, and your grandpa's not the only one who can get his Irish up. I learned worse words at my daddy's knee. But that's neither here nor there. Why didn't you tell me?"

"Tell you what?" Winter was slow to catch on, too baffled by her grandma's use of the word "fuck." It was historic. She wondered if her grandpa had ever heard it come from his sweet wife's mouth.

"That the horrible man they call The Preacher is back?"

"He's not b—"

Beth stopped Winter's lie dead, vibrating in fury. "Don't."

The one word was enough, more than enough with the anger that crackled from her in waves, but Gramma Beth's tears clinched it. They shimmered in her blue eyes and over-flowed, smudging that papery, lavender-scented skin with ruined makeup.

Winter caught her breath on the lie before she could finish it.

"I'm sorry." Her regret was immediate and profound. Gramma Beth *did not cry.*

"Don't apologize."

Beth stiffened her shoulders. Scrubbed angrily at the tears on her face like a child trying to hide a tantrum.

Winter and her grandmother were more alike than she'd realized. She'd always thought she took after her Grampa Jack, with his rough manners and quick wit. Calm and steady, with a boiling temper just beneath the surface that came out when provoked.

But while Grampa Jack seemed to be fading, Gramma Beth was coming into sharp focus with a quickness that almost scared Winter. And the feeling seemed to be mutual. At the very least, it was making both of them extremely uncomfortable.

They eyed each other like she-wolves from across the table.

Winter could see now that her beloved grandmother also hated to cry. While Winter sympathized, Beth had never shown emotion after her daughter and son-in-law were killed, and her only grandson taken by a monster. She'd been calm and mothering and everything Winter needed, but she'd never grieved.

At times, it had been like she hadn't cared at all. Beth had just packed them up—her orphaned granddaughter and her grieving husband—and had done what was necessary to move them all on with their lives.

She'd been warm about it, but somehow still cold. The thought highlighted a distance that had been between them all along. Now, as Beth struggled to control her tears unreasonably, flames began to lick at the kindling of Winter's own temper.

"I'm keeping you safe."

The bitchiness of the snapped words was harsh in the silent room. But it put them both back on equal footing, somehow.

Gramma Beth's lips firmed, her eyes hardened.

"I can see that. I met your *protection* this afternoon," Beth shot back. "I met Officer Felcher this morning. Sweet woman and likely very capable. Fat lot of good that would've done your grandpa and me, though, if The Preacher had decided to sneak in the back door tonight and murder us in our beds."

Blood. Dripping on the floor from one outstretched finger. Her mother's ravaged face—

Winter felt like she'd been slapped. Hard.

But the barrage continued.

"You think you're so smart. You think your grandpa and I need your protection, but you don't need jack shit to keep *you* safe. You're invincible. A superhero FBI agent so wet behind the ears, it's laughable. You think that we—*I*—am just an old lady who doesn't know any better. Who can't figure out what's going on when she sees it happening right in front of her face."

Forget slapped. Gramma Beth had just slapped, shot, and gutted her. Now, it felt like Winter's battered emotions were being kicked while she lay writhing on the floor.

"Gram," Winter started to say, wanting to deny it all. To apologize.

But she got no further than the first word.

"You just shut the hell up. Shut up right now."

Beth, hearing the guttural words coming out of her own mouth, slapped a hand over it.

She paled and suddenly looked her age.

"My God. Winter." She sat back down. Slowly. Shaky, like she was afraid she'd collapse. She looked as shell-shocked as Winter felt, though it wasn't much comfort. "I'm so sorry. I don't know where that came from."

Her world was going through a polar shift, and her internal compass was spinning.

Gramma Beth and Grampa Jack had never raised their voices to her. She sounded like a spoiled brat, just admitting that to herself, but it was true. She'd come to them, traumatized and alone. Gramma Beth had scooped her up like a wounded chick—clucking and hovering—her Grampa Jack always a protective mountain somewhere nearby.

They'd never shown any kind of regret that they'd been forced to alter their lives permanently. That *she* had caused them their own pole shift.

Taking on a child—a *teenager*—under the conditions they had would have been enough to throw anyone. But they'd taken her in, already well-set in their golden years. Winter felt like caving underneath the guilt that suddenly seem to press down on her with the weight of a mountain.

Gramma Beth—the pretty, fragile, songbird-like old woman across from her—looked as beaten and bedraggled as Winter felt. It was shocking. As indomitable as she seemed, Beth was elderly. So was Grampa Jack.

Beth was her grandmother still, but only under a technicality. She'd been passed the baton of motherhood back from the second she'd opened the door to the police that night.

Now, Winter could see the daughter in her too.

Her own mother. Jeannie Black. It hurt too much for words.

"Why didn't you tell me you felt this way?" The words were quiet. Penitent.

"Well," Beth almost whispered, "I certainly wish I would have just texted you. The neighbors are probably dialing 911."

Winter was afraid to roll her eyes, still adjusting to the vision of a whole new Gramma Beth.

"Most of my neighbors *are* 911."

"Oh, no." Gramma Beth's eyes widened. "They're going to think you have a crazy grandma. That I have Alzheimer's or something."

That teased the smallest of smiles onto Winter's lips. "If you don't come over here and sit down and tell me what the hell is wrong with you, I'm going to call your bridge club and tell them you *are* crazy and you *do* have it."

"You wouldn't." The menace was back.

"Try me."

Instead of calling Winter's bluff, her grandma rounded the sofa promptly and plopped down. "That was underhanded. You know Bertha is dying to get her cousin in on Bridge Night. To do that, she'd have to take me down, first."

"I always wondered where my mean streak came from." Winter smiled slightly. "And stop trying to change the subject."

"Well," Beth sniffed. "I suppose you know now. We don't need to elaborate on it."

"I think we do. I don't want you blowing up at me again."

"I won't." Beth looked tired. "I have a temper, but it wears me out. My fuse is long, but—"

"There's a powder keg on the other side. I get it. And I've been wrong." Winter let go of some anger she didn't realize she was hanging on to in that moment. Beth looked frail and old. Her grandpa obviously wasn't well. It wasn't time for that.

It was time for vengeance. Her own hurts could wait.

"You're right. It's The Preacher. He's back."

"Winter Morrigan Black," Beth cried out, sounding hurt and angry all over again. "I knew, but why didn't you tell me?"

Winter shook her head slowly.

"Because he's mine."

Beth shot to her feet. "You can't mean to do this."

"Gramma Beth." Her voice sounded stiff and stilted, even to her own ears. "I'm going to do this. He's gone on long enough. He's like an old wolf, and another reason you shouldn't pass judgement on someone just because of their age. This wolf may have lost all of his teeth, but he's still rabid."

"It's not for you, child." Her face crumpled. "Let someone else do it. Noah would do it for you. Or that Aiden."

Now, it was Winter's turn to growl.

"Noah is a friend. Not a white knight. Not my protector. Not my savior. I don't need Noah. As for Aiden and the rest of the FBI, I don't need anyone to solve my problems for me."

"You couldn't have changed anything that night." Gramma Beth's eyes glittered with sorrow, but also strength. "You were only a child."

"I'm not a child anymore."

Just saying the words out loud tightened the resolve in her belly.

Beth looked at her for a long moment. Winter wanted to squirm under the scrutiny, but urgency pushed and nibbled at her.

"Gram, I have to. He's mine."

Long seconds stretched, pulling at each of Winter's nerves.

Finally, Beth nodded. Her lips quivered once and then firmed. Holding her arms out, she pulled Winter in for a tight hug. Tears flooded Winter's eyes, but she didn't let any of them fall. Just put her hand on the delicate ribs of her grandma's back. She seemed so fragile, but the intensity of the hug almost hurt.

"I know you do, sweetheart. Just be careful."

She pulled away just as quickly, with a bitter and fierce light of hate in her eyes that reflected the glint in Winter's own.

"Let him find you and then put the bastard out of his misery."

28

As he swept his gaze over the briefing room, Aiden kept the motion measured and even. He did not let his attention linger on any one person for longer than another, especially not her. Not Winter.

With the possible exception of Bree, The Preacher case had pushed the already strained relationships of each person in this damn room to their absolute limit. One wrong move now, and those bonds were liable to shatter into countless shards like a piece of tempered glass. Once they were broken, there would be no putting them back together.

Aiden tried to tell himself that the cost of his ambition did not matter. After all, he had finally done it. After more than a decade of relentless pursuit, after he had become all but certain he would be forced to contend with his own failure, he had finished what the murder of the Black family had started.

The Preacher had a name, and Aiden aimed to ensure everyone in this room, in this building, in the entire Federal Bureau of Investigation, knew who had found that name.

When the trepidation about the price he had paid

bubbled to the surface of his thoughts, he beat the notion back and cleared his throat. He did not have to look to know that Winter's intense stare was fixed on the side of his face.

As he squinted down at his laptop, he wished he had been given enough time to throw together a few photos and locations for a visual aid.

"All right. We're all here." He snapped his attention away from the screen and to the three agents.

Bree's patient focus was already on him, her slim hands folded together atop the table. The man to her side, however, had only just shifted his gaze away from the ceiling and to the front of the room where Aiden stood.

As Noah Dalton's green eyes met his, Aiden didn't miss the glint of malevolence. He should have felt a measure of grim satisfaction at the obvious sign of envy, but like his effort to rationalize the underhanded tactics he had employed so liberally over the last few months, he could not drum up so much as a twinge of pride. For the second time, he pushed aside his uncertainty and forged ahead.

"Midland City, Alabama. February fifteenth, 1927. Melvin Kilroy is the third child born to Mary and Joseph Kilroy. Then, three years later, July second in Rich Square, North Carolina. Nellie Banks, the first child born to Eileen and Kenneth Banks. Fast forward nineteen years, January. Hiltonia, South Carolina. Nellie Banks marries Melvin Kilroy. Nine months later, November twenty-second, 1949."

He paused to glance from person to person. Despite his disciplined avoidance earlier, he let his gaze linger as soon as he met those familiar, icy blue eyes. Time ground to a halt, and he was sure his stare was locked on Winter's for at least a full minute. He could hear the rush of his pulse in his ears, but he ignored the unexpected rush of adrenaline and pried his eyes away from hers.

"What happened on November twenty-second?" The flat

tone of Agent Dalton's query reminded Aiden of the precarious position of their collective emotional states.

"I'm glad you asked," was Aiden's sardonic response. "November twenty-second, 1949. Fort Lawn, South Carolina, Nellie Kilroy gives birth to their first and only child, Douglas Kilroy. Now, Douglas was born happy and healthy, or at least healthy, but the pregnancy was a complicated one. It would have been manageable in this day and age, but back in the late forties, Nellie was lucky to survive. I didn't find any definitive indication that the difficult pregnancy resulted in infertility, but based on the fact that Nellie and Melvin didn't have any more children, it's a safe bet."

"It's not like birth control was widely available in the early fifties," Bree put in. "Especially not in the South."

Flashing her a quick smile that was mostly genuine, he nodded. "Right. Now, Nellie and her husband, Melvin, they were what we'd probably refer to now as religious fundamentalists. To say they were old-school would be a drastic understatement. There may be a lot of people now who like to reminisce about the 1950s, the 'good old days,' but in the '50s, there were plenty of people who thought the same thing about the decades before them. And these guys, the Kilroys, that's exactly how they thought.

"Melvin Kilroy dragged his wife and son around the South with him so he could try to spread his agenda, so he could amass a following that would go with him back to the 'good old days.' He taught little Douglas the trade right along with him, and finally, when the kid was about fifteen, he picked a spot to stay and open up shop. McCook, Virginia. It's a little rinky-dink town, almost right on the Virginia-North Carolina border."

When Aiden paused this time, he was sure there would be no interruption. By now, each man and woman in the room knew the direction his announcement was headed. Palms flat against the edges of the polished wooden podium, he leaned forward. The move was made to ease the strain on his healing leg muscles, and the dramatic effect was an added bonus.

"Holy Trinity Baptist Church," he pronounced. He could almost hear their eyes widen, and he fought against a self-assured smirk. "Founded by Melvin Kilroy in the early nineteen sixties, toward the beginning of Vietnam, right in the middle of the Civil Rights movement. Now, if you take a look back through Melvin and his family's traveling days, it's a little tough to find every stop they made. But at every single stop I found, a woman went missing. Some were found years later, murdered, not much more than a skeleton left. But for the most part, they just disappeared."

"Holy shit," Bree murmured.

Aiden bit back a sarcastic pun and cleared his throat instead. He might have been elated by the discovery of The Preacher's identity, but the fact remained that they were hunting the same man who had butchered Winter Black's entire family.

When he dared another glance to the stoic woman, her eyes glittered like a pair of glaciers.

"A couple years after they settled in McCook, Nellie Kilroy died. Her death was ruled an accident, and sources said that she was thrown off a horse and then trampled. But the buzz around the area was that there was foul play. While Melvin was traveling around the country, he didn't stay in one place for long enough for people to put together the fact that he was a grade A creep. But he'd been in McCook for half a decade at that point, and people had started to talk.

"Between losing a hand around the church and all the rumors that were flying around town about Nellie's death, the congregation stopped coming. Melvin and his son, Douglas, gave sermons to rows of empty pews. And then one day, Melvin threw in the towel. Right here." Aiden paused to press his index and middle fingers against the underside of his chin. "One shot from a .38 Special, and that was the end of the Holy Trinity Baptist Church."

"Jesus Christ," someone muttered.

Aiden nodded. The comment was fitting.

"This was just before the Tet Offensive was over," Aiden went on, "and people were questioning the information that'd been fed to them about Vietnam. The hippie counter-culture was in full swing, with lots of sinning going around. I'd be willing to bet that all those events were motivation for Douglas Kilroy to take up his father's work. All the social upheaval, the departure from the nuclear family of the '50s. Never mind that the '30s were long dead too. Douglas Kilroy, The Preacher as he's been dubbed, was on a crusade."

"Murdering bastard," came from Bree.

Aiden nodded again. Also fitting. Before anything else could be said, he continued.

"Obviously, there aren't any CPS records from the middle of nowhere in Virginia during the '50s, but I can say with some certainty that Douglas Kilroy was raised around plenty of violence. From an early age, his father taught him that violence was an acceptable method for him to express emotion and assert himself. Douglas carried that thought process with him when he was drafted to Vietnam after he turned eighteen. He served over there as a Green Beret, which explains where his physical prowess comes from."

"What—" Noah started, but sick of interruptions, especially from him, Aiden gave the big man a hard stare. Jaw tight, the agent leaned back in his chair.

Turning his attention back to the group, Aiden refocused on his train of thought. "Given the limited amount of time I've had so far, I haven't been able to find out much about his combat record, just that he served for around four or five years. In that four or five years, my guess is that Douglas used Vietnam as a sort of training ground. It's not unheard of for serial killers to get their starts in active combat zones, especially conflicts as bloody as Vietnam. And once Melvin was gone, Douglas had even more motivation. He wouldn't fail where his father had. He wouldn't kill himself before his work was done."

Without another glance to the little group, he snatched up the remote for the television mounted to the wall at his side. As soon as he pressed the power button, a magnified image of a man's driver's license lit up the expansive screen.

His well-kempt white beard, rounded cheeks, and easy smile all would have conveyed a calm comfort were it not for his eyes. They were black, the iris all but indistinguishable from the pupil. But it was not the color that unnerved him.

Those were dead eyes.

The look behind those eyes was the same cool apathy Aiden had seen on the faces of some of his generation's most notorious killers.

Sociopaths, people who operated by their own definition of right and wrong. People whose moral compass was crafted by their own set of twisted ideals. Though they weren't ideals as much as they were rationalizations or excuses for men like Douglas Kilroy to carry out their macabre fantasies. To inflict pain and suffering for their own ends, to make others hurt so they could get off.

"That's him." Winter's quiet proclamation snapped him out of the reverie.

Shifting his gaze to her, he offered a slow nod. "Douglas Kilroy, a handyman by trade. It explains how he gets into all the houses so easily. Alarm systems, locks, he works on all of them. Seems like he keeps up with technology, at least in that respect. Public records indicate he's lived in Virginia for the last two decades. Local police raided his last known address as soon as I called in the APB last night, but they didn't find a damn thing. He's in the wind.

"There's an all-points bulletin out for him, as well as any truck matching the description of the red and green beater we've heard about. As of right now, it's safe to say that Douglas Kilroy is one of America's Most Wanted. As soon as someone spots him, we'll be the first to hear about it."

The silence that descended on the room felt like a suffocating shroud, but try as he might, Aiden could not come up with a way to break the spell. Any words he thought to vocalize would only have made the eerie quiet more noticeable.

Until Bree heaved a sigh and leaned back in her chair with a squeak, the only sound was the distant din of the HVAC system. Whether or not her intent had been to garner the attention of the room, all three sets of eyes snapped over as she stretched her legs.

"I didn't say anything," she said as she spread her hands, a hapless look on her face.

"What's our next play?" To his surprise, the question was posed by Noah. The usual cheer had vanished from his demeanor, and his countenance was flat, almost tired.

Maybe the deadpan look should have brought Aiden some manner of satisfaction, but instead, he felt the first pinpricks of unease on the back of his neck. Rather than answer Dalton's question, he glanced over to Winter.

She paid no attention to his scrutiny as she narrowed her eyes at the photograph on the television, looked back down to her notebook, and scribbled another line of text. She was brooding, he noted.

Well, that probably wasn't good.

When Aiden, Winter, Bree, and Noah had taken the time to combine notes on the differing angles with which they had all approached the same case, he'd hoped the mind games and the secrets were at an end.

Hope in one hand, shit in the other. See which one fills up faster.

He had never entirely understood the old adage—why in the hell would anyone *want* to shit in their hand? But he was not naïve enough to believe that all the lies and all the manipulation that each occupant of this room had employed in the alleged interest of bringing down The Preacher would just disappear.

That damage would last. He knew from personal experience that those wounds did not close easily. He hoped—there was that damn word again—that the same manipulative tactics he had used to secure himself a position in the grand finale of this case would not become the new norm for Winter.

He had been sure he was ready to pay any price necessary to see to the removal of the single blemish on his otherwise spotless record. He had been sure there would be no price too steep, but now, he wondered how much of the sentiment had been his rationalization. After all, he had become adept at discovering the inner workings of those who rationalized all manner of despicable acts, hadn't he?

Yes, he had. And he knew desperate rationalization when he saw it.

Grating his teeth together, Aiden shook his head to pull himself from the moment of introspection.

"We wait, Agent Dalton. All of us. We know who he is, and we know he's still in the country. This is officially a manhunt, and Douglas Kilroy is officially a fugitive. We'll find him. There's no question of 'if.' Now, all that remains to be seen is 'when.'"

29

For the remainder of the day, Noah made a concerted effort to focus on the menial tasks associated with The Preacher case. He had taken on the dreaded paperwork, dotting i's and crossing t's so he would have a head start once the bastard Douglas Kilroy was finally in custody.

During any moments of downtime, Noah had even gone so far as to force himself to contemplate the sheer number of notorious serial killers who had terrorized the 1970s and 1980s. Ted Bundy and the other bastards who go off on other people's pain and suffering.

He'd tried, but he'd failed.

Sure, he might have a solid start to his paperwork, but he hadn't been able to push the morning meeting from his mind. Neither Aiden nor Winter had noticed his scrutiny, but Noah had not missed the glint behind her eyes while she watched the SSA provide them The Preacher's origin story.

On more than one occasion, he had bit back a passive aggressive remark about whether or not she needed a tissue to deal with the drool on the side of her face. With the outright hostility that had marked not only his and Winter's recent interactions, but Aiden and Winter's interactions, he'd almost forgotten how long the two had known one another.

Over a decade. For over a decade, she had been able to confide in him, had been able to rely on him for emotional support in her darker moments. Which would have normally brought him a measure of comfort—after all, he had not lied to Winter. He cared about her. If she had another friend in whom she could trust her secrets, in whom she could confide, then he was sure he could have shoved aside any pangs of jealousy to encourage her to pursue her own happiness, no matter the source.

But that friend, that confidante, was Aiden Parrish. Aiden was ambitious and manipulative to the point that any sort of relationship with him was outright treacherous. Did the man even *have* a conscience? A moral compass? Did anyone mean more to him than just a steppingstone toward fulfilling his own ambition?

He knew Winter was smart, and he knew she was capable of spotting the borderline sociopathic traits that were evident in Aiden Parrish's interpersonal relationships. At the thought, he heaved a sigh and rubbed his eyes as he leaned back in the driver's seat of his pickup.

The idea that he knew better than Winter what was best for her hovered precariously between the realms of "concerned friend" and "paternalistic asshole."

Whether or not he wanted to admit it, he was jealous of Winter's lengthy history with Parrish. Of the look of reverence that had flitted over her pretty face during the morning briefing.

He'd felt the chances for anything beyond a rocky friendship with Winter begin to slip through his fingers. Tension in the conference room that morning had been so palpable he thought he could taste the strain between him, Winter, and

Aiden. Everyone was on edge, and their paranoia was not just the result of the madman they chased.

Whether their motive was to erase a black mark on their record, to avenge the death of their family, to keep a dear friend safe, or merely to bring a killer to justice, they had all resorted to lying and manipulating one another in their pursuit.

Bree must have thought they were all insane.

At the sudden realization, Noah felt the laughter build up in his throat. The sound was dry and bordered on irascible, but he could admit that the thought *was* funny.

Poor Bree. By the time they slammed the iron bars on The Preacher's cell, Bree was liable to request a transfer to the other side of the damn country—to California, Oregon, hell, maybe even Hawaii. If he was honest with himself, he could not blame her. If he was the witness to a bunch of paranoid agents and their secret wars with one another, he would be inclined to go home to pack up his apartment in preparation of the move.

With a self-deprecating chuckle, he shook his head and turned the key over in the ignition. He was unsure how long he had been sitting in the dim parking garage, and he didn't want to pique anyone's interest.

As he pulled out onto the street, he stifled a yawn with one hand. He was tired, but it was not the type of weariness that could be chased away by an adequate night of sleep. No, he was tired of the immature competition with Aiden Parrish to earn the affection of Winter. Maybe the stupid contest was all in his head, but either way, he decided today was the day he would lay the lingering anxiety to rest.

The time did not feel right. Emotions had been scraped raw, and their limits had been pushed to the point of breaking, but he had to do something. If he didn't, if he left the pieces scattered as they were right now, who knew what trick, what lie, Aiden might have up his sleeve.

He had to tell her. If he put off the conversation in the interest of permitting them all time to rebound from the tumultuous few months, he might never get a chance.

At the least, he had to tell Winter how he felt so he could stay honest with *himself*.

FOR THE MOST PART, Winter enjoyed spending time around friends and family. She liked to be around people, but as soon as she closed and locked the door to her apartment, she wasn't so sure she ever wanted to see another person in her entire life.

When she made her way down the dim hall to change into a pair of yoga pants and a hooded sweatshirt, she half-expected a fellow federal agent to hop out of the closet to ask her how she was doing.

People needed time alone, even if they were sociable. She needed to recharge, to command her own space for longer than a trip to the ladies' room. She wanted to drink a Coke and burp aloud without the obligation to offer up a panicked apology afterwards. And as she pried open the refrigerator, she decided that was exactly what she would do.

After the opportunity to finally mellow without the prying eyes or concerned gaze of her co-workers, she would have a clear mind to approach the bizarre image of the red coat.

As she stretched her legs across the couch cushions, she took a thoughtful sip of her soda. It might have been her imagination, but she swore the beverage tasted better when no one was around to stare at her while she drank. Or, maybe she had a newfound appreciation for the flavor now that The Preacher was on his last leg. Like Aiden had said, there was no *if* anymore, there was only *when*.

Aside from one prominent Mexican drug lord, Douglas Kilroy was the most wanted man in the entire United States of America. To be sure, she had not let down her guard. She was painfully aware of the sick bastard's newly stoked obsession with her.

But what did a red coat have to do with The Preacher's intent to come for her? Was the color symbolic of the blood he had spilled since he came out of his so-called retirement?

No, the visions were not symbolic, they were literal. If her brain had shown her a red coat, then The Preacher's plans involved an actual red coat. Parsing through the clues left in the wake of the intense headaches was convoluted enough. She didn't need to contend with symbolism as well.

As she tapped an index finger against the cool, metal can, she tilted her head backwards to fix her vacant stare on the ceiling. Maybe she didn't need to discern the meaning of the stylish garment, she thought. After all, Douglas Kilroy was the second most wanted man in the country. The *entire* country.

Around the state of Virginia, law enforcement agencies— everyone from the local police departments to the US Marshals—were on high alert. Douglas Kilroy's suspected body count neared the hundreds, and even though he had passed his physical prime, he was still clearly a danger.

If he tried to flee the country, he would be done the second he showed his face at an airport security checkpoint. This was the beginning of the end for Douglas Kilroy, so why did Winter have a nagging feeling that the red coat was significant?

It was significant. It had to be significant. But what in the hell did it mean?

With a resigned sigh that sounded closer to a groan, she

slumped down farther in her seat and took a long swallow from the can. She felt like she was in college, back in calculus as she stared down a problem like it would wither under her gaze and reveal the answer. To her chagrin, that was not how math worked.

Apparently, it was not how visions worked, either.

Her haphazard spot on the couch made her body feel like it had aged ten years. No, scratch that, she thought as she pushed herself to stand. Fifteen years. Definitely fifteen years.

The trick to calculus problems had been to step away from the textbook and the calculator for a short time, and then to come back with a new viewpoint. Physical activity helped the brain process information, so she plopped down on the scratchy carpet to go through her usual yoga regimen. In the meantime, she mentally stepped away from the puzzle and forced all the lingering thoughts from her head.

Over the past few months, ever since The Preacher case had taken off, she had done her body no favors. Lack of sleep alone could cause a litany of health issues, and her diet was closer to what she would expect from a college freshman or a middle schooler, not a fully grown woman. Mid-stretch, she paused and pursed her lips.

She had run herself ragged in the pursuit of the vengeance that had shaped her, that had directed her entire life. But how could she expect to enact that vengeance if she was half-asleep and half-dead?

"Damn it," she sighed.

Scooting forward, she retrieved the Coke and took another sip. It was okay, she told herself. Half-asleep, half-dead, fully asleep, mostly dead, it was okay. They had found him. There was no *if*, only *when*.

As she pulled a deep breath in through her nose, she nodded to herself. *When*, not *if*.

Just as she was about to return her focus to stretching her tired muscles, a muffled knock on the door jerked her attention to the nearby entryway. Her pulse rushed through her ears, and the first pinpricks of adrenaline flitted up her back.

"Who is it?" Her voice sounded harried even to her own ears. As she glanced to her matte black service weapon beside the can of Coke, she grasped the edge of the coffee table with one hand to haul herself to her feet.

"It's me." Like the knock, the visitor's voice was muffled.

"Noah," she muttered to herself.

So much for a few hours of quiet contemplation.

30

B ree wouldn't have used the term "insane" to describe her teammates, but they were...odd. Intense. Maybe even troubled. Without irony, she figured the little group would benefit a great deal from the calm reassurance of a professional counselor. The thought was entirely without malice, but she wouldn't dream of vocalizing it to any of her tentative friends. Not everyone held a positive attitude toward mental health professionals.

In fact, some even took a psychiatric recommendation as a personal affront.

Then again, once The Preacher was behind bars, Bree wondered if she would have to seek out a counselor to talk through the stress of the past few months.

Mental health was much like dental or physical health. The brain was a person's most complex part, and brains required upkeep. Just like teeth, just like eyes, and just like muscles. That was the purpose of counselors—to help their patients keep their brains in the same healthy shape as the rest of their bodies. Any time Bree heard a disparaging remark about those who sought mental healthcare, she was pretty sure her eye twitched in annoyance.

Once the case was over, maybe she would drive around the city to collect brochures from psychiatric and counseling offices. Then, she would dump a pile of the pamphlets on the desks of each of her co-workers.

At the thought of their befuddled expressions, she raised a hand to stifle a laugh. If she couldn't laugh about life's little oddities, she wasn't sure how she would survive.

As she retrieved her phone from the nightstand at her side, she thought a viable alternative to the pamphlet idea was to try to cut the tension with a butter knife the next time they were all in a room together. She could picture the scene, and she felt another fit of laughter in the back of her throat.

Without a word, she would produce the little knife from her pocket to saw away at the conference room air. Someone would ask what in the hell she was doing, and she would advise them that she was trying to cut the tension. Now, this was all provided she could keep a straight face. More than likely, she would wind up cackling like a maniac, and they would all be convinced that she was the one whose cheese had slid off its cracker.

Her quiet laughter continued as she unlocked her smartphone to check for a text from her friend.

Shelby was out of town for work, and with The Preacher investigation in full gear, Bree figured her fiancée's absence was for the better. If Shelby was at work, that meant she was among co-workers and friends. And if she was among co-workers and friends, she was safe. At the thought of someone as twisted as Douglas Kilroy coming within even a hundred yards of Shelby, Bree's mouth felt like it had been stuffed with cotton.

Bree had been in long-term relationships before, but her bond with Shelby was different. When she was around

Shelby, she could be herself and didn't worry that her quirks were off-putting. After all, Shelby had quirks, too, and Bree loved every single one of them. Well, except maybe Shelby's tendency to return a box of Triscuits to the cupboard when there were only three crackers left.

There had been no indication that Douglas Kilroy planned to lash out at anyone other than Winter, but Bree still felt better with Shelby out of the man's reach. As she glanced down at the newest text message, Bree felt her lips curl into a smile. Her fiancée was safe, and Douglas Kilroy would be behind bars by the time Shelby returned.

Sounds great! We'll be at The Lift by 7:00, her friend Julia had written.

Bree hadn't been to The Lift in ages. The restaurant and bar was one of her favorites in the entire city. Snowboards and skis, photos of snowcapped mountains, and even vintage signs for ski resorts decorated almost every available wall. Contrary to the bar's namesake, the décor made the space feel warm and comfortable.

Perfect! I'll see you soon! As she typed the response, her smile widened.

She needed a few hours off—as in, *off*. Away from any other agents, away from any thoughts that might steer her even remotely close to The Preacher case.

Though each crime scene had been more gruesome than the last, Bree thought she would have had a stress-free handle on the investigation if it wasn't for the tense vibes emitted by each of her fellow agents. Bree might have been curious by nature, but she didn't want to pry into the reason for each person's vendettas with the other. That was a job for a counselor, not a special agent with the FBI.

As she slid away from where she lounged against a series of pillows on her spacious bed, Bree sent a quick text message to Shelby to tell her about Julia's proposed trip to The Lift.

I miss that place! The reply was almost instant.

We'll have to go when you get back. After she added a couple smiling cat emojis for emphasis, Bree sent the message to her fiancée and stretched her legs.

A few drinks, some good food, and some good company would work wonders for the mounting stress of her co-workers and The Preacher. SSA Parrish told them their investigation had effectively become a waiting game, and Bree saw no reason why she should stay at home to do her waiting.

Bree slid her phone into the back pocket of her slim-fitting jeans and made her way to the master bathroom. As she tucked a few wayward curls back into place, she hummed the rhythm to a song Shelby had introduced her to before she left for her work trip.

White light from the fixture above the wide mirror glinted off one silver earring, but as she turned her head to check for the second, it was gone.

"Really?" Rolling her eyes at her reflection, she unclasped the little hoop and set it down beside the sink. There was a reason she never spent more than ten dollars on a pair of earrings. Whether it was the way she fastened them or her regular physical activity, Bree had made a habit of losing earrings since she was in high school.

The obvious solution was to forget about the jewelry altogether, but Bree *liked* earrings. She had a collection, much of which was comprised of cute pieces she hadn't been able to part with after she lost one of the pair. Blowing a few pieces of hair from her face, she opened the top drawer of the vanity to retrieve a pair of black and silver post earrings.

She remembered from her trip home that evening that the weather was unseasonably chilly. Bree was not a fan of the cold, but she was glad for the excuse to wear her favorite coat.

When she picked it off a rack at a local boutique, she had wondered if the bright color would be too off-putting. Even after she tried it on, she still hadn't been convinced. But the garment was warm, comfortable, and cheap. Plus, she had been looking for ways to add a bit more color to her wardrobe.

Smoothing her hands over the red fabric, she grinned at her reflection in the foyer mirror. She was glad for the impulse purchase, and she dubbed it as one of the few random buys that had panned out in the long run.

RED HAD ALWAYS BEEN my favorite color. Even when I watched the blood from Momma's head splatter across Daddy's white dress shirt, it was still my favorite. It was almost like he painted a picture when he dealt her that final blow. I'd been just off to the side in Daddy's workshop when it happened.

There had been a table saw right behind me, and I remember wondering what it'd look like to run someone's arm or leg through it. *I bet it'd make the red spatter from Daddy's hammer look like nothing.*

I was scared at first. After all, I was only fifteen, and I didn't know what kind of mission God had planned for me. But by the time Daddy asked me to grab Momma's feet to carry her out to the field, I wasn't scared anymore.

Daddy told me it was all part of the plan, told me that this was what God wanted us to do. I was like him, he said. I had a mission. A purpose.

I knew right then that I was going to make my daddy proud.

Without folks like me, my daddy said the whole world would plunge into darkness. There weren't enough of us, but as long as we were there, we'd keep fighting. We'd keep pushing back against the tide of sin, and we'd keep reminding people that this was God's country. One way or another, we were going to take this land back, and while we did it, we'd make sure those sinners were punished. That was my purpose.

Momma had been a good, proper woman, but somewhere along the line, she lost her way. That was why Daddy had to send her to meet God. We didn't make the final judgements, Daddy said. That was up to Him. All we did was carry out our orders.

The police and the folks out around McCook never did believe Daddy's story that Momma got trampled by a horse. I remember hearing one of them say something about how the damage to her head was too focused, too specific. I'd seen her face when we dropped her out in that field—there wasn't nothing left. Her dark eyes were gone, smashed into the bloody mess and broken bones of the rest of her head.

I wasn't surprised when Daddy told me that Momma had lost her way. Women were like that, treacherous, sinful by their own nature. Even the very first woman, Eve, proved that to be the truth. But when Daddy lost his way, well, that was a different type of disappointment.

He called me into the dining room one night, and I could still remember how warm it'd been in that house. The humidity was oppressive, almost like it was about to turn to sludge, and it felt like all the fans did was push it around. We'd had an air conditioner once, but after our church started to lose its following, Daddy had to sell it so he could pay the mortgage.

When I walked into that room, I saw it right away. Set neat and proper on the table in front of my daddy was a .38

Special. We had a couple long guns, a shotgun and a hunting rifle, but the .38 was the only handgun. I pulled out my chair, and it almost looked like the overhead light glinted off the wooden grip when I sat down. Daddy hadn't touched the weapon yet, though, so I knew it was my imagination.

He started to tell me how proud of me he was, and that's when I knew what was about to happen. For a minute, I thought he might shoot me, too, but when he started telling me about how I was going to carry on our family's work, I knew he wouldn't.

"God has called me home," he said. When he tucked the barrel of that pistol under his chin and pulled the trigger, I didn't even flinch.

And maybe God had called him home, I still wasn't certain. Part of me always thought that Daddy was just too weak for our work. That wasn't his fault, though. It was the way he had been made. Daddy was a preacher, not a soldier. Not like me.

A month after my eighteenth birthday, I got drafted. Maybe I should have been scared like some of the other guys my age, but I saw it as a sign. I'd never doubted my Daddy's words, but that draft card was like proof that I had been chosen.

Vietnam was filled with women who needed to be reminded of their place in this world, in a man's world. Everyone was too busy trying to survive to notice when I'd head out in the middle of the night to punish one of the women in a nearby village. I wasn't sure how many of those women I sent to God in the three years I was over there, but by the time I came back home in 1971, I knew it was my time.

Women back at home had forgotten their place, not to mention all the squawking about oppression and equal rights. Someone had to do something, and that someone was me.

A flicker of movement from the house across the street snapped my attention back to the present. I'd been gathering wool again, but at least my old brain could still recognize when something important happened back here in the real world.

The woman stepped out onto the dim porch, but a motion sensor brought the golden light overhead to life as soon as it caught her movement. Her back was to me, so I took a quick second and slumped down in the seat of my new van. She was FBI, after all. I couldn't let her catch on to my presence while I followed her out to wherever she was headed.

Her movements were fluid and graceful as she hurried to the silver sedan that had pulled up to park just behind the mailbox. The bright red of her coat stood out in stark contrast to the shadows left in the wake of the setting sun. I felt the corner of my mouth turn up in a smirk as she pried open the passenger's side door.

That coat was a lovely shade of red, my favorite color.

I knew right away that it was a sign. My girlie was close, and this lady in the pretty red coat would bring Winter to me. Manhunt or no, I was about to complete my mission.

31

Aside from tucking away her service weapon, Winter put forth no effort to make her apartment feel welcoming. She didn't even bother to hide the look of exasperation as she pulled open the heavy door to admit her visitor.

When she noticed the trepidation behind Noah's green eyes, she felt some of the irritability dissipate. His typical cheerful demeanor was gone, and in its place was anxiety, even a pang of sadness.

Had it not been for the unusual expression, she would have been inclined to close the door as soon as she had opened it. Stepping aside to permit him entry, she waved a hand to the living room.

"Come in," she offered.

"Thanks." His reply was quiet, and if there was one thing Noah Dalton was not, it was quiet.

Even as she opened her mouth to pose the question, she knew the answer. "Is something wrong with the case? Did they find him? Did they find The Preach..." She cleared her throat. "I mean, did they find Kilroy?"

Whenever someone called Douglas Kilroy "The Preacher," Winter felt like it gave the man some otherworldly power. Now that he had a name, the façade was over.

"No, it's not about that." The words were still soft, and she turned to offer him a quizzical glance.

"What's wrong?" She made sure to keep any lingering irritability out of her voice.

If there was something wrong in his life, she didn't want him to think his decision to confide in her was a burden. After all, how many times had he been there to listen to her? His timing might have been inconvenient, but after all the damage that had been done to their friendship over the span of the Kilroy case, she wanted to make sure he knew she was still there.

As he scratched the side of his unshaven face, he offered her a half-smile. "That obvious, huh?"

"I'm your friend. It's my job to tell if something's wrong." For emphasis, she flashed him a matter-of-fact smirk. "Do you want something to drink?"

"Sure." With a nod and another strained smile, he moved to follow her to the galley kitchen.

"So, what's up?" She didn't wait for his request before she handed him a bottle of beer.

Leaning against the counter, he shrugged as he twisted off the cap.

If he didn't start talking soon, she would have to fish around in the cabinets for a bottle of hard liquor. Did she have shot glasses? She couldn't remember. If she didn't, then she would just fill a coffee mug halfway with whiskey and shove it in his hand. She knew how chatty he got after a few too many drinks.

At the thought, an unbidden recollection of a distant, drunken night surfaced. Their outing had been punctuated by jokes and laughter, a far cry from the grave undertone with which they now interacted. Even though he lived only a few doors down from her, she had drunkenly offered for him to crash on her couch.

Only, she hadn't yet bought a couch, and if he had accepted the offer, well…if the light kiss before his departure that night was any indication, they wouldn't have managed much actual sleep.

Without warning, her cheeks felt like they had been set on fire. As she raised a hand to rest her cool fingers against the flush, she shot a quick glance over to Noah. He was on his own plane of existence, his green eyes fixed on the countertop across from him.

How long had it been since either of them spoke? A minute? Two? Three?

Coughing into one hand to clear her throat, she shot him an expectant look. "Well?" She forced her voice to remain light. "Do you want me to start guessing, or are you going to tell me what's bugging you? Because right now, I feel like I'm trying to talk to a rock. A rock that's drinking my beer."

His charming smile appeared so suddenly that she almost took a step backwards in surprise. From brooding to down-home Southern charm in zero point two seconds. The man had a gift.

"Now you know how I feel, darlin'." The grin didn't waver as he inclined the bottle toward her and took a long swig.

With a huff of feigned exasperation, she crossed both arms over her chest. "I'm not *that* bad."

"Okay." He half-laughed, half-snorted. "Whatever you say, sweetheart."

As she took a short step forward, she jabbed an index finger at him. "You're deflecting, Dalton."

"Yeah, yeah," he muttered before taking another sip.

She wanted to rip the bottle from his hand. "Well? Out with it."

"Winter, I'm really glad you're my friend. I just want to get that out there first. I know this is shitty timing, but by now I'm starting to wonder how much longer I can keep this to myself before my damn head explodes."

Though she made an effort to keep her expression neutral, she could hear the sudden rush of her pulse as her breath caught in her throat.

He met her gaze, and the vulnerability in his made her heart ache, but she said nothing while he took another sip of his beer before going on.

"The way I feel about you, Winter, it's gone beyond that. Beyond friendship. I think maybe it's been that way for a while, but it seems like these last few months, with everything that's happened, with watching how hard this has been for you, I think it just sort of drove it home. And now, if I keep it to myself like I have been, then it's like I'm lying to you. Maybe even like I'm lying to myself. I feel something for you, and I'm sorry if this is the wrong time. I just, I had to tell you."

She didn't know when she had moved so close to him, but she swore she felt the heat from his body. His presence had always been a comfort, even on the days when he frustrated her, even after he had gone to Dr. Ladwig. The act felt like a blatant violation of trust, but at the end of the day, his intent hadn't been to divulge her secrets, but to figure out a way to help her. Aside from Gramma Beth and Grampa Jack, Noah was the only person who cared enough about her to take the risk.

If she told him she didn't share the feelings, would he still be her friend? And was she really so sure she *didn't* share those feelings?

She took a deep breath. Well, there one way to find out.

Before she could pause to consider the absurdity of her

so-called test, she stepped forward to close the remaining distance between them, raised a hand to touch the side of his unshaven face, and tilted her head to press her lips to his.

If he was surprised by the sudden gesture, he didn't show it.

She expected a wave of clarity, a lightbulb to tell her whether or not she had ventured in the right direction. Maybe an overwhelming sense of contentment or a pervasive desire for more. But aside from the warmth on her cheeks and the rapid beat of her heart, nothing changed. That was not to say she didn't enjoy the drawn-out kiss. She savored every sweet second of it, but the pieces didn't snap into place like she'd hoped.

Romantic relationships were not Winter's forte, she knew. By and large, she had steered clear of any lasting bond that wasn't strictly platonic. Admittedly, much of the hesitation had been borne from her early infatuation with Aiden Parrish.

There weren't many college-aged boys who could measure up to a grown man with his own office in the Richmond FBI building. Even now, there weren't many grown men who could compare to the tall, handsome Aiden Parrish. Part of her hated it, but part of her would have it no other way.

At the thought of Aiden, the first chill of adrenaline pulsed through her veins. Shit. Aiden. What in the hell was she doing?

Dropping one hand to rest over Noah's button-down shirt, she pulled away from the heated gesture. As she opened and closed her mouth in an attempt to summon up words to explain her impulsive action, his green eyes went wide. It was like he could read her mind.

In a split-second, any hints of contentment on his face were replaced with unabashed dread.

"Oh, shit," he managed. "What the hell just happened?"

"Oh my god," she stammered. Reaching to cover her mouth, she shook her head. "I don't know what that was. I didn't mean to, oh my god, I didn't mean to do that. I'm so sorry. I don't know what I'm doing."

She could almost hear him bite back a sarcastic response as he clenched and unclenched his jaw. As his eyes darted from one kitchen fixture to the next, he heaved a sigh and gulped down the rest of his drink. When Winter licked her lips, she could taste the craft beer.

"It's just, it's not a good time." The words were quiet and weary, and she fought to keep her gaze from dropping to the floor. He didn't respond, and she took her cue to continue. "For a second, I thought I was losing you. I thought I was losing my friend, and I just, I don't know. I panicked and I kissed you, and I'm sorry. That wasn't fair to you, and if you want to tell me to go to hell while you walk out the door right now, I think I'd understand."

She waited for him to say something. Hoped like hell that he would say something. But he just stood there, waiting for her to go on.

So, on she went. "If I'm being honest, I don't know what I want right now. Other than this case, other than seeing Douglas Kilroy dead or in prison, I've got no idea what I want anymore."

He scrubbed his hands over his face. "Winter, I—"

She held up a hand, hating how her fingers trembled. "I really hope you'll stick with me while I figure it out, but after what I just did, I wouldn't blame you if you decided not to. You're basically my only friend, Noah, and I don't want to risk screwing that up unless I'm one-hundred-percent sure I'm doing the right thing. But I guess that's all provided I didn't just screw it up, huh?"

Though his laugh was strained, she was relieved to see some of the usual humor return to his handsome face.

"No, Winter, that's all right. Thank you for being honest. That's all you can really do, you know?"

"I guess." She felt deflated, like someone had just poked a hole in her side to let out all the air.

"Okay, well," he pronounced. With a hapless shrug, he held up his hands. "I feel like an idiot. I'll just get that out there right now. I'm not going to turn into a jackass just because you don't have the same feelings that I do, but that doesn't mean I'm just going to bounce right back. Right now, I'm going to go out to the living room, grab my coat, and then slither into the darkest hole I can find."

"You and me both," she muttered.

She wanted to turn his offhand remark into a reality. She wanted to go grab her coat, drive to a hardware store to buy a shovel, and dig a hole. Maybe she didn't need a hole, maybe all she needed was a camouflaged coat. Then, instead of lying in the dirt, she could hide in a bush until her awkward embarrassment abated.

Just as she was about to make a comment about leaving to buy a camouflaged coat, the realization dawned on her.

"What?" she heard him say.

"The coat." The words were scarcely above a whisper. "The red coat, holy shit. You remember the red coat? That coat I wore to catch that rapist asshole a while back?"

"The one Bree lent you? Yeah, what about it?"

"I saw it. That vision, or whatever you want to call it, that's what it was. It was Bree's coat."

He perked up at the mention of a vision, and he set his jaw to flash her a determined look.

"He's going after Bree." Even as the words left her lips, she brushed past him and hurried down the hall to her room. She donned a pair of dark jeans, boots, and exchanged her hoodie for a worn leather jacket all in record time. After she snatched up her keys and tucked her service weapon beneath her arm, she glanced to Noah and nodded.

Neither of them bothered to speak as they all but sprinted into the chilly evening. Just as she approached the passenger side of Noah's pickup, she spotted a flicker of color in her periphery.

"Hold on." She took in a deep breath and shifted her gaze to the source of the red glow. The mailbox. *Her* mailbox. Without a word of explanation, she stalked toward the glimmer.

As she turned the key over to pull open the metal door, she felt like each movement was made through molasses. She had gotten her mail after she returned home that afternoon, and a photo was the only item in the little cubby.

"What is it?" Noah's voice grew clearer as he approached, his foot falls quiet.

She took in a sharp breath as she held up the Polaroid to the white glow of a nearby streetlight. Wrists zip-tied together, a black bandana tied around her face. Her eyes were closed, and her mouth was agape.

"Shit," Noah growled. "Is she dead?"

"I don't know." As she shook her head, Winter glanced up to her friend. "But we need to go."

With a solemn nod, he turned and made his way back to the parking lot, Winter less than a couple steps behind.

32

Bree's thoughts shifted back and forth between the realm of unconsciousness and the waking world, but every time she tried to speak, her voice was muffled by a wad of fabric. The ache in her head was exacerbated by each bump, and she squeezed her eyes closed against the throbbing pain. She didn't know where she was, but she could tell that she had been loaded into a vehicle, and the vehicle was in motion.

Last she could remember, she had stepped outside the bar to make a phone call.

Shelby'd had a long day at work, and she was about to head to bed. After Bree excused herself from the little gathering of friends, she had picked her way across the bar and out through the front entrance. There was a group of college-aged kids not far from the double doors, so she decided to move around the corner of the building to a quieter, darker area. The conversation with the love of her life had been short, but before she took a step back toward the sidewalk, she felt a sharp pinch on her neck.

Before she could blink, the world went black.

Her careful recollection was cut short as the vehicle rolled over what she assumed was a pothole. For a split-second, she felt like she was airborne, though discerning her body's position was difficult through the lingering haze of whatever had knocked her out. When her head smacked into the floorboard, she heard a startled groan escape her lips.

"You're awake," the driver commented.

There was an unmistakable Southern drawl in his soft voice. He didn't sound surprised or angry. There was no emotion in his voice, and even through the cobwebs in her throbbing head, Bree knew who he was.

The icy rush of adrenaline pushed away the rest of the drug-induced fog as she glanced down to her bound wrists. The tips of her fingers were cold and tingly, and she flexed her hands in an effort to restore the circulation. He had used industrial grade zip-ties to tie her wrists together, but the binds were not inescapable.

Back when she and Shelby had still been dating, Bree explained the detriments of a long-term relationship with a federal agent. Specifically, an agent who worked in the violent crimes division.

Bree and her colleagues hunted down the worst of the worst, and she reminded Shelby that the subjects of their investigations would have no qualms hunting down and kidnapping an agent's loved ones if it meant leverage.

Shelby had not balked at Bree's warning. Instead, she had asked Bree to teach her some of her "FBI badassery." Aside from time at a shooting range and lessons in self-defense techniques, she had taught Shelby the fundamentals to escape a variety of binds, including zip-ties.

"Well, we can't have this now, can we?"

In a split-second of panic, Bree thought he had read her mind.

"Going to have to give you another dose. Internet said

that one'd be enough to last a couple hours, but you know how the internet goes, don't you? Can't trust nothing you read on there."

After the light click of the turn signal, the vehicle slowed until it lurched to a stop. A ruddy orange streetlight glinted off a stainless-steel handgun as the man unbuckled his seatbelt to turn to face her. When he flashed her a smile, Bree felt the hairs on the back of her neck stand on end.

There was no mirth, no amusement, and no self-assuredness. There was just...nothing.

"Now, I might be an old man, but I'll have you know that my trigger finger's just as fast as it was in Vietnam. I'm goin' to stick you with this needle right quick, but if you move like you're goin' to put up a fight...well..." As he pulled the plastic cap free from a syringe, he shrugged.

With speed that should have eluded someone his age, he leaned toward her, his weapon in one hand, needle in the other.

Squeezing her eyes closed, Bree clamped her hands so tightly that her nails dug into her palm. She knew who he was, and she knew he wouldn't hesitate to put a bullet in her head if she made an effort to overpower him now. Though she did not know his plans, did not know where the dingy van was headed, she had to trust that she would have another opening. A better opening.

She would be smart, and she would bide her time until she knew she had a fighting chance.

EVEN THOUGH SHE knew the woman wouldn't respond, Winter had sent two text messages to Bree's phone. She didn't pause to wait for a reply before she pulled up Aiden Parrish's contact information. With a sideways glance to

Noah, she pressed the button to dial the SSA's number. They didn't have time for whatever territorial pissing match Aiden and Noah had started. Bree had been kidnapped by a psychopath, and her life hung in the balance. Their awkward feelings could wait.

"Agent Black." Aiden's greeting was curt, and his tone bordered on irritable.

Winter didn't bother to address his attempted slight. "The Preacher, I mean, Douglas Kilroy took Bree. He took a picture of her and left it in my mailbox. I can't tell if she's dead or just unconscious, but either way, we need to find him, and we need to do it now."

"Shit," Aiden spat.

"We're on our way to her house to see if there's anything out of place there, anything that might point us in the right direction."

"We?" he echoed.

"Yeah, me and Agent Dalton." She didn't bother to conceal her own annoyance, and she raised the volume of her voice as she met Noah's wide-eyed stare. "You know what, SSA Parrish, you two can save the dick measuring contest for when this is over, all right? I don't want to hear a word from you, *either* of you. I'm so unbelievably sick of watching you each direct all this passive aggressive bullshit toward one another. This isn't about you finally closing the door on the case that still haunts you, *Aiden*. And it's not about trying to be a knight in shining armor, *Noah*."

"Now, you listen—"

"Shut up," she said, unwilling to listen to him say another word. "It wasn't ever about that, and it sure as hell isn't about that anymore. Now, it's about Bree. If I can put aside my vendetta with Douglas Kilroy to focus on doing what's necessary to get Bree home safe, then you two damn well better be able to do the same. And, if you can't, then maybe you aren't fit to carry around a badge!"

It was about time someone said it, she thought. She had drawn the conclusion during the conversation with Gramma Beth, and she wanted to make sure the two men came to the same understanding.

Though she had devoted her entire life to seek revenge for the brutal slaying of her family, Winter could admit to herself that her half-cocked plan to personally take over the Kilroy investigation had been misguided, to say the least. She would get her revenge, but the fact remained that her parents would not come back if Douglas Kilroy was dead or behind bars. Winter could gut the man herself, but no amount of Kilroy's blood would bring back what he had taken from her.

What should have motivated her, what should have motivated them *all* was the desire to prevent another poor girl from returning home to find the mutilated remains of her parents. They could not change the past, but they could change the future, and they could change the present.

Instead, for three months, they'd all behaved like a group of petulant children. All of them except for Bree, and now she was the one who would pay for their mistakes.

Winter half-expected Aiden to berate her for the heated observation, and she half-expected Noah to launch into a spiel to defend his motives. If either man decided to take that route, then she would find Bree by herself.

To her relief, any hint of condescension had vanished from Aiden's voice when he replied, "I'll check on her phone activity and see if I can find anything, and I'll make a couple calls. You two check her house and see what you can find there. I doubt he just knocked her out so he could send you a picture, so she's probably not there. I'll get back to you as soon as I've got something." His grim determination became more noticeable as he went on, and she could almost picture the look in his eyes as he regained his composure.

"Thank you," she replied, her shoulders almost sagging in relief. "I'll call you if I think of anything else. Otherwise, I'll let you know once we've had a chance to check her place."

"All right. Watch your back, Winter."

"Yeah, you too."

The red glow of a stop light glinted off the screen as she swiped a thumb to disconnect the call. She could feel Noah's intent stare on the side of her face.

"What?" Tucking the smartphone back into a pocket, she snapped her head over to narrow her eyes at him.

With a strained, self-deprecating chuckle, he spread his hands and shook his head. "Nothing." The engine hummed as the red glow switched to green, and he pulled away from the intersection.

"I don't believe you," she said. "If you're going to say something, then spit it out. Speak now or forever hold your peace, Noah."

"No, I wasn't going to say anything. You were right, darlin'. We've all been acting like a bunch of angsty teenagers ever since this thing started. We've been acting like this was something we all had to do on our own, like we all had something to prove. It's stupid, and I'm just glad someone finally had the guts to say it."

Her mouth dropped open in surprise. "Oh. Well, thanks."

"This is her street." With one hand, he gestured to a shadowy side street as he used the other to flick on the blinker.

Winter straightened in her seat and turned her focus to the road.

"Shit." He ground out the word. "That's her car."

Before they had even pulled into the sloped driveway to park, Winter unbuckled her seatbelt and reached for the door handle. Noah had not yet shifted the pickup out of drive when she pushed out into the chilly night. One hand tucked inside her leather jacket to clasp the grip of her service weapon, she cast a hurried glance to the familiar gunmetal Audi. Nothing stirred, and she spotted no red glow.

As he strode to her side, Noah's green eyes flicked to hers as he inclined his head in the direction of the modest front porch. She nodded, and their footsteps were all but silent as they hastened up the short set of stairs. When she spotted the gap between the wooden door and the frame, she took in a sharp breath.

The matte black handgun was in her grasp before she realized she had retrieved it. She looked over to see that Noah held his own weapon. The look on his face was grim as he nodded his agreement to her unspoken question.

Glaring down the sights of the 9mm, she shoved the wooden door inward with one hand before she returned her iron grip to the handgun. Wordlessly, Noah gestured to a staircase before he made his way to the landing.

The barrel of Winter's service weapon led the way as she crept from one dim room to the next, but she didn't spot so much as a stray piece of paper that looked out of place.

When she circled back around to the bottom of the steps, she had to suppress a groan. A light creak from the side directed her attention over to the wooden stairs.

"Upstairs is clear," Noah advised.

"Yeah, it's clear down here too." With a sigh, she tucked the handgun back beneath her jacket.

"Did you see anything?"

"Nothing." She looked around the small room. "You weren't kidding when you said she was a clean freak. What about you?"

"Nothing. You should probably come up here too. You

know, catch anything I might have missed." He raised his eyebrows for emphasis.

"Right." The tingle of adrenaline brushed down her neck as she hurried to the second floor. Before she even spotted the faint, red glow, she knew she was about to find something significant.

Less than three steps into the hallway, her eyes were drawn to a glimmer of red along the otherwise blue-gray drywall. To the side of an eight-by-ten photo of Shelby and Bree on a dance floor was a screw where another picture should have hung.

"There's a picture missing." As she brushed her fingers along the bare spot on the wall, Noah muttered a string of curses under his breath.

"Kilroy was here." His utterance was not a question.

And Winter knew that his statement wasn't wrong.

33

In the midst of a frantic search to find a missing Federal Agent, Aiden figured the last place anyone else would be was on the line with a customer service number. Then again, the ability to think outside the so-called box was no small part of the reason for his advancement within the BAU.

He didn't know what had possessed Bree Stafford to use her work email on her PayPal account, but tonight, he was grateful for the little quirk. Accessing the government issued email account of an agent he technically outranked was far easier than requesting a summary of Bree's online activity from one of the Bureau's tech agents. Not only was it easier, it was faster.

As Winter had pointedly reminded him, the hunt for Douglas Kilroy was no longer a personal affair for any of them. Not that it should have ever been a secretive vendetta in the first place, he thought. Winter was right. In pursuit of their own ambitions, they had each lost sight of the real reason they were after Douglas Kilroy.

Douglas Kilroy was a madman who had brutally raped and slaughtered close to a hundred women. He was a sociopath, and he was not fit to walk freely among them. The man was a scourge—the worst of the worst—and their duty was to put an end to his rampage before he claimed another victim.

"Uber customer service, how can I help you?" The cheerful voice snapped him out of the solipsism, and he bit back a sigh as he rubbed his eyes.

"Hi, yeah, I think I've got an unauthorized charge on my account."

"Oh, I'm sorry to hear about that. Could I have your first and last name, and your email address, please?"

Without hesitation, he rattled off Bree's email address and advised the representative that he was Bree Stafford. Aside from a slight pause, the young man gave no indication of doubt.

"It's a charge for seventeen dollars and sixty-eight cents." Eyes fixed on the text of the email receipt for the payment, Aiden scratched the side of his face and leaned back in his office chair. "It was made tonight, just a little bit ago. Sometimes, my fiancée uses my account, and I was wondering if you could tell me what the address was? I'd hate to go through all the trouble of filing a claim just to find out my fiancée was the one who made the payment."

As the rep read the street address to him, Aiden typed the location into an online mapping service. According to Bree's Uber payment, she had ordered a ride to a restaurant and bar called The Lift. The inspiration for the name and the décor was a ski resort, though Richmond was not known for its snow-capped mountains.

"You know what, that address sounds familiar. I think I'll ask my fiancée if she made that payment before I file a claim on it. Thank you for all your help."

"No problem, sir. I, I mean ma'am."

At the panicked correction, Aiden felt the start of a smirk

tug at the corner of his mouth. He wasted no time before he pulled up Winter's number.

"Yeah?" The line had hardly rung once before she answered.

"I saw your message about her car still being there," he started. "She took an Uber to a bar called The Lift. The receipt said she paid for the ride about an hour and a half ago."

"Wait, how'd you find all that?" He didn't miss the skepticism in her query.

"It's called social engineering." There was a patronizing tinge to the simple statement, but his patience had already worn too thin for him to care. "I tricked someone at Uber into giving me the address. It was faster than trying to get one of the tech guys to go through her internet history or track her phone. Look, that was the last charge. That means she went to that bar and either didn't leave, or someone showed up and took her."

"There was a picture missing in the upstairs hallway at her house. It was Kilroy. It had to have been."

"No doubt," he agreed. "I'll text you the address. In the meantime, I'll look to see if there's anything I can dig up about where he might have gone. Call me after you've had a chance to canvass the bar."

"Okay, I'll do that. Talk to you soon."

"Yep," was his laconic response. With a clatter, he dropped the smartphone to the surface of his desk. He doubted he would be able to unearth any solid leads for Kilroy's location from where he sat in his office, but he knew for certain he could not sit by and do nothing.

He would not, *could not*, have the blood of a fellow agent on his hands. They had to find Bree. There was no alternative.

As Noah pushed through the set of double doors, the smell of fried food and beer wafted past him. On a normal day, the scent would have been enough to make his stomach grumble, even if he had just eaten. Tonight, however, a growing pit of dread made the idea of eating all but laughable.

He swallowed back the bout of nausea and started toward the cluster of patrons crowded around a horseshoe shaped bar. Mouths gaped open and eyes went wide as he flashed his identification to clear a path for him and Winter. In an effort to assuage their trepidation, he offered what he hoped was a charming smile.

"We're just here looking for someone," he started. Along with the pleasant expression, he turned up his disarming folksy drawl. He watched the unease vanish from the faces of a college-aged couple as he held up his phone to show them a picture of Bree. "We've got reason to believe she might be in danger. Have y'all seen her here tonight?"

The young man and woman shook their heads in response.

"All right, thank you for your time. Enjoy your evening." As he tipped an invisible hat to the duo, he wondered if the gesture was too over the top.

"Hey," a voice called.

In tandem, he and Winter turned to the source.

"Let me see that picture," the bartender asked. Wiping her hands on a white towel, she peered up at him with eyes that glinted like a pair of emeralds.

"Have you seen her?" One elbow resting atop the wooden bar, he held the phone up for the young woman.

As she brushed a piece of auburn hair from her fair face, she shifted her gaze back to his and nodded. With one hand, she gestured toward a circular table in the far corner of the open room.

"She only had one drink, maybe two. She was hanging out over there with those folks before she went outside."

On a normal night—a night that did not involve the kidnapping of a fellow federal agent—he thought he might have turned the charm up to eleven. Her skin was like flawless porcelain, her dark, auburn hair a stark contrast to the pale shade. Moreover, the silver band she wore on her left hand was on her middle finger, not her ring finger.

But tonight was not a normal night.

"How long ago do you reckon you last saw her?" Returning the smartphone to his coat, he dared a quick glance to Winter. Her lips were pursed, and her blue eyes shifted between him and the bartender.

Between the dim lighting and the couple days' worth of scruff on his face, he hoped Winter could not see his face flush. Was this really how he was going to act? Was he really going to abandon any hope for a future relationship with a woman he considered his *best friend* just because they'd had one awkward moment?

Suppressing a groan, he returned his attention back to the bartender.

As her green eyes flicked from Winter to him and then back to Winter, she shrugged. "Honestly? It's been a busy night, man. I haven't been looking at the clock. Could have been anywhere between a half-an-hour and three hours ago." With a shrug, the woman returned the towel to the counter at her side. "It looked like those people over there were her friends, though. Might have better luck asking them."

"Yeah," he agreed. He offered an appreciative nod. "Thanks for your help, darlin'."

In response, she made a sound that hovered somewhere between a snort and a laugh. "Any time, Agent Mulder."

Without another glance, she beckoned the nearest patrons forward.

"That was helpful," Winter muttered as they started to pick their way across the crowded room.

"Actually, yeah, it was. Unless you knew where to look for Bree's friends?"

"Between a half-hour and three hours? Really, Noah?" There was an unmistakable tinge of irritability in her voice, and he noted with some resignation that the exasperation was also visible in her expression.

"Well, hopefully Bree's friends were paying a little more attention to the time."

As he offered her a pleasant smile, the ire dissipated.

"Evening, y'all," he pronounced. Waving a greeting with one hand, he held up his identification with the other.

Four sets of eyes snapped over to them at the announcement, and the cheery conversation lapsed until the only sound was the din of the bar.

"Is something wrong?" one of the women asked. Her amber eyes shifted from him to Winter and then back as concern etched its way onto her face.

"We're not sure. We're hoping not. Any of y'all know Bree Stafford?"

"Bree, yeah." The woman nodded. "She was just, wait, where is she? Jeff?" As she turned her expectant glance to the man at her side, Jeff, he shook his head.

"I don't know," Jeff answered. "I think you were at the bar when she went outside. She said she was going to call Shelby to tell her good night."

"Oh my god." The woman's eyes widened. "How long ago was that? That was like an hour ago, wasn't it?"

"Shit." Noah and Jeff spat out the word at the same time.

"She's been gone for an hour?" Winter surmised.

"Close to, yeah." With a sheepish nod, Jeff picked up his glass of beer and took a long pull.

"All right, thanks. Here." Pausing, Winter retrieved a white business card from her jacket and set it atop the table. "If you hear anything from her, please, call me as soon as you can."

"Of course." Julia's voice was just a step below fervent. "Is she okay? Is there anything we can do?"

"I'm sure she's fine," Noah replied. "We're just having a little trouble getting ahold of her. You know, work stuff."

With a look that insisted she was far from convinced, Julia nodded. "Okay. When you see her, have her send me a text, could you?"

"Sure thing." After another smile he hoped was convincing, he and Winter turned to make their way back to the doors.

34

As she climbed into the passenger seat and closed the door, Winter heaved a sigh. She was not sure what she'd expected to find from a last-ditch trip to a bar, but she must have hoped for more than they learned.

"So, what've we got?" Turning the key over in the ignition, Noah's green eyes flicked over to meet hers.

"A whole lot of nothing," she muttered. "Bree went to call Shelby about an hour ago, and she never came back. The—I mean, Douglas Kilroy left a picture in my mailbox of her either unconscious or dead. What time did we leave my place? That was about a half an hour ago or so, wasn't it?"

"Forty minutes," he answered.

"All right, forty minutes. So, he grabbed her from here, dragged her to his vehicle in the middle of a crowded parking lot, and then took a picture of her with an old-school Polaroid camera. While he was on his way to wherever in the hell he's headed, he stopped by my place to drop off the picture. It's obvious he wants us to go after him, but he's not doing us a lot of favors if he wants us to actually find him."

The first twinges of a headache pulsed with each beat of her heart, and she squeezed her eyes closed to massage her temples.

Without warning, a pop sounded out through her aching head. Not the report of a car as it backfired or a gunshot, but more akin to the satisfying sound of Bubble Wrap. One, then two more pops followed, each louder than the last.

The ring in her ears was the same tone that followed a gunshot in a cramped area. She was aware of Noah's voice at her side, but through the ring, she could not make out his muffled words. The sensation was so unlike any she had experienced, that for a split-second, she thought she had been shot in the head. There was no pain, so maybe she had been dispatched to the afterlife.

Then, she opened her eyes.

"What is it?" she finally heard her friend ask.

"What the *fuck?*" The words were scarcely above a whisper.

Rather than the parking lot of the ski lodge themed bar, she stared out the windshield to a looming building cloaked in shadow. A flash of lightning split the inky sky and lit up the wooden cross at the peak of the dilapidated roof. More shingles had rotted or been washed away by the elements than remained, and in the darkness, the shrubs and vines from the ground looked as if they intended to swallow the structure whole.

All at once, the building shot forward until she could see through the shattered wooden doors. With a yelp of surprise, she leapt backwards in her seat, both hands raised to shield herself from the unexpected movement. Had the church moved closer to her, or had she moved closer to it?

"What the hell?" She wheezed out the question as much as spoke it. "What is this? Am I...am I dead?"

"What do you see?"

She was not sure from where the query emanated, but to her, it sounded like the man might have been hidden in the dark clouds.

"It's...it's a church," she started. "It's old. No one's used it in a long time."

She squinted through the shadowy doorway as she rubbed her arms in an effort to ward off a sudden chill. Before she could open her mouth to elaborate, she was whipped forward through the entryway and to the center of a vaulted room. As she took in a sharp breath, she clamped both hands over her mouth to stifle the sound.

Rotted pews lined either side of the aisle like a regiment of decaying soldiers. Overhead, a flicker of light shone through the various holes in the arched roof as thunder rumbled throughout the space. Then, the air was still, and all she could hear was the incessant ring in her ears. This was it, she knew.

"It's his church," she managed.

She thought she heard the voice ask "Whose?"

"Melvin Kilroy's."

From the corner of her eye, she spotted a flicker of color. Red, the same coat she'd seen the previous day. When she glanced to the bright garment, the hairs on the back of her neck rose to attention. Suspended amidst nothing, the red coat floated beside an altar.

"Bree's here," she said.

And then, just as soon as it had come to life, the world went black as the first waves of searing pain rolled over her. Agony, at its worst.

She'd found Bree, and for that, she would be eternally glad. But right now, she was sure she was about to die.

❄

Aiden narrowed his eyes as the agent's name flashed across the screen of his smartphone. Though he had expected the call, he had expected to hear from Winter, not Noah.

Swiping the green answer key, he raised the device to his ear. "Yeah," was his laconic greeting.

"We know where Bree is," Noah said. His voice was hurried and strained.

"But…?" Aiden pressed. He had already pushed himself back away from the desk as he prepared to rise to his feet.

"Winter's unconscious. Look, I don't know what the hell happened, but it wasn't the same as her normal headaches, or her visions, whatever you want to call them. It was bad. But she saw Melvin Kilroy's church, and then she said that Bree was there. After that, she was just…out."

"Shit," Aiden hissed. "His church was just outside McCook. That's two and a half hours away from us, Dalton. We need to leave, like, yesterday."

"Winter's *unconscious.*" The other man's voice was flat. "This isn't like what's happened to her before, you hear me? Something about this one was different. She was awake for the first part of it, but it was like she was somewhere else. Like she was walking through a damned horror movie or something."

"She'll come out of it. She always does."

"You'd better be right, Parrish," Noah grated.

What other options did they have? With Bree in Kilroy's custody, they didn't have time to swing by the emergency room on their way out of town to make sure that Winter had not fallen victim to a stroke or an aneurysm. It was just another vision, he told himself. She would be fine. She was always fine.

"We don't have time for this shit, all right? We need to get moving, but we can't go down to what may well be a trap with a couple Glock nine-mils and our coats. We need Kevlar and we need heavier firepower." Aiden used his shoulder to press the phone to his ear as he snatched his coat from the back of the chair.

"No argument here," Noah muttered.

"Which means you need to come inside. SSA or not, I can't check out a rifle for you, Dalton. Meet me at my car in the parking garage, first floor. At this time of night, it ought to be one of the only ones in there."

"What about Winter?"

"Bring her with you. We'll get her situated and make sure she's good, then we'll head to the armory."

"We're just going to leave her in your car?" His tone was incredulous, almost haughty.

"She's unconscious, Dalton!" Aiden snapped. "She's not going anywhere. It'll take us five minutes, ten tops. If you want to face off against Douglas Kilroy with the iron sights on your nine-mil, then be my guest. But I'd rather have something that's a little more precise over a longer range. He might be old, Dalton, but he was a Green Beret for four years in Vietnam. I don't have to tell you the kind of shit Green Berets can do, do I?"

"No," Noah ground out. "But—"

"If you really want to sit down there in a locked car, in an FBI parking garage *filled* with security cameras, then be my guest. But I'm not going to risk my damn job just to get you a rifle, you understand? And honestly, for Bree's sake, I think you ought to drop the savior act for a second and come get a fucking rifle so you can back us up when we get there."

"Yeah," Noah sighed. "All right, Parrish. I'll meet you down there."

Without a word of farewell, Noah disconnected the call.

Aiden flicked off the light to his office, eased the door closed, and strode down to the elevator as fast as his healing leg would allow.

They loaded Winter into the back seat of Aiden's car without incident, and neither man spoke as they hustled down to the armory of the Richmond FBI office. Three Kevlar vests, three jackets with the Bureau's insignia printed in bright yellow on the back, and two M4 carbines later, Aiden tossed his keys to Noah.

"You want me to drive your car?" the taller man asked, one eyebrow arched as he flashed Aiden a skeptical look.

"If we take yours, we're going to have to stop four times for gas," he muttered. "My leg's still fucked up, and I can't sit in the damn driver's seat for two and a half hours. I've got insurance, Dalton. We'll be fine."

"Full coverage?" The questioning expression turned amused as Noah opened the driver's side door.

"Yes." With exasperation that was mostly feigned, Aiden rolled his eyes.

35

As he set the cruise control to just over eighty miles per hour, Noah shifted in his seat. He glanced up to the rearview mirror to check if Winter's condition had changed. Head propped atop a bundle of a couple FBI jackets, another coat draped over the top half of her body, she lay just as still as she had the last time he'd looked. Her pale face was serene, an expression so rarely seen when she was awake. Especially now, especially over the last few months.

Had anything gone right, he wondered? Had there been one, single clear-cut victory in the entire investigation into Douglas Kilroy? Just once, had they spotted an anomaly and come away with a greater understanding of the man after whom they sought?

No, he did not think they had.

He didn't have to ask the opinions of tenured agents to know that the Douglas Kilroy case was the type of investigation that drove good cops to turn in their gun and badge. When the worst the world had to offer surfaced and they were powerless to stop it, what then? When they could not drag the darkness into the light, what did they do?

Gritting his teeth, he forced his attention away from the bleak thoughts. The drive to where Douglas Kilroy had holed up with an FBI hostage was not the time or the place for a philosophical debate. Besides, he still had to puzzle over Winter's bizarre gesture of affection earlier in the day.

As he thought of the unexpected kiss, he glanced over to his unlikely passenger. The SSA's lips were pursed, his countenance grim as he listened to the tinny voice on his phone.

"All right," Aiden said. "Let me know the second anything changes. All right. Thanks. Goodbye." Shadows cast by the passing lights shifted along his face as he clenched and unclenched his jaw.

"Any luck?" Noah asked.

"None," Aiden all but spat. "Their nearest SWAT team is an hour outside McCook as it is, and right now they're all busy with an active shooter turned hostage situation in the opposite direction of where Kilroy is. They've got backup people, but they'll have to call them in. It'll take them close to three hours to get their team together and get them there."

"We might not have three hours." Rather than accusatory, his words were quiet and strained.

"That's what I told them. Looks like it's just us versus Kilroy. Anyone that can help us will be about thirty minutes to an hour behind."

"Glad you talked me into getting that M4," Noah muttered.

"You and me both."

Another silence descended on them, and Noah's thoughts drifted. Now, he wondered even more whether or not he should have merely called Kilroy's location into a different department, maybe the US Marshals, rather than load Winter in the back of Aiden's car to undertake the task himself. If she'd awoke in a hospital bed to learn that The

Preacher had been gunned down by a marshal while she was unconscious, how would she react?

More than likely, petulance would have flashed behind her blue eyes as she leapt to her feet to demand to know what in the fresh hell had crossed his mind when he decided to pawn Kilroy off on another law enforcement agency.

Putting Douglas Kilroy away might have been a personal affair for Noah and Aiden at this point, but Kilroy's actions had shaped Winter's entire life. The only reason she was an agent in the FBI was because she had vowed to track down the man who massacred her family. Compared to what had been taken from her, could he or Aiden claim to have any idea how she felt?

Then again, he was reminded of an old saying. *When you seek revenge, remember to dig two graves.* As he glanced to her still form, he felt a chill rush down his back.

Was Kilroy worth it? Was Kilroy worth her livelihood?

No, he told himself. *This isn't about you anymore. This isn't about her anymore. This is about bringing Bree home safe so no one has to show up on her fiancée's doorstep with a folded flag in their arms.*

Three hours. The SWAT team was three hours out, and now, they were only two hours out. Whatever his motive for loading Winter into Aiden's car, for following the SSA to the armory to retrieve an automatic rifle, they were now the first line of defense for Bree Stafford.

Though he had been leery when Aiden first advised of his intent to enlist the aid of a local law enforcement agency, he bit back any doubts and let the man make his calls.

For Bree's sake, he could not justify leaving any potential for rescue off the table. This wasn't about them anymore.

On any given day, Noah could not stand Aiden Parrish, but he could admit that the effort to reach out to a closer group of law enforcement officials had been the right call.

With Bree's life in the balance, he was sure even Winter would agree with his assessment. How selfish would they have to be to throw away the opportunity to save Bree's life just so they could satiate their desire for vengeance?

But now, there was no one to swoop in to save the day. No one except for the three of them.

Three FBI agents with enough tension between them to choke out a heavyweight wrestling champ, and they were going to save the day. One had run herself so ragged that she hovered precariously close to emaciated and another had played his fellow agents like they were pawns in a damned chess match, and then there was himself. He had been bound and determined to save a woman who quite clearly did not need to be saved.

Hadn't there been a movie made about a situation like theirs? *The Replacements*? No, *The Replacements* had been about the second string of a professional football team.

Close enough, he thought to himself.

They were a mess, and he could admit as much. But, like the players in the film, they were good at what they did. As much as it irked him to give the man credit, Aiden's suggestion—his demand—that they take a couple high-powered rifles had been smart.

The military's training regimen for Special Forces soldiers, also known as Green Berets, may have changed since the days of Vietnam, but Noah doubted the men of the specialized warfare faction had been any less formidable during the '60s and '70s.

Plus, when it came to dealing with the unknown, more firepower was always better.

I KNEW my girlie was close. I could feel it.

It was almost time. Just like God had told me, just like my daddy never could—I was going to make it. Winter would be here soon, and there was no chance I'd be forced to turn my pistol on myself like Daddy had. Once I'd gotten a chance to punish her, my mission would be complete.

As I shifted in my seat, I stole a glance to the little lady I'd picked up outside that bar. What a filthy place for a woman, I thought. Then again, this wasn't an ordinary woman, was it?

She'd turned her back on her God and embraced the life of a sinner. I mean, a woman married to another woman? What had this world come to?

This wasn't the country I remembered, but that was fine. I'd make it right. Once my girlie got here, I'd set these sinners straight. I'd punish both of them, first the lesbian, and then my Winter.

She was pretty that one, just like her momma. That long black hair and those crystal blue eyes.

I'd have her watch when I punished the other gal, show her exactly what I did to her momma all those years ago. Every movement, every cut, I'd make sure she saw it all, from start to finish.

I glanced over to where I'd propped that other woman up against the front of the old altar. There was a light sheen of sweat on her forehead, and it felt like any time I looked away, her eyes were back on me.

I'd have to watch out for her. This one was slippery, and she wasn't about to lay down and accept the punishment for her sins. I'd have to make her, but in the meantime, I'd have to keep a close watch on her.

When she turned to look at me, I didn't miss the way her blue eyes flashed. I paused, staring. Could it be? Those were Winter's eyes.

The distant light caught polished metal as I pulled a

hunting knife free from its sheath inside my jacket. Was she here? Had my girlie been here the whole time?

As the woman shifted in her seat on the dingy wooden floor, her gaze flicked from mine to the knife and back.

I shook my head. No, her eyes were dark. They weren't blue. I'd picked this one up because she was one of my girlie's friends. One of those FBI agents, but more importantly, she was a godless heathen. A woman who'd forsaken men, who'd laid down with other women, who'd fucked other women.

Now, that wouldn't do.

I'd been seeing my girlie everywhere, and I knew that was a sign too. A sign that we were close to the end. This was a test, wasn't it? God was using this woman to test me, to see whether or not I could be patient to complete my task. That's why I kept seeing those damned blue eyes, and that long black hair.

The last mission was never easy, and I reminded myself to be patient.

Winter was close. I could feel it. She'd be here soon, and then I could finally carry out the work I'd waited so long to finish.

36

W inter heard his thoughts as clearly as if he'd spoken them at her side. Though he was unhinged and dangerous, Douglas Kilroy was predictable. His intent was to use Bree as a lure to pull Winter into what he thought was a trap.

What he did not know was that when he landed that blow on the back of her head on that fateful night, he had sown the seeds to his own undoing. When he swung to kill that teenage girl, he had provided her the means to find him to take him down.

Was that irony, Winter wondered? Karma? Or just random chance?

No matter the reason, Douglas Kilroy didn't know that she had seen through his eyes. She had seen Bree as she rested her back against the splintered altar, both hands zip-tied in front of her. Bree's red coat was dusty and stained with dirt from the road, and in the depths of Winter's unconscious mind, the color looked dull and listless.

Though matted curls stuck to her forehead and her eyeliner had been smeared, Bree's face was calm, almost unreadable. Winter did not have to venture closer to her to know that she had a plan.

She was reminded of Bree's age then, and she wondered if the woman had been taken captive at any other point during her FBI career. Maybe for Bree, the position as Douglas Kilroy's hostage was just another day at the office.

Shadows swept up from the edges of her vision, and darkness engulfed the scene in the dilapidated church. She was not sure how long she floated in that eerie pool of black, but the sensation was not laden with the anxiety she had expected.

The waves of nothing were a comfort. For the time she spent suspended in the warmth of the inky darkness, none of the problems of the waking world rushed up to greet her. She knew they were there, but while she was in this corner of her mind, they seemed less burdensome.

Bree would be okay. Though Winter did not yet know how, she knew she would reach the fellow agent before Kilroy could cut her throat. As long as Winter got there, Bree would be okay.

Kilroy had approached the final hours of his reign of terror. After fifty years of running unchecked from state to state as he murdered men and women alike, Douglas Kilroy was finally about to meet his maker.

Without warning, she was jerked away from the calm nothingness, almost like she had been yanked through the fabric of space and time. As she took in a sharp breath, she snapped open her eyes and sat bolt upright.

When the dim scene before her came into focus, she wondered for a moment if she was still unconscious. Had she left one colorless void only to venture to another? With both hands, she rubbed her eyes before she blinked repeatedly to clear the film from her vision.

She was awake, and she was in a moving vehicle. A white

streetlamp rolled over the back seat and briefly illuminated the jacket that covered her lap like a blanket. Bright against the dark fabric, block text on the back of the coat read "FBI."

"Winter?" The familiar voice cut through the remaining haze like a gust of wind.

"Yeah, Aiden, it's me," she replied.

"Holy hell." This time, the outburst came from the man in the driver's seat. Noah. "Are you all right?"

"I'm, yeah, I'm fine. I feel fine, almost like I just woke up from a full eight hours." Rolling her shoulders, she shifted to the side to stretch her legs. The eerie calm of the colorless void still hung in the air, but as she met her friend's green eyes in the rearview mirror, the lingering serenity started to fade.

Why had she been so damn calm, she wondered? What kind of vision had that even *been*? Bree was still in danger, and even though Winter's unconscious brain assured her that they would reach the woman in time, should she really take the prediction to heart? Was she really about to stake Bree's life on the accuracy of a feeling she'd had in an unconscious haze?

No, she told herself. No, she was not. They were in a moving car, and she didn't have to ask to know they were headed to the rinky-dink town of McCook, Virginia.

"Did anything happen while I was, you know, out?" She shifted her eyes from the driver to the passenger and then back. Neither man returned her scrutiny, but Noah nodded.

"Yeah, sort of." From the mirror, she watched Noah offer her a slight shrug. "We're headed to McCook right now, to that church that you saw before you went under while we were still outside The Lift."

"Is anyone else on their way there?" When her first inclination was to hope they had undertaken the journey without the aid of a fellow law enforcement department, she winced.

This isn't about us anymore, she reminded herself. *It'll be about us once Bree's safe. But right now, it isn't. It's about getting her out of there before that sick bastard can hurt her.*

"No," Aiden answered. "Not for lack of trying, though. The closest SWAT team to that town is an hour out, and right now they're dealing with an active shooter turned hostage taker. It's all over the news right now, everywhere from here to California, even all the way over in the European Union. Seven dead so far, and seventeen hostages. Two shooters, both with military backgrounds, both wearing SS armbands. It's ugly, and it just keeps getting uglier. To say they've got their hands full would be an understatement.

"They aren't about to pry people away from that to send them down after a throwback serial killer. I actually got a text from ADD Ramirez to tell me that they're sending some of our people from the Richmond office out there to help. She told me that this is all us. We might get some backup, but it won't be until at least a half-hour after we've gotten to that church. I think I speak for all of us when I say that we aren't about to pull up and wait for backup while that piece of shit has Bree."

"Agreed," Noah said with a nod.

Winter bit back a sarcastic comment about their sudden accord and turned her attention to the window. "Bree's there," she said instead. "He's using her to get to me. She hasn't been hurt yet, but we need to get there before that changes."

"We will." The note of determination in Aiden's voice was unexpected. Of the three of them, she figured he would have been the last to put aside his personal vendetta with the Douglas Kilroy case.

Then again, Noah and Aiden likely thought the same of her.

They had all made a mess of the investigation, but they

could still salvage it. Aiden had already gone through the protocol to request backup, but since the life of a federal agent hung in the balance, they were more than justified to go in without a SWAT team at their backs. Kilroy was volatile, and now, if her vision was any indication, the man could hardly distinguish reality from fantasy. She had seen through his eyes, had felt his certainty when he looked over to Bree and saw a flash of blue in her gaze.

The possibility that Kilroy would finally fall off the deep end—that he would see Winter where Bree sat—was a real one. No matter his plan to wait for Winter to arrive, if he was sure Bree was Winter, then Bree would die.

"How much longer do you think we've got until we get there?" she asked. It was all she could do to force out the words in anything other than a growl.

"Half-hour," Noah answered. "At least according to the GPS. Why? Something wrong? I mean, aside from the obvious."

"He's losing it. If we don't get there soon, he's going to kill Bree." Her response was quiet, but sure.

"I'm already going fifteen over," her friend advised.

"Make it twenty." To her surprise, the suggestion had been uttered by Aiden.

"We ain't going to do Bree a damn bit of good if we're all dead by the time we get there. Unless y'all have some sort of regenerative iguana powers that I'm not aware of? Do you?" Noah flashed a quick, irritated glance to Aiden, and then to her. "Not to mention, yeah, sure we're FBI, but if we get pulled over, how much time do you suppose we'll lose? Fifteen minutes? Twenty? All the cops might be at that hostage situation, but I'd be willing to bet there're a few Staties between us and McCook."

Silence returned to them, and she could see the tendons in Noah's hand shift as he tightened his grip on the steering wheel. She kept her eyes fixed on the eerie blue glow of the dashboard clock as the seconds ticked away.

"You're right." After the prolonged bout of quiet, her soft words sounded like the crack of a whip.

Of course, Noah was right. Noah was always right.

BREE HAD MENTALLY RECITED the chorus of the old Rick Astley so many times, she was certain she would forever associate the melody "Together Forever" with a concerted effort to alleviate anxiety. From the moment she awoke in the abandoned church, she had repeated the lyrics in her head to drive the heavy air of impending doom from her thoughts.

Now, how long her "forever" was, she did not know. Kilroy had risen from his seat at a splintered pew to pace back and forth. His booted feet had already worn visible tracks through the dirt and dust that coated the tarnished wooden floor, and she wondered how much longer he could walk the same path before he fell through to the subfloor.

Since she regained consciousness at the base of the altar, the man had uttered a grand total of five or six words. The utterances had been made mostly under his breath, and Bree still wasn't sure what he had said, though she thought she heard the word "winter" muttered at least once.

Kilroy was a man of few words, much to Bree's relief. She wanted to wait until she had a clear opening, and focusing on the task would be markedly more difficult if he spent the hours blabbing about whatever bullshit rattled around in his head.

Both her wrists were bound one over the other, and the skin beneath the durable zip-ties had been rubbed raw as she adjusted the binds. She had not undertaken the painful task for comfort, she reminded herself. Flexing the fingers of both hands to return a portion of her circulation, she focused her attention on the flicker of movement in her periphery as Kilroy paced.

She had to time her movement right, and she didn't want to let on to her intent observation of his strides.

He arrived at the end of his trail, spun on one foot to face her direction, and then started toward the other end. One, two, three steps, and then his back was to her. She watched him go through the motions one more time for good measure.

As soon as she saw the back of his olive drab jacket in the corner of her eye, she snapped her hands up to rip out one post earring. She forced an expressionless look to her face just in time for him to turn. His steps were rhythmic and unperturbed, which meant he had not noticed her movement. Good.

She had moved the zip-ties in place so she could press the earring into the clasp to loosen the bind, but she needed a distraction. She could free herself in less than a few seconds, but his pacing didn't allow enough time for her to both free herself and duck into cover. If she tried, he would notice her well before she had freed herself, and that would be the end.

But she was the only other person here, so how in the hell was she supposed to distract him?

Glancing to the rubble at the base of the altar, she sketched out the beginnings of a plan. As long as he continued the impatient pacing, she would gradually loosen the ties around her wrists, all while she maintained the appearance that the binds were still in place. Then, she would pick up a piece of splintered wood and hurl it off into the distance as far as she could manage. When he went to investigate the sudden disturbance, she could run to cover.

She had no idea where in the hell they were, but she would take her chances alone out in the night.

ONCE HE SHRUGGED into the black FBI jacket, Aiden accepted the rifle from Noah Dalton's outstretched hand. More than a mile away from their destination, Dalton had killed the headlights and slowed their speed to a veritable crawl. The road had once been covered with gravel, but rain had washed away much of the rocky surface. Now, the path was as much dirt as it was gravel.

In the center of the road, Aiden noticed the faint impressions left from a set of tires that had only recently disturbed the earth. If there had been any doubts flitting through his head, he could officially put them to rest.

From where they had parked on the other side of a slight hill, only the cross at the peak of the church roof was visible. The clouds had parted, and though the moon was a quarter of the way into its waning phase, the meager light was enough to silhouette the cross against the night sky. Considering the demon they were about to face, Aiden thought it would have been fitting if the cross were inverted.

"Really wish I had been awake to get one of those," Winter muttered. Her blue eyes flicked back and forth between Aiden and Noah's rifles.

"Two M4s should be fine," Aiden replied. With one hand, he eased the trunk closed as he shouldered the carbine with the other.

"All right, we don't know much about the layout of that building, so what's the plan?" Noah wondered.

Just as Aiden was about to open his mouth to respond, he felt a faint disturbance as his phone vibrated in his pocket.

Holding up a hand to forestall the discussion, he retrieved

the device and unlocked the screen. The text had been sent by ADD Cassidy Ramirez, and the body of the message was followed by a blue hyperlink. Even in a text, Ramirez still cited her sources, he mused.

However, any bemusement at the ADD's formality and professionalism vanished as soon as he started to read. He could feel the haunted expression on his face, but he made no effort to conceal the look.

"What?" Winter and Noah asked.

"That was ADD Ramirez." His voice was hushed as he turned the volume off and pocketed the phone. "They killed one shooter and apprehended the other. Right now, they're estimating that thirteen people are dead, and another ten are injured. They executed six of the hostages before SWAT got to them, and the only reason there weren't more deaths is because one of the guys they had as a hostage was an off-duty police officer."

Noah took in a sharp breath, and even in the low light, Aiden could see his knuckles turn white where he gripped the shoulder strap of his rifle.

"Oh my god," Winter breathed. "That's terrible."

"Yeah." He left off the final part of Ramirez's message. According to the takedown team, the surviving shooter had cited Douglas Kilroy's "work" as part of their motivation to undertake the plan. Their goal had been to come as close to Kilroy's body count as they could, but fortunately, they had been stopped well before they reached the obscene number.

Now was not the time to discuss the motivation of a couple neo-Nazis. There would be plenty of time to parse through the lunatics' reasoning once they had gotten Bree to safety and stuffed Kilroy in a jail cell.

"It could have been a lot worse." Aiden made the statement as much to pull himself back to the present as he did to reassure Noah and Winter. "Local LEOs did their job, and they did it well. Now, it's time for us to do ours. They've had a busy enough night, so let's go in there and get Kilroy so they won't have to do any more work when they get here."

"Agreed," Noah said. "What's the plan, then? Best as I can tell, that place has two entrances: one at the front, and another around back."

"He wants me." For emphasis, Winter poked herself in the Kevlar vest. "I should go in first and get his attention."

"What?" Mouth agape, Noah turned his incredulous stare to the woman at his side.

"You? Why?" Aiden managed to force a hint of irritability into his tone.

"He wants *me*," she repeated.

"So?" Noah's brows drew together as he narrowed his eyes.

"Believe it or not, I'm with Dalton this time. You're out of your mind, Winter. The fact that he wants to murder you seems like a pretty good reason for you *not* to go in there and walk right up to him."

Crossing both arms over her black jacket, Winter shook her head. "No, that's not the way he works. He's a serial killer, and he has a specific ritual he adheres to whenever he kills a victim. Just trust me when I say that I know what's going through his head. He's a serial killer, right? By definition, he has a really specific ritual he sticks to. His ritual isn't to shoot me in the face as soon as he sees me.

"And he knows something about my brother. I *know* he does. If we barge in there and go all sharpshooter, I'll never know what that is. I'll never even know where he's fucking buried! And it's not just me, you two know that, right? How many unnamed victims do you think are out there? How many families has he ripped apart?

"I'm going to go in there first because he won't shoot me, and because I know I can get him to *talk*. I can get him to tell me what happened to my brother, and then we can take him out of here in cuffs so all those other families can get the closure they need too."

She let her intense stare linger on Noah first, and then she turned those vivid blue eyes to him.

He felt like that look had suspended him in time. It was a look he had seen before, a look of cold determination that bordered on blatant stubbornness. He hated that steely resolve as much as he fucking loved it, dreaded it as much as he admired it. But in that moment, he realized the feeling that clamped its hand around his throat was more than admiration.

His effort to keep in contact with Winter over the years had been borne from more than just his desire to erase a blemish from his file. Maybe that was what drove his initial decision, but relationships—professional or otherwise—were rarely static. And how could they be static when so much had changed over the past decade?

No, he thought. What he felt for her now had gone far above and beyond a professional admiration, or even a platonic friendship. He didn't know what hole he had fallen into, but he would deal with it later.

"Are you sure?" He had no idea how much time had elapsed between the end of her proclamation and his question.

For all he knew, they might have stood there with their eyes locked on one another for an hour. Maybe while they watched one another, Noah Dalton had gone to the church, killed Douglas Kilroy, and brought Bree back to the car. For a split second, the outlandish scenario felt so likely that he glanced over to make sure Bree was not beside Noah.

Agent Stafford was not there. Instead, he spotted a flash of annoyance behind the taller man's green eyes.

"I'm positive," Winter replied. "Look, I can't explain it,

but, when I was passed out, it's like I saw what he's got planned. The reason he took Bree was because he wanted to get to me, and the reason he's here at this church is because he feels like he's bringing this whole 'mission' of his full circle. He's ending it all where it started, or at least that's what he thinks.

"And you know what else I'm sure about? I'm sure that if either of you two walks in there and he sees you, he's going to shoot first and ask questions later. I'm the one he wants, so I'm going to make it seem like he's about to get it. You two need to stay out of sight. If he sees you, he *will* kill you."

After another abrasive silence, Aiden nodded.

"What?" Noah guffawed, disbelief and ire both prevalent on his unshaven face.

"She knows more about Kilroy than either of us, Dalton." As Aiden spoke, he turned his head to meet Noah's glare head-on. He brushed past the venomous look and continued. "I get that this isn't a personal thing for anyone anymore, or maybe it's even more of a personal thing for *all* of us, but listen to me, Dalton. She's right. You know she's right, and I know she's right. He won't open fire if she walks in there first, but if either of us tries to, he will."

"You don't know—"

"And these weapons." Aiden plowed on, pausing to gesture to the carbine over his shoulder. "These weapons are way more effective than a Glock nine-mil at a range. I know you knew that, and I know you know that they make us the best option to hang back and provide backup in case something goes wrong. Our help is thirty to forty-five minutes out, and that's a generous estimate. If we don't go in there now, then we're gambling with Bree's life. And I don't know about you, Dalton, but I *will not* be responsible for an agent's death, do you understand me?"

Noah's jaw was like granite. "Yes, sir."

Aiden wasn't finished yet. "We don't have the luxury of time to sit out here and skim through blueprints so we can make our entrance as effective as possible. We need to make the best out of what we've got right now, or Bree is going to fucking die. None of us, Winter and Bree included, want Winter to get hurt. And she won't. Winter leads, and then Dalton, you find somewhere in there to post up. You're a better shot than either of us, and you've got a weapon capable of precision from a greater distance than a handgun. As long as we back her up, she's going to be fine. As long as we work *together*, we'll all be fine."

Aiden thought he might have spent an eternity staring down the former Marine. With a blustery sigh, Noah finally rubbed his eyes and nodded his assent.

"Yeah," Noah started. "Yeah, damn it. All right. You're right. Both of you."

"Winter, you go through the front entrance. Dalton and I will go through the back, and we'll stick to the shadows. We don't want him to know we're there. Winter, you keep him distracted and we'll get Bree, and then before he notices she's gone, we take him down, one way or another. We do whatever we can to make sure we take him alive, but we aren't going to risk anyone's life to do it, understood?"

Winter nodded. "Understood."

37

The crunch of dirt and debris beneath Winter's booted feet was quiet, but to her, the sound might as well have been a series of firecrackers. As she neared the end of a wide hall, she flattened her back against the peeling drywall and crept to the edge. For several agonizing seconds, she held her breath to strain her hearing. She thought she might have caught the distant scuffle of a footstep, but the likelihood that the sound had emanated from the crumbling building was just as high.

Flexing her fingers against the textured grip of her service weapon, she grated her teeth together and scooted until her shoulder was flush with the door frame. A wide ray of white light fell along the splintered floorboards of the hallway, and she narrowed her eyes as she looked to the source—a battery powered work lamp. The light had been positioned just on the other side of the wall to illuminate the doorway.

It was smart, she thought. The rest of the church was bathed in darkness, but as soon as someone walked through the entrance to the main room, they would be lit up as plain as if they stood in the afternoon sun.

The light might have been smart, but it only meant that she had to be fast. As long as she kept her eyes away from the fluorescence, her vision would be clear by the time she slunk back into the shadows.

With one last deep breath to steady her nerves, she spun around on one foot and snapped up her arms to level the barrel of her weapon in the direction of the altar. Her shuffle to the side and out of the halo of light was quick, and she didn't let her aim falter as she moved.

At the front of the church, she spotted one shadowy figure, and then another. Clarity returned to her vision in short order, and before she had a chance to take in the scene, she lined up her sights with the man's head.

With *Kilroy's* head. *The Preacher's* head.

The glow from the work light caught the polished steel of a handgun as Kilroy pressed the barrel to the temple of the woman he had grabbed to use as a shield. *That* was why the light had been there, she realized. He hadn't expected the brightness to throw her off so much as he had wanted to buy himself time to snatch up Bree.

"Well, well." The corner of Kilroy's mouth turned up in a self-assured smirk as he clucked his tongue. "'Bout time you showed up, little lady. I was startin' to get impatient, even wondered for a second there if you were goin' to come at all. It's been a long time, Winter. And my, my how you've grown into such a lovely young woman."

His gaze was like a spider crawling up her skin, and as much as she wanted to hurl insults at him, lash out at him, her mouth was dry as bone.

This man killed her parents.

This man took her little brother.

This man changed her life irrevocably, at his demented whim.

"It really is a shame, you know that?" he went on after licking his dry lips. "A shame you decided to follow that same sinful path as your momma. Now, your momma, *there* was a beautiful woman, I tell you what. And you, girlie, you look just like her."

At a pace that was barely perceptible even to her, Winter crept forward and tried to adjust her aim to the creep's forehead. Bree's dark eyes were wide, but as she followed Winter's movement, she was calm.

"If you get a shot, take it." Bree's voice wasn't panicked, not even strained.

"Yeah," Winter replied through clenched teeth. She knew that ensuring Bree's safety was their primary focus, but she couldn't let Kilroy off that easily. One way or another, she *had* to find out what had happened to her brother.

And now that there was a gun to Bree's head, she had to do it fast.

"You ladies sure about that?" Kilroy chided. Though quiet, his chortle was eerie and unsettling.

"What, you think I need someone's permission to blow off your fucking head?" Winter snapped, happy to hear the strength in her voice she didn't feel. "You know that's a federal agent you've got in front of you like a human shield, right? You know what the penalty is for killing a federal agent? Well, just in case you don't, I'll tell you."

"Death," Bree added for her, then tightened her jaw when the gun pressed harder against her temple.

Winter's heart thumped wildly in her chest. "She's right," she said. "It's death, Kilroy. Death by lethal injection. And since it's a Federal offense, that means Virginia or North Carolina's death penalty laws don't have any bearing on it. It doesn't matter where it happens, they're still going to be able to jam a needle in your arm after you're convicted. And, let me tell you, Douglas, other cops don't take kindly to the death of their own."

"Maybe." His smirk widened as he chuckled again, that same, disquieting sound. "But I reckon you'd have to take me out of here in cuffs if you want any of that stuff you just said to come true. And here's the deal, girlie. Maybe you get that shot you're after. Maybe I stick my old head out just a little bit too far and you take your shot. Well, what then?"

Winter gritted her teeth. "Do it," she countered.

"You see this?" As he paused, he gruffly jammed the steel handgun even harder into Bree's temple. "My finger's already on the trigger, ya'see? Now, maybe I'm just an old timer, and maybe my reflexes aren't quite what they used to be back in 'Nam, but I'm not quite old enough for them to be slow. You go ahead and pull that trigger when you get a shot, girlie, but I can already tell you what'll happen. In that last split-second before I die, my hand'll seize up, and then your friend here will go right down to that floor with me."

Winter cursed under her breath because she knew he was right.

The bastard chuckled. "Now, maybe you'll get lucky, and you'll make that one-in-a-million shot. Do you know the one I'm talking about?" With his free hand, Kilroy tapped a gnarled finger against Bree's pursed lips. "Right there, girlie. That's where you've got to hit me if you want all the nerves in my body to shut down right away. You see, right here, that'll blow my brainstem out the back of my head. No twitching, no nothing. It's the same shot they train snipers to make in the military, and I'd be willing to bet that it's the same shot they train your federal agent friends to make too."

He was right. Winter knew he was right—she could recall the lesson from her time at Quantico.

"Not very ladylike to be waving a gun like that around,

anyway, is it? I tell you what, girlie. You drop that weapon, set it on the floor nice and slow, you got it? You've got 'til the count of five or I blow this little lady's head clean off her shoulders."

Winter didn't need her enhanced sensory ability to know that Kilroy would follow through with his threat.

"Fine," she snapped. Both arms raised, she eased her finger away from the trigger as she crouched down to set the handgun on the floor.

As she lowered the weapon, a flicker of movement from just below Bree's stomach caught her eye. The motion slow and measured, Bree slid one wrist free of her binds and wiggled her fingers like she was a baseball catcher signaling their next play.

No wonder she hadn't been panicked, Winter thought.

"There you go, Kilroy," Winter sneered. "Now, let me ask you something, huh? All the women you've murdered over the last few months, sure seems like you were trying to kill *me*, doesn't it?"

He opened his mouth to object, but she cut him off.

"No, don't deny it, Kilroy. You're losing it, aren't you? Maybe those reflexes of yours are just as catlike as they've always been, but I don't think you're all that sharp anymore, are you? You legitimately thought that you were killing me when you went for those women, didn't you?" With a mocking laugh, she shook her head. "You did. How senile are you, old man?"

His face went cold as stone. "I'm not—"

She laughed, cutting him off. "You know, you've always been like this otherworldly monster, but let me tell something I just realized. You aren't an otherworldly monster. You're just an old man, past his prime, trying to cling to whatever he can to preserve his relevance. You're scared, aren't you, Kilroy? Scared that time's going to forget you, that come tomorrow, no one's going to remember your name."

Did his bottom lip tremble? Winter watched him closely for another tell.

She sneered, looking him up and down. "Or, if they do, they aren't going to remember you as The Preacher. No, not at all. See, they'll do an autopsy of your body after you die here tonight, and they'll be able to see all the abnormalities in your brain. That's the only definitive way to diagnose Alzheimer's, did you know that, Kilroy? An autopsy, where they slice up your brain like bologna. Is that what you think they'll find? Because that's what I think they'll find."

"I—"

She didn't let him finish. "And then that'll get out to the press, and that's all anyone will remember you as. You'll only be known as that old, senile man who went after women in their sleep because he was too fucking scared to confront them otherwise. That's why you're doing this all, anyway, isn't it? Because, deep down, you're scared of women. You grew up with such a strong hatred of women that now you've got to take out all that rage on us because somewhere in the back of your mind you're worried that you're not good enough."

"Enough!" Kilroy's shout echoed through the high ceiling with so much force she thought the roof might cave in. He was pissed—livid, even.

In a blur, Bree clamped one hand down on his forearm, pushed his aim away from her head, and snapped her elbow back into his face. Even from where she stood, Winter heard the satisfying crunch of popping cartilage as the blow connected with his nose.

Before the roar of pain escaped the old man's lips, Bree had taken hold of his hand and jerked his wrist backwards. With a clatter, the stainless-steel handgun fell to the floor.

As soon as Bree scooped up the weapon, Winter closed the distance, arced her right arm backwards, and swung for the bastard's face with all the strength she could muster. The force of the blow ached along her tensed muscles, but she pushed the sensation from her thoughts as she reared back for another swing. When her fist connected with his cheekbone that time, she felt a sting as her knuckles split open from the collision.

"Winter," a voice, Bree's voice, called. "I've got a shot if you move out of the way."

"Hold on!" Winter shouted. He couldn't die. Not yet.

"Don't," Kilroy wheezed. "Don't you want to know what happened to your brother, girlie?" With one olive drab sleeve, he made a vain attempt to stop the flow of blood from his ruined nose.

"Do you really think you're in a position to bargain right now, Kilroy?" Winter's voice was so cold, she hardly recognized it as her own.

"Do you think he's still alive?" The question brimmed with mocking derision, and for a split-second, she wanted to yell at Bree to take her shot. She wouldn't, though. For Justin's sake, she would keep this sick bastard alive until he finally told her the truth.

She clamped her hand down on the front of his shirt to hold him in place as she prepared to land another concussive blow. The rage that flooded through her veins with each beat of her heart was all-consuming. Her mind was devoid of rational thought as she clenched her hand back into a fist.

So, this was what it meant to see red.

"Your brother," the man growled.

"What?" she retorted. "Speak up, Kilroy!"

"What if I told you he's still alive?" Even when his face was shattered, even when he desperately tried to wipe the stream of crimson from his nose as he braced himself for the impact of the next right hook, his tone was ripe with ridicule.

"What?"

All at once, she was thrown back to that night, to Justin's goofy smile, to his adorable lisp.

Don't let the bed bugth bite.

She could hear him as well as if he stood at her side.

"Damn it, Winter!" Bree exclaimed. "Get out of the way! He's got a—!"

"I'm fine," Winter shot back. "I can handle this! What the hell are you talking about, Kilroy? What did you do to my brother? Where is he?" Her voice was just below an outright shout, but she still didn't feel the question had been loud enough.

He sneered. "Come a little closer, and I'll tell you."

She spotted the red glow beneath Kilroy's olive drab jacket at the last possible second.

As she stepped aside to avoid the blade, fire rippled from beneath her armpit and up into her shoulder, hitting the vulnerable flesh that the Kevlar didn't cover. She grasped at the source of the pain, and when she pulled away her hand, the distant work light glinted off the syrupy blood that coated her palm.

"No!" Through the haze of adrenaline, Bree's exclamation sounded distant and tinny. "I can't get a shot."

Winter knew why. The bastard kept moving in front of her, using her in a reverse sort of shield. Bree's gun was a .45. Unless they were lucky and it was loaded with hollow points, if she shot him, the bullet would go straight through his head and straight into Winter's.

"If you can get a shot," Bree shouted. "I suggest you fucking take it!"

She was shouting to Aiden and Noah, Winter realized, wondering where they'd taken up station.

"No!" Winter screamed. "Not yet."

Kilroy took advantage of her distraction. She felt more than saw his movement. Moving quickly, she took a swift step backwards and felt a slight breeze as the blade whipped past her chest. She could handle this. Douglas Kilroy knew about Justin, and one way or another, she would make him tell her.

But he was faster. Much faster than a man of his age should have been.

Light glinted from the blade as it arced through the air. She dropped but instinctively knew it wouldn't be enough.

Bang!

The retort of a gunshot cracked through the night air like a clap of thunder. Before she could register what had happened, a fine mist of dark crimson exploded from the side of Douglas Kilroy's head. The hunting knife clattered to the ground, and a puff of dust rose around the silver blade as it hit the floor.

"No," she cried as the murderer dropped an instant later.

When she whipped her head around to regard the source of the shot, her eyes met Noah's as he lowered the rifle tucked against his shoulder. Though her rational mind insisted he was not to blame for the loss of Kilroy's secrets, she wanted to take hold of his jacket and shake him until his teeth rattled in his head.

"No," she repeated, but much softer this time.

Winter's baby brother was alive, but thanks to a single gunshot, she would never learn more than that.

38

Three months, Winter thought as she glanced down to her steaming mug of coffee. Douglas Kilroy had been dead for three months, almost to the day.

The investigation of Douglas Kilroy, also known as The Preacher, ended much as it had begun—with more questions than answers. Crime scene techs had scoured any address where he had been known to reside, but they came away from each search empty-handed. According to the news, criminological experts had expected more than just the trail of bodies. They had anticipated a manifesto, a collection of trophies, a journal, something.

Instead, there was nothing.

Some reporters and journalists were still convinced that law enforcement agents would unearth a veritable treasure trove of information about the inner workings of Douglas Kilroy's twisted mind. Winter could not say she cared either way. The man was dead, his remains cremated and buried in an unmarked grave. If there were answers to the multitude of questions, they had been burned away with the rest of Kilroy's body.

Douglas Kilroy, also known as Barney Fife, Jared Kingston, and a whole host of other aliases, was dead.

Winter told herself repeatedly that she harbored no ill will toward Noah for firing the fatal shot into the side of Douglas Kilroy's head. And, if she did, she *shouldn't*. Kilroy's knife-wielding arm had been raised, and if Noah had waited even a second longer, he would have sunk the blade through Winter's heart. For the second time in their tenure with the FBI, Noah Dalton had saved her life in the nick of time. And for the second time, the former Marine had killed a suspect in the line of duty.

Aiden Parrish's last-minute decision to collect a couple rifles for the venture to McCook had been a wise one, as had Bree Stafford's decision not to risk a shot at Kilroy while Winter stood just behind him. The weapon Bree had forcibly taken from Kilroy had been one of the most powerful handguns of its caliber on the market. Kilroy was not clad in a Kevlar vest, and the shot would have undoubtedly ripped through him and then into Winter.

Aside from a handful of murders where some form of DNA evidence had been present, the majority of Kilroy's suspected killings were still open cases. To Winter, the closure of the double homicide and kidnapping of the Black family had seemed watered down and meaningless when it was compared to the grief countless others faced.

Biting back a resigned sigh, she gingerly picked up her mug to take a sip of the steaming beverage. A flicker of movement from the corner of her eye drew her attention, and she offered her grandma a quick smile.

"How is he?" Winter asked, her voice hushed.

Whether due to her beauty regimen or good genetics, Gramma Beth rarely looked her age. But in the warm glow of the late morning sunshine, the lines on her fair face seemed more pronounced as she sat down across from Winter.

"He'll be fine, honey," Beth replied. "The golden years aren't always so golden, I'm afraid. It'll be okay, don't you worry."

Winter didn't believe her, but with a solemn nod, she returned her attention to the cup in her hands. "How about you, Gramma? How are you? Is there anything I can do?"

"Oh, you're so sweet for asking, honey. You're doing plenty just by being here. I hope you know I don't take that for granted. I'm so glad you're here." A ghost of a smile passed over Beth's face as she scooped up her empty mug and pushed herself to stand. "Do you need a refill, dear?"

"No, thanks, Gramma." Winter returned the warm look as well as she could. "My mug's still pretty full."

"Sounds like you'd better drink faster, then."

"I'm not sure about that. If I chug a cup of coffee, I'll probably get all jittery and antsy."

"How are you liking the hot cocoa and coffee combination, anyway?" Gramma made her way back to her seat, freshly filled mug in hand.

"Uh, I love it," Winter chuckled. "It's the closest to a mocha I can be bothered to make on my own. It's genius, honestly."

As they lapsed into silence, she heard the birds chirping from a large, shady tree in the backyard. She'd tried to climb that tree a couple times when she was younger, but to no avail. Once, she had even made an effort to display her climbing prowess to her little brother. Maybe now that she had grown into her lanky limbs and tacked on a bit of muscle mass, she could finally make it.

The flash of her phone's screen pulled her from the contemplation, and as her eyes fell on the preview of the text message, she heard her pulse rush in her ears.

For the entirety of the three months she had been with her grandparents, Winter had not even replied to an email from any of her co-workers. Not from Bree—though the woman had not made an effort to reach out until she was, by her own admission, coaxed to do so by Aiden and Noah. Even though she appreciated Bree's candidness, Winter didn't reply. She had ignored Aiden and Noah with the same adamancy she might have used to keep herself off the radar of a debt collector.

Gradually, the attempts to reach out to her had dwindled in frequency. For the past two or three weeks, she had not received so much as a professional email from either man.

After she had avoided them for so long, how was she even supposed to reestablish contact? What would she even say? "Sorry, guys, my grandpa's sick and Kilroy's dead so I think I'm just going to sit over here and lose my mind for a few months?"

Yeah, I'm sure that'd go over great, she thought.

But the newest message from Noah was unlike any of the previous. *I'm going to call you, and you NEED TO ANSWER. THIS IS IMPORTANT, WINTER.*

As she read the words, she could almost picture Noah's stern look of disapproval. Disapproval, disappointment, she honestly couldn't tell the difference anymore. She had enough of her own feelings to deal with. She didn't need to be beholden to someone else's feelings too. Not even if that someone was the person she'd once referred to as her best friend. Not even if she'd kissed that same someone in a panic because she thought she was about to lose them.

This time, she couldn't help the weary sigh as it slipped from her lips.

"What's wrong, Winter?" Gramma Beth's eyes darkened with a sudden rush of concern.

"I don't know, Gramma," Winter replied. "But I think I'm about to get a phone call."

"Honey, they're your friends." Beth's voice was gentle, but

unwavering. "You should at least let them know that you're okay. Just, you know, make a Facebook post about it or something."

With a chortle, Winter shook her head. "I gave up on Facebook years ago."

"Yeah, that's always been your grandfather's wheelhouse. Not mine."

"Grampa Jack *Facebooks?*"

Now, it was her Gramma's turn to snicker. "Oh, he used to play those silly little farm games. I had an account at the time, and he'd always send me requests to log in and send him crops or something. I got sick of it, so I closed my account."

"No way." Winter laughed. For the first time in weeks, the mirth in her voice was genuine. She wanted to ask Gramma Beth what other sorts of mobile games Grampa had taken on over the years, but before she could open her mouth to pose the query, she jerked her attention back to the table at an obnoxious buzz.

So much for that. Though she snatched the device from the wooden tabletop, she made no move to swipe the green answer key.

"I think I should take this," she started. When she glanced across the table, her grandma offered a wistful smile and a nod.

"Do whatever's right for you, sweetie."

As she rose to stand, Winter returned the sad look and nodded. "I'll be right back," she said. After a warm clasp to her grandma's shoulder, Winter pried open the sliding glass door and stepped out onto the deck.

In what she was sure was the last possible second, she slid her thumb across the screen. The caller ID had shown Noah's name, but in the ensuing moments of quiet, she wondered if the other end of the line was staffed by a robo-caller.

"Hello?" a familiar voice finally said.

Winter bit down on her tongue to steady her voice before she answered.

"Yeah," she managed.

She expected her friend to launch into a tirade about her lack of communication, to ask what in the hell went through her head when she left three months earlier without so much as a word of farewell. She expected him to rip her a new one for abandoning him, but he did none of the above.

Instead, his voice was crisp, cool, and professional. "Parrish and I have been looking into your brother, Justin Black."

"W-what?" The stammer of disbelief was all but involuntary.

"If you'd answer your phone, you would have been the first person we told about it." His response was flat, and she felt a twinge of guilt.

For the second time, she expected him to go off on a tangent about friendship. And for the second time, she was disappointed.

"We found something about Justin," he said, his voice softer this time.

The sting of tears burned in the corners of her eyes as she turned her attention to the shimmer of green as the oak tree swayed in the summer breeze.

Once upon a time, on a day much like today, she had told her little brother to "watch and learn" as she made a valiant effort to climb up the trunk of the old oak.

It was her day to do the same.

Watch and learn.

The End
To be continued...

Want to Read More About Winter?

Want to discover out what happened to Justin? Find out in Book Four, Winter's Rise. Now available! Find it on Amazon Now!

ACKNOWLEDGMENTS

How does one properly thank everyone involved in taking a dream and making it a reality? Let me try.

In addition to my family, whose unending support provided the foundation for me to find the time and energy to put these thoughts on paper, I want to thank the editors who polished my words and made them shine.

Many thanks to my publisher for risking taking on a newbie and giving me the confidence to become a bona fide author.

More than anyone, I want to thank you, my reader, for clicking on a nobody and sharing your most important asset, your time, with this book. I hope with all my heart I made it worthwhile.

Much love,
Mary

ABOUT THE AUTHOR

Mary Stone lives among the majestic Blue Ridge Mountains of East Tennessee with her two dogs, four cats, a couple of energetic boys, and a very patient husband.

As a young girl, she would go to bed every night, wondering what type of creature might be lurking underneath. It wasn't until she was older that she learned that the creatures she needed to most fear were human.

Today, she creates vivid stories with courageous, strong heroines and dastardly villains. She invites you to enter her world of serial killers, FBI agents but never damsels in distress. Her female characters can handle themselves, going toe-to-toe with any male character, protagonist or antagonist.

Discover more about Mary Stone on her website.
www.authormarystone.com

facebook.com/authormarystone

instagram.com/marystone_author

goodreads.com/AuthorMaryStone

bookbub.com/profile/3378576590

pinterest.com/MaryStoneAuthor